Grace and Baby

Peggy Leon
2014

ISBN: 1496171209
ISBN 13: 9781496171207
Library of Congress Control Number: 2014904713
CreateSpace Independent Publishing Platform
North Charleston, South Carolina

JUNE

*g*race emptied the bottle of pain pills into the mortar. She stared down at the heap of pills. Dilaudid, a morphine derivative, she guessed. It would be enough. She picked up the pestle to begin.

From the living room, the television blared, ceaseless, comforting: Barney Fife's strident warble, Andy's accented murmur, the tinny answer of the laugh track. A "*Ha!*" deep and loud over the chattering laugh track: that was Baby. "Hohohoho!" Grace smiled. Baby and that Christmas laugh of hers. Grace leaned back slightly to peek around the doorway. Grace's sister, Baby, a mass of flesh and polyester house dress, sat in her straight-backed chair, huge shoulders hunched, massive elbows on slippery knees, intent on the screen a foot and a half in front of her. Butler, their fat, black Corgi, slept on her toes, snoring slightly. Beyond, the TV glowed in shades of gray. Reruns of *The Andy Griffith Show* reflected on Baby's thick glasses.

On the screen beyond Baby, Barney Fife, gun drawn and shaking wildly, worked his trembling way through some brush. Baby's gray head trembled with expectation. She and Grace both knew that in about thirty seconds, Andy would come up behind Barney and startle him. Barney would shoot his gun in the air, and a remarkably large limb would drop at their feet. Grace turned her attention to Baby, watched Baby's lips move in a silent mimicking of Andy's quip about the tree limb. "Ho, ho, ho, ho, ho." Baby's entire body shook with pure joy. In response, Butler lifted his nose, sneezed, and resettled with a loud sigh.

Grace grinned. She suspected that Santa Claus and Baby were the only two people on the earth that laughed like that. *I was the lucky one,* Grace thought. No waiting for Santa in this old house. She had the real thing, the one, the only. She had Baby.

The smile slipped from her face. Grace looked at the pestle, felt its sudden weight in her fingers, felt her fingers cramping, cramping as if she had been holding this piece of cold marble for years.

"*Ha!* Yellow!" Baby bellowed from the living room. "Grace! Grace! Yellow!" Baby spoke in colors, colors and names—names of her favorite people, laughter, moans. In the seventy-two years of living with her sister, Grace had never heard her utter another kind of word. Yellow was good; very, very good. Brown was equally as bad. Between, a rainbow of primary hues marked the experiences of their lives, a vibrant conversation, lacking only in vocabulary. Grace was the interpreter, the keeper, the protector.

The laugh track burbled. Baby chuckled, radiating pleasure. She turned to see Grace watching from the kitchen doorway, grinned, and waved. "Andy, Grace! Ha!" She turned back to the TV and hunched in concentration.

Grace smiled and hollered over the noise, "Pretty funny stuff, there, Baby!" She felt the hard, sharp tug of love in her chest and nearly gasped at its pull. She clutched the pestle fiercely. She was the protector. She would do her job.

The pills cracked and split beneath the pressure of the pestle, but then they resisted further reduction, escaping from beneath its curved bottom to be chased around the mortar bowl or shooting out to ricochet from the edges with a sharp ping. Grace caught and crushed each piece with dogged deliberation. One large chunk shot out and across the kitchen, skidding to a stop beneath the table. Grace moved to retrieve it, squatting to slap about beneath table for the bit of pill, wincing at the sharp pain in her gut that the movement caused. Finding the piece at last, she eased herself up to standing and continued her task, grinding the pills to a fine powder.

4

On the stove, the timer buzzed; then, from the other room, the familiar jingle of a commercial, the groaning complaint of Baby's wood chair as she shifted positions. Grace turned off the timer, lifted the lid on the cooking pot. Steam billowed. Grace took a big spoon and stirred the brightly colored liquid. Thick, sluggish bubbles broke the surface and sputtered. It was ready. Grace turned the flame off under the pot. Behind her, the kitchen floorboards creaked and clicked lightly. Unsurprised, Grace felt Baby's breath on the back of her head, Butler's soft fur at her ankles. "Pudding," Grace told her.

"Yellow." Baby bent down, face close to the pot, came up with glasses coated in steam. "Ha!"

"Yes. Your favorite. Lemon pudding." Baby reached for the pot. Grace intercepted her. "That's for later, Baby. Too hot now." Baby crossed her arms and frowned. "You can't bully me, Baby. I said later. You'd burn yourself now." Baby remained, solid, frowning. "Don't you worry. You can eat as much as you want later. Go on." Baby remained. "I promise, Baby. Wait! What's that? I think Andy's back on!"

Baby turned. "Ha! Andy!" She engulfed Grace in a hug, then scuttled off toward the living room. Grace watched her go before she stirred the pot once more, then set it aside. It would have been easier to use one of those instant mixes, Grace thought, but Baby always liked it the old-fashioned way: homemade from scratch, cooked, cooled, then chilled, thick and creamy, lots of food coloring for effect—a spoonful of yellow heaven. Nothing was too much effort for Baby.

Grace placed a dish towel over the mortar. Used more than sixty years ago for dosing the cows, idle since, the mortar had been their father's. The thought made her grimace. She turned her back on it and rinsed the pestle in the sink. She would wait until the pudding was thoroughly cooled before she mixed the pain-killers in. She wasn't sure what effect the heat would have on the potency. She worried, too, that the lemon in the pudding would not mask the bitter pills. She decided to whip up some cream, make it sweet. When the time came, she'd add a great dollop of it on top.

Grace had spent that morning waiting at the specialist's office on the third floor of the hospital. The appointment had been for 9:00 a.m. Grace had been prompt, but then she'd sat for forty-seven minutes in the mauve-and-light-blue waiting room. It was a long time to leave Baby unattended except by Butler the dog and the morning reruns of *Bewitched* and *I Dream of Jeannie*, but Grace had to know, or rather needed to have confirmed, what her insides were telling her. She had been a nurse once, for a short, few weeks and long ago, but she could still recognize the signs, had even checked one of her old textbooks. Beyond book knowledge, there was this: she and her body were old friends. They told each other everything. Lately, the headlines had been bad.

From the reception room, Grace was shown into the doctor's office, not to an exam room. Grace nodded with grim satisfaction, a confirmation of what she had guessed. The doctor sat behind a desk of extraordinary messiness. He was the same young man who had examined her weeks back, run her through murmuring machines, took samples of her from disparate spots with that long, pinching needle. He was dark, with deep-set, quiet eyes. Grace liked his eyes. She saw her own headlines echoes there. There were words, of course, too, offered gently, with regret; smooth, hard, scientific words too heavy to carry that dropped like river stones onto the messy desk between them. What else could he offer? A scheduled return visit, a prescription for pain pills, a mention of hospice, an unspoken acknowledgment of the shortness of time. Grace caught herself nodding, her head trembling slightly. She held herself still. The doctor asked her if she had any questions. She looked into those gentle, dark eyes. There was a question, the central question of her life. He could never guess, never help her with the answer. *What about Baby?* She shook her head, rose from her chair. "I'll figure it out," she told him. "I've been doing it since I was tiny. It's my job."

The answer came to Grace while she waited at the only stoplight in the village. Pain tugged in her belly. She glanced at the prescription lying on the seat next to her, glanced back at the red light. "That's my

6

pancreas," she told the warm interior of the Buick. "I was right about that."

She had been right about many things, right about her sister, Baby, right from the start. She had freed Baby, cared for her, raised her even, though Baby was the older of the two. They were tied together, Grace and Baby. Different minds, matching dresses. A complicated knot, thought Grace, of love, hurt, frustration, bodily functions, and a good amount of fun, to boot. They were a history; their endings intertwined. She looked again at the prescription, the thin, white slip with the doctor's scrawled orders. Overhead, the light turned green. Grace stared at the prescription, noticed the slant of the doctor's letters, the roundness of the capitals, blue ink, not black, his signature, a jagged line with three slashes through it. Certainty settled inside her, a gentle weight that rested on, and perhaps even eased, the pain resident there.

Behind the old Buick, a polite tooting sounded. Grace checked her mirror: three waiting cars. She peered up at the light, saw it change from yellow to red. It was too late; she was committed, already moving. She proceeded through the red light and on her way.

Baby would not eat the pudding. Not even the whipped cream helped. Grace wondered why she had thought it would ever be easy. Baby loved lemon pudding. She loved yellow in all its forms. But not this yellow. She had taken one taste and pushed the bowl away. "Augh!" she announced and pushed the saliva and pudding out of her mouth with her tongue. The mess slipped down her chin and plopped onto the wood table. She fixed Grace with a hurt, bewildered look and kept working her tongue, pushing bitter saliva out. It caught in the slight fuzz of her chin, then dripped to the table.

"Baby. Shame on you." Grace furrowed her brow. "Go on. You love lemon pudding. Yellow."

"Augh!" Mouth still open, Baby made the same noise and furrowed her brow back at Grace.

"Stop that racket." Grace stood and crossed her arms over her heavy breasts, leaned over the table toward Baby, pressed a scowl into her features. "You eat that pudding."

Baby heaved to her feet, too, crossed her arms, pulled all the lines in her face down and stared down at Grace. In her housedress of faded pink flowers that matched Grace's exactly, Baby was a furiously drawn enlargement of the original. "Augh."

Grace felt her control slipping away, her plans scattering in black dots before her vision. Grace sucked in air. She reached over and spooned the pudding, thrusting it into her own mouth and swallowing. "See!" She gagged. "It's good! Now you eat every bit of this pudding. Don't make me come around this table and make you!"

Baby took the spoon, scooped the mixture, and threw the spoon and contents across the room. Grace stepped back, upsetting the chair, which fell with a loud smack. Baby recoiled at the noise. Her own chair crashed backward. The kitchen echoed. Butler shot out from beneath the table and fled the room. The hard lines of Baby's face dissolved, and she began to shake violently. "Brown," she moaned. "Brown, brown, brown, brown." Repeating it over and over, she scrabbled to pick up the fallen chair. She clattered with the chair to the corner of the kitchen, smacked it at an angle against the wall, and then stood it there. Intent, she rushed back to snatch another chair.

"No, no, Baby." Graced watched the frantic, trembling movements helplessly. "Baby, it's OK. Please. No more pudding...no more pudding." The last chair Baby culled was the one lying on the ground behind Grace. Grace stooped to stop her. "Baby. Baby! Please. It's OK. You don't have to do this. Please!"

Baby jerked the chair from Grace's grasp and scuffled back to the makeshift pen. With the last chair scraped into position, she sealed herself in and slid down to the floor behind her construction, a puddle of faded pink flowers, flesh, and tears. "Brown," she sobbed, hands over her ears, eyes lost behind misted glasses.

Grace came over and collapsed into one of the chairs, slid her fingers through the laddered back. "Baby. Baby." Grace wiggled her fingers so that Baby would notice.

Baby watched the fingers, her vision blurred by tears that welled and slid over the tight, fat cheeks of her face. Finally, she reached out with both hands and clasped Grace's proffered fingers through the bars of the chair, across the long-remembered barrier, the ancient hurt…"Brown."

"Shhh. I know, Baby. Everything will be OK. I'll make it OK," Grace murmured. *How?* "Brown," Grace whispered, and she and her sister nodded together.

Grace put Baby to bed, taking comfort in the rote motions. She took out Baby's dentures and put them in the cleaning solution, brushed the remaining teeth way in the back on the top, and helped Baby use the toilet. She helped Baby struggle into her nightgown. The gown's blue nylon periwinkles stretched, blooming over Baby's tummy. Grace walked her to bed and tucked her in, turned on the nightlight on the side table and the one on the dresser.

She clumped into her own room and closed the door against the hall light. She slid between the sheets, noticing a slight relenting in the tight fist of pain in her stomach. That bite of bitter pudding had been worth something.

The door creaked open. Baby stood there, solid, undeniable against the light. "Andy?"

"Tomorrow. Go to bed now." Baby remained. "OK, come on. Shut the door." Grace sighed and pushed herself over. The mattress eased under Baby's weight.

After a minute or two, the door nosed open again. Butler padded in low to the ground, executed a surprisingly agile leap onto the bed, circled twice, and flopped over, rabbiting Grace with his squat legs to make more room. "Butler," Baby, still awake, informed Grace.

"Yes, indeed," Grace told Baby. "What a day. Oh, well, always tomorrow, huh, Baby? Sleep tight." She was too tired to go shut the door. She lay there, listening to Baby's sudden snoring, Butler's sighs. Beneath her the bedsprings groaned. She wondered how it carried all their weight.

Grace's first memory is of the cage. She is four. Behind the double-gauge chicken wire, a pair of blue eyes just paler than Grace's own look back. Older eyes, yet younger.

"Gub," the girl in the cage says.

A tiny blossom opens in Grace's mind. The world is full of wonders. "Mama, Baby just said my name."

"Nonsense." The woman thrusts the red wool hat onto Grace's dark curls. The hat is so far down on Grace's head, her eyelashes are pushed into her eyes. A red wool scarf is winding tightly around her neck. Mittens attack her hands. The kitchen is moist and warm from baking bread and bubbling soup. Grace struggles up from a sea of red wool.

"But—"

"Outside."

Grace is pushed into a world that is white and chest high. She can hear her brothers and sister laughing and calling off to the left. A snowball thumps the wood of the screen door near her ear. "Gracie, over here. You're on my side!"

Later, her cheeks matching the red of her scarf, Grace stands before the cage. She puts a wet mitten against the chicken wire. The girl inside reaches out, touches the red. "Gub."

Grace is yanked away. Mama whacks the frame of the cage with her heavy, metal spoon. The kitchen vibrates with the blow; the wire zings. The girl in the cage recoils. Grace, blinking from the moist, narrow space between hat and scarf, watches her ten-year-old sister's face break apart, dissolve.

TWO

*I*n her periwinkle nightgown, Baby sat at the kitchen table drawing on her pad of paper, crayons at her elbow; Butler, as always, on her toes. Morning sun slanted through the kitchen window and down onto the table. Behind her hunched back, on the wall where Baby's pen once stood, was a mural, one of Baby's: an exact replica of the view from the window across, but in vivid shades of magenta and lime green. Baby rubbed her nose and showed her pad to sunslant, to window, to sleeping Butler, turned to show mural, then pulled it back, and, glasses almost touching the pad, she continued her faces. She mumbled to herself, nodded, drew, and waited for Grace to come in from the barn to feed her eggs.

These were Baby's colors, her people. She knew the weather or the mailman's mood in browns and blues, in reds and greens. Yellow was the best. A yellow day was sunshine, silly chickens, and cool, prickly grass under her seventy-six-year-old feet. Yellow was Sheriff Andy Griffith and *Get Smart*. Maxwell Smart was yellow, yellow, yellow. Agent 99 was not. Baby was jealous of 99. It was plain that Agent 99 loved Baby's Maxwell Smart. Every time that 99 used her soft, wheedling voice on Max, Baby would sit up in her chair, cross her arms, bristle, and fume. Agent 99 was brown, worse than brown. Andy Griffith was pink, soft like a sweater that Other Sister Kate had once. "Keep your mitts off." Other Sister Kate was not pink.

Other Sister Kate and Larry. They had Peter, Paul, Luke, Rachel, Rebecca. Peter and Karen. They had Jenny and Mikey. Paul and Tina. Tina

11

was lost. Tina was lost with Baby Sam. Dark blue, almost brown. Rachel and Bob. Rachel got rid of Bob, but she still had Adrianne, whose hair was orange and whose heart was bright green like spring. Brother Bud and Doris had Little Bud, who was big; Callie, and Sissy. Sissy and John. They had Steven. Other Brother Bill. All alone. Dark blue. Other Brother Ted and Fay. They had Teddy, Susan, Lily, Nick, and Sarah. Teddy used to have Gail. Teddy and Charlene. Sometimes Christopher when Gail said OK. Susan and Paul. Another Paul. They had Little Paul. Another, Another Paul! Nick alone. Dark blue. Sarah loved Mark like Agent 99 loves Max. That was OK. Lily had Walter, nobody else. Lily was light gray, like morning mist hiding yellow sun. Walter had sunshine hair and water eyes and a grin with holes in it. Grace and Baby. Baby had them all. Yellow.

In the barn, Grace searched for errant eggs and put down kibble for the barn cats. The barn cats were good-for-nothings, torturing Butler the dog and holding seemingly amiable conventions with the rampant mice. Grace filled two big bowls, one with Friskies, one with the last of yesterday's milk. "Come get your breakfast, you damn, useless creatures," Grace called to the cats. She noticed two eggs nestled down in the hay and stumped over to collect them. Rising, she felt the knife-edge in her gut. The eggs rolled from her fingers and smashed at her feet.

"I have cancer," she told the cats. "I have cancer, and I tried to kill Baby last night. It didn't work, though. I bet you could have guessed that. You know Baby." Grace in the barn, with the cats cleaning the eggs from her feet, took stock. With her mind, she probed the soft, inside tissues. It was there, all right, growing bolder. Grace felt her heart beating fast, ticking like a clock. What was she going to do now? Grace felt a sandpaper cat tongue at her ankle. "We'll just have to try again, that's what. But first, breakfast for Baby," she told the sleek tabby.

The cat blinked up at her, the long, satisfied blink of a cat that has dined and is now open to other suggestions.

"And it won't be eggs," Grace told him.

Baby waited, the sunlight reaching across the table to her. Her gallery of family faces grew. She labeled them in her mind. Ted, Paul, Sarah…Baby had them all. "Lily, Lily, Lily," Baby whispered to herself.

She pulled out her crayons and sharpened each carefully in their box. She colored the faces in bold shades: sky blue, sea green, melon.

Grace came in carrying the two bottles of milk the neighbor had dropped off, still warm and frothy from the cow. "No eggs, Baby." Baby's eyes went wide, the canary yellow crayon poised over Lily's eyebrows. She dropped the crayon's front end, giving Lily a sharp question mark on her forehead, then crossed her arms stubbornly on her wide chest. "I dropped them. I'll make oatmeal. Feel. The milk's still warm." Baby turned her head away. "With brown sugar and butter?" Grace knew she shouldn't.

Baby was unmoved, behind her glasses inscrutable.

"Rainbow sprinkles?" Baby smiled. "First the finger stick, then the rainbow." Baby considered hugely, sighed, and stuck out her hand.

As Grace waited for the glucometer reading, she thought. *I could do it this way. Too much insulin…not any…*Baby hated the shots, anyway. How would it be? A slow slipping away, a sleep that deepened beyond waking? Grace pulled insulin from the vial through the slender needle. *No!* Some part of Grace revolted. *Wrong way.*

The insulin shots, the trips to the toilet, the baths, the dressing and undressing, the brushing of teeth and hair, the wipings of nose and butt, the careful, measured plying of the right foods, the daily exercise, the central tasks of her life. Like breathing out, breathing in. Stopping was unthinkable. Her job. Her. Taking care of Baby. Not doing was unthinkable. *No.* It would have to be done another way. There was time, surely. Her heart ticked in response.

Grace hiked up Baby's nightgown and pulled down her pink panties, exposing a vast hip pocked with needle pricks and mottled, bluish-green bruises. Baby tensed and moaned. "Shh," Grace comforted and slid the needle in, depressed the plunger, and pulled the needle out. She rubbed away the bead of blood and laid her hand on the hip, willing it not to hurt.

"Hooo, hooo, hooo." tears rolled down Baby's face. Baby's crying and laughing were almost the same noise, differing only in texture, in quality of air released. Grace shook her head. Baby cried every time, twice a day for forty years. She cried every time.

Grace boiled the oatmeal in the milk, added butter and brown sugar, divided it into two bowls, and then, after a brief hesitation, finished with a heaping spoonful of rainbow sprinkles on Baby's. "What the hell. Go to town." Grace plopped the bowl down in front of Baby and patted her back. "You know what you are, Baby? A tyrant. Who's going to take care of a tyrant?"

Baby stirred her oatmeal, joyfully watching the rainbow sprinkles melt in crazy-color swirls. "Hohoho," she chuckled and stuck her fingers into the streaks of yellow, blue, and green in her bowl.

"Humph!" Grace countered. The oatmeal nauseated her. She pushed it away and thought of the leftover lemon pudding stashed in the freezer. That's what she needed, she thought, a little frozen pain relief. Later, maybe, when Baby was out of the kitchen so the sight of the bowl and its contents wouldn't start her off again.

Grace reached for Baby's pad of paper. "What's all this?" Grace scanned the tiny, many-colored sketches. She recognized each face: the tilt of a head, the shape of a cheek or nose, the way a set of eyes looked out at the world. She shook her head, thinking, *Baby can do this.* Something wrong with her from birth—that's what her parents had said. *But no,* Grace thought, *not wrong...different.* Baby could do this. She was that good. She could not tie her sneakers or turn on the TV or utter a simple sentence, but she could do this. This was Baby. She had caught them all. "You're not going to see these people until the Fourth. That's a whole month. Don't you start bugging me about family."

Grace wondered briefly if one of this crew would take Baby. "Maybe this pink one here would look after an old tyrant like you. What do you think?" Grace knew the answer already. Frankly, she couldn't understand Baby's attraction. She never said a word beyond bluegreenblueblue and a few names to them, and they ignored her like a giant pimple on somebody else's nose. Don't be caught staring. Well, Grace admitted, most of them anyway. "Maybe this yellow and gray one, huh, Baby?"

Baby, her face blank and oatmeal on her chin, blinked at the sketches Grace held. She began her litany of names and ended, smiling, "Lily, Lily, Lily...Grace...Andy!"

"Andy? Who the hell's Andy? Oh, I see where you're heading. Now we're back on track, aren't we? Well, it's not Andy this morning. It's *Green Acres*. In ten minutes. So we better get you upstairs and dressed." Grace reached across the table. "Let me wipe that face."

"Green!" Baby hooted. "Green, green! Orange!" *Green Acres* was orange, like the flowers that bloomed at the bottom of the garden against the gray stone wall. After the wall were willows, greengray then white in the wind, hiding the pond. Brown water. Brown. Baby's bottom lip began to tremble.

"Orange?" Grace blurted. "Orange Acres. Whatever you say, Baby." Baby laughed as Grace hauled her up off the seat and herded her upstairs.

Grace would have been happy to give the man who had thought of a cable network devoted to old TV shows a wet, sloppy kiss right on the mouth. She suspected he wouldn't want some old bird doing such a thing, but she was willing and waiting. Space. That's what the TV Land channel was. A little bit of space throughout the day. There was waking and insulin and breakfast and dressing. Then TV. Then the bathroom and a walk, across the street in the wood and through the fields, Butler far ahead of them clearing the path. Or sometimes, for a change, they walked in town. Then lunch and the bathroom. TV. Glucometer. Then Baby fed the chickens. Then errands or maybe shopping. The bathroom. TV while Grace made dinner. Insulin. Then they sat and went over their magazines.

Grace liked the *Enquirer* with its doctored pictures and wild gossip about the Hollywood stars. Baby's perennial favorite was the *Weekly World News*. Grace had fifteen years of back issues of the defunct paper stored shelf for Baby's viewing pleasure. Baby hid her face and peeked through smeared glasses and fat fingers at the grotesque figures that appeared on the covers: *BAT BOY JOINS THE ARMY!*, *WOMAN'S CHILD HALF DOG!*, *TWO THOUSAND POUND MAN MISSING AGAIN! MR. FUR-FACE SHAVES!* Grace read her the stories, Baby nodding avidly. What a world. After the magazines, bathroom, TV, bathroom, bed. A day, a life, partitioned by Andy Griffith, *Green Acres*, *Get Smart*, *The Brady Bunch*, by Mr. Fur-face and the Two-Thousand Pound Man.

Upstairs, Grace stripped Baby, helped her into voluminous, bright blue panties and orange bobby socks, then finally hooked the old, white bra behind her back while Baby sat immobile on the edge of her bed. Grace opened the closet door with a flourish and closed her eyes. "OK, Baby!"

Baby lurched up, trembling with excitement, and with a clumsy mimicking of stealth, shuffled over to examine Grace. Baby's toothpaste breath on Grace's face. Satisfied, Baby went to the closet, peeking over her shoulder girlishly before choosing a dress. She held it up across her chest, the hanger poking her cheek. "Hohohohoho, Grace!"

Grace opened her eyes and summoned astonishment from the talcum-and-urine scented air of Baby's bedroom. "Baby! You're dressed just like me! I thought I was seeing myself! Looking right in a mirror!"

"Hohohohoho." Baby's eyes crinkled. She stomped her feet in delight, the dress moving like agitated water across her body.

"Well, we better get that on you, then. Almost time for *Green Acres*. I just don't know what people are going to think, Baby, when they see us! You think they'll take us for twins?"

"Hohohohoho!"

Grace knew exactly what people were going to think. *Strange*, that's what they were going to think. The village would never be used to the sight of two old, fat ladies, dressed identically, both pushing the shopping cart or standing at the bank window, Grace's shoulder to Baby's elbow. Sometimes they walked down Pioneer Street along the line of staid, white-with-black-shutters houses, arms linked under the oaks and maples. Butler, low and wide, strutted along on six-inch legs, the gentleman always proud to be escorting his fine old gals through town. *Look at us*, his jaunty gait said. *Aren't we grand!* People stared, or didn't, on purpose. *BAT BOY! MR. FUR-FACE! WEIRD OLD LADIES WALK LEGLESS DOG!*

Grace eased the dress over Baby's head. "You look stunning! Just beautiful. Everyone that sees us is going to say, 'That tall one, she's the pretty sister. She's the looker, all right!' That's what they're going to say!" Baby slid her hands over the material, touching each white-and-orange flower delicately. Daisies clustered down her arms, spread and bloomed hugely across her tummy and down her hips. She was a garden. The beginning of another perfect day. Yellow and Grace.

Never mention her. That is the rule. She is Our Shame, Our Cross. Grace can tell they know about her in town and at school. The kids whisper in small groups, their eyes cut across the playground at her. Monster in a cage, whispered near the jungle gym; monster, murmured by the swing set. Grace follows her older brothers and sister around, but they are used to this game. They are tough. "Go on with you." They push her away. "Go play."

The new girl wants to be friends. She has hair the color of lemony sunlight that falls all the way to her waist. Even the older boys stop to watch her brush it back from her neck. Grace figures the new girl doesn't know about Our Shame. She hasn't heard about Our Cross. Not yet. She stands in a group of admirers and smiles at Grace across the expanse of the blacktopped basketball court.

The new girl invites Grace over to her house. It smells of new paint. The new girl shows Grace all of her shoes, pairs and pairs of them. "Now it's your turn," the new girl tells Grace as they walk to the front door. "I want to come to your house." Grace's father waits in the pickup at the curb.

The new girl is persistent. Grace picks a day when they can play outside, when her mother is away at a church meeting, Ted and Bud at football practice; Kate, as always, in her room with a book. Grace shows the new girl around. The cows stink. The cats are scrawny. The piles of raked leaves might be dirty. Finally, the new girl stops in the middle of the backyard, puts her hands on her hips. "I want to see it."

"What?"

"What you have in the house. In the cage."

Grace looks over hills behind the farm, mostly gray and brown now with just a few patches of late maples holding on, offering a far-off brightness. The new girl always gets her way.

They stand in front of the cage. Baby sits against the back wall on the floor. She sways to an interior wind and gently knocks her head against the plaster. Seeing Grace and the new girl, she scrabbles forward. "Gace."

The new girl steps back. "She stinks. Worse than the cows."

"She wears a diaper."

"But she's almost grown." Her voice is outraged. The new girl turns her head away and shivers.

Baby watches the new girl's hair ripple and float in the dull afternoon kitchen. She sticks her fingers through the wires and wiggles them, trying to reach the hair. "Yeb."

17

"*Disgusting.*" *The new girl marches to the door and out into the yard. Grace follows, helpless and silent.*

In the house, Baby calls, "Yeb! Yeb!"

Grace closes the back door.

"*I want to go home now. Tell your dad.*"

At school, the new girl is huddled with the others. A mass shudder runs through the group, its wake lapping back from the jungle gym all the way to the sandpit. The new girl turns her head, looks through Grace standing off by the fence. Grace knows not to respond, not to wave or smile or blink. She is still. But inside, she hates the new girl, hates Baby. It is sudden and huge. She hates her, hates her, hates her, loves her! From across the vastness of the playground, Grace sees. The new girl flicks her river of golden hair.

Yeb.

THREE

On their walks, Baby touched the trees along the path. Sometimes she pushed a bit into the woods to reach the right tree. She had to do it. She felt each trunk, sliding her fat, soft hand along the bark, then giving each an encouraging pat, a hug. Each had a color. There were one hundred twenty special trees, just like the crayons in her Big Box of Crayons. One crayon for each tree. The color was inside, but Baby could see it through the rough bark, deep in the cracks, or glowing just below the moss-slick surface. Baby could see it just by looking. Grace never looked. So Baby told her. The first tree past the gate was *asparagus*. Baby welcomed the tree, laid her cheek against the cherry's gray, curled bark. She could see the crayon color, feel it, hear it pump up through the heart of the tree to the stretching branches. *Asparagus*. Baby patted the tree, opened her lips to say the tree's secret. "Green!" Baby crowed, her face falling with annoyance. *Asparagus*. She knew this word, written just this way, and one hundred nineteen more, knew just which sharp cone pointing up from the box was *asparagus*. She could hear Grace's voice from the very first time, the very first Big Box, enunciating *asparagus*. "Green," Baby could say. But Baby knew. The tree knew, too. Baby knew colors, the first forty-eight and all that came after, boxes and boxes. They were hers, from *burnt sienna* to *purple piazza* to the latest, *banana mania*. *Burnt sienna* was not *brown*. Grace had given her the colors and the words. Now when Baby looked around, she saw the colors everywhere, behind people's eyes and shot through

19

the sky, in the shadows on the wall, in Andy as he sat behind his sheriff's desk on TV, and even pumping up through the trees in her forest. She knew the secret color of everything, but she couldn't tell Grace. A *midnight blue* feeling.

The first Big Box. Grace and Baby at the kitchen table, smooth, round-faced Grace with crisp, black hair that turns blue in the sunlight from the kitchen window. Grace is grown up. Baby knows grown up. Grown up is to go away. Kate and Bud and Bill and Ted are grown up and go away. They come back for fireworks, bright in the sky. Noise. The other two are gone, the brown woman who owns the cage, the sad man at the table. They have grown up for good. Grace grows up and goes away. Comes back! Yellowyellowyellow. Baby stays. Baby never grows up. No color there. Now it is just Grace and Baby and the kitchen table and the box that Grace holds out.

"Open it, Baby. Go on, you can." An explosion of vivid points of color. Grace and Baby at the kitchen table, heads together, Grace pulling out each color, naming the shade. "Forty-eight crayons for you, Baby." Grace has already given Baby redyellowbluegreen. That was long ago. Then came black and white, orange. Baby has always known brown. But now all this! "Melon," says Grace, passing it on to Baby.

Melon. Baby stares at the bright cone. Melon. Baby opens her mouth wide. "Orange!"

"That's OK. Close enough," Grace says and hands her the next crayon. "Look at this one. Cornflower. Isn't that a pretty thing!"

Cornflower. Baby nods, opens her mouth wide. Cornflower. "Blue!"

"Yup," says Grace.

Baby with Grace at the kitchen table and the sun making black hair spill blue light and colors. They are close enough.

FOUR

---

race had hoped to use this walk to talk to Baby. She needed Baby to understand just a little about what was happening, about what was coming. She wanted Baby to know she wouldn't leave her behind with nothing but the TV and the unknown. Baby would be coming, too. Grace reached down into the bag that hung just inside the garage and collected two handfuls of sugar cubes for the cows in the field across the road. Grace suspected that no one had ever thought of spoiling cows, couldn't see past the dirt, the dumb stare. To most people, they were disappointing creatures. Grace approved of them. They lived by a schedule just like she and Baby did: morning milking, food, a little outing in the field, food, milking, bed. They clomped along the path with sure, accepting steps. They saw more than people suspected. Grace knew them by their markings and the look in each pair of eyes. Baby knew them by color, not a single black or white among them.

Grace hurried across the road and up the path to catch up with Baby. She could hear her calling from around the bend. "Orange! Orange, Grace!"

"Hold up, Baby!" Grace cupped her arms under her belly, tried to carry the pain and ease the jarring. Baby waited next to a stand of slender birch, her arm wrapped around a leaning trunk. As soon as Grace stopped in front of her, panting, her face pale and tight, Baby hurried to the next tree. "Wait, Baby! Wait. I need to talk to you!"

"Blue!" Baby called from up the trail.

"Baby! Stop!"

Baby waited at a huge old oak, her glasses askew, her face pressed, nose first, into the heavy, mossy bark. She sighed happily, "Yellow." She could hold this tree forever.

"Baby, listen. Stop your running off and listen to me," Grace gasped. "Things are changing for us, Baby."

"Yellow," Baby murmured.

"No. It's not yellow. It's not yellow at all. It's bad. It's going to be real bad." She didn't want to say the word, but she did anyway. Baby needed to understand. "It's going to get brown."

Baby hugged the tree tight, pressed her face harder into the bark. The tree whispered, *dandelion*. "Yellow," she confirmed. Grace was wrong. Baby waddled off to the next tree, Butler rushing in front. He knew every tree she went to. He liked to reach them first, lift his leg, and mark them so that they would be ready for her.

Grace watched Baby and Butler go. *Hell*, she thought, and followed. Never easy. Up ahead she heard, "Red, red, red!" Dragging herself up the steepest part of the trail, Grace tripped over a root and fell hard. The pain in her gut washed out from her center in shock waves. She carefully rolled over and lay staring up at a river of pale sky flowing along the trail above the sun-striped trees. She breathed carefully, waiting for the pain to subside a little. The earth turned beneath her.

It had been days since she had given up on scraping away at the frozen, toxic pudding. It was easier to take two aspirin and try to ignore the rest. There was still enough lemon pudding in the freezer to kill an ox.

Baby's face suddenly swam into the air above her. "Grace!" Baby sounded outraged. What was Grace doing? There were trees waiting.

"I tripped and fell." Grace gathered her breath. "I'm dying."

Butler, launched from somewhere, landed like a furry cannonball on Grace's chest and began washing her ears and chin. Grace tried feebly to push him away. "Ho! Butler, Grace! Ho, ho, ho!"

Grace struggled to sitting, Butler still churning in her lap. Baby lifted Grace to her feet. Grace was light. What color? *Mauvelous*, Baby thought, Grace is *mauvelous*. Grace is changing too. Baby hugged Grace. Grace held on. "I'm dying, Baby. Like Papa did. Like Mother."

Baby struggled from Grace's hold. What was wrong with Grace today? Saying those words. Earlier she had said *brown*, and now those other two words, those two names Baby had erased from the list long ago. Grace was not *mauvelous*. What color was Grace today? *Timberwolf!* "Gray!" she barked at Grace and stomped off up the trail, pointing imperiously.

Grace, with the pain still liquid and turbulent inside her and the weight of dying pushed firmly back into her own arms, laughed. Gray. There was an answer for her! What had she expected? An "I'm so sorry to hear that, Grace," a "Don't worry, I'll be fine," or better yet, "Don't worry, I'll take care of you!"? Grace hooted. She howled. She laughed so hard, the sugar cubes in her pockets rattled. Butler nipped gently at one calf. *Come on, Old Gal! What about our walk?* Grace brushed the dirt from her backside and, still chuckling, trudged off behind Baby. "Gray!" she hollered to the quiet woods.

"Pink!" Baby answered from up the trail.

The cows were waiting when they emerged from the trees into the field. The land dropped steeply in every direction. To the left, through trees, then fields, a road, more fields, the river, finally to the village and the lake. Straight ahead, the spine of the hill arced downward toward the Millers's farmhouse and barn, hidden in pines. A cow trail, deep and sure, marked the shortest path to the milking shed. To the right, the field dropped quickly through rough, open ground strewn with rocks and June wildflowers to the road and then to Grace and Baby's house, vivid in the morning sun.

This was Grace's favorite spot. She loved to stand here and look out over the land, the hills wrapped in late spring, the spires of the village churches, the finger of lake. It was worth the long climb, even lugging the cancer, the pain. This was their field, Baby's and hers. Farmer Miller rented it for his cows, paid them in milk and a little besides. Grace had always thought that if their house had been up here, pierced by the cleansing wind and open to all this view, this light, her family, Baby, their whole history might have been different.

The cows nudged closer, and Grace fished in her pockets for the sugar cubes. "Greenbluepurpleredorangeyelloworangeredpurplebluegreen."

Ten rainbow cows. Baby chuckled. *The Partridge Family* was rainbow, too. "Partridge!"

Grace snorted, "Sure, Baby." The cows' empty udders swayed as they jostled for position. Grace handed out their treats. Every fine morning was Halloween on top of the hill! "That's it. That's it. That's all there is, girls. Go," Grace told them. The cows stood still and blinked at Grace. "All right, then, you ignorant beasts. I'm counting to five. If I were you, I'd get a head start." The cows placidly held their ground, running their tongues around their mouths to trap the last of the sugar. "Butler," was all Grace needed to say.

Released, the squat corgi shot at the cows. In response, they rolled their eyes in mock surprise and wheeled like planets lurching and changing course, scattered, and trotted off, tails high in offense. Baby clapped and laughed at the show, the streaking rainbow cows split like a prism.

"Cows..." Grace shook her head. "They never think ahead, do they?"

Think ahead. The words seemed to hang in the air and shimmer in the sun. *Things are going to change, Baby*, she had said in the woods. Grace breathed in the view and allowed her vision to darken. *Is that what it will be like*, she wondered, this slow, deliberate blotting out until there was nothing to focus on, no light, no color? Grace shut her eyes tight, then opened them. Her vision brightened before her. First, Baby's wide back, resplendent in dark pansies and tiny red rosebuds, then their field, steep, rocky...beckoning. Now? Grace's hands moved on their own, inched up toward Baby's back. Oblivious, Baby watched a van crawl along the road. "Blue," she murmured.

Grace's hands were out in front of her, her palms suddenly moist with intention. A quick, sharp thrust, that was all it would take. *Watch out now, Baby! You be careful, you could break your neck.* How many times had Grace said that? Grace's whole body trembled. She took a deep breath, tensed to push.

"Grace! Grace! Ho!" Baby was pointing, excited. "Blue! Blue!"

Grace's hand dropped, useless, heavy with guilt. The blue van had pulled into their driveway. "Now, who could that be?" Grace gasped, shaking.

Baby squinted, pushed her glasses up her nose, squinted some more. Out of the smear of blue, two small figures emerged. Baby concentrated. Little smudges of movement. Baby could see their colors radiate. Light gray, like morning mist. *Pearl*, that was the tall one, and the other, the little one, that was easy. "Yellow! Gray, yellow! Gray, yellow! Lily Walter!" Colors coming! Baby let gravity launch her. She lumbered down the hillside, a floral-print boulder set loose. Barking and nipping, Butler raced in tight, tense circles around her chaotic path.

"Baby! Baby! Slow down! Be careful, you're going to break your neck!" Grace hustled to catch up, to catch Baby, if need be.

From a safe distance, the rainbow cows watched and chewed.

The first word.

Grace is sitting at the kitchen table, staring out the window. Fall colors on the hillside, sunset behind. Fifth-grade math, long division, too much work. Behind Grace, Baby roams restlessly, endlessly, the precincts of her pen, rubbing a head and shoulder against the back wall, trailing fingers along the chicken wire with a sound of far-off running feet, then back to the wall again. Finally, she stops at the wire and holds on. Her jaw works. "Grrraaace..."

Grace blinks at the transformed scenery, a rupture of hues. She turns and stares at Baby. "What?"

Baby's jaws tense and chomp. Saliva collects at the corners of her mouth. "Graaace." Baby grins wetly.

This is all that Grace sees, all new: Baby is tall in her cage; her smock is too short for her and tight; she has breasts. When? Baby's hair is black, like Grace's but finer, thinner, not so curly. There is a large baldness across one side just above the ear where Baby rubs her head along the back wall. Why? Her blue eyes are smiling; so is her mouth. Somebody needs to brush Baby's teeth.

"Graaace."

"Yes," Grace agrees and jumps up to tell the world. She meets her mother pulling grocery bags from the pickup. "Baby said my name. Plain as day."

"Just your imagination," Mother says. Her lips are tight. "She's as God made her, Grace. Leave it." Mother stuffs escaped celery and cauliflower back into a brown paper bag. Her strict fingers keep the vegetables in line.

"No," *Grace calls back as she runs toward the field across the lane. "Plain as day! Now we can let her out."*

Grace charges up the hill to where her father is bringing in the cows. She follows him. "Papa, Baby said my name! She said Grace!"

Papa clicks his tongue at the cows; the cows, understanding his language, begin their slow, solid, careful progress down the steep slope. Milking time. From the crest of the hill, Grace watches him go, the last pink rays of the sun illuminating his back, his hat, slipping away. Grace stays at the top of the hill, watching the last of the color drain from the sky. She knows she has been chosen. From all the others, from the whole family, Grace has been chosen.

Why?

She gathers creamy Queen Anne's lace and black-eyed Susans, stocks of blue chicory and tall sprigs of golden grasses, adds two brilliant maple leaves. She will bring the outdoors in. For Baby.

FIVE

ily stared up at the glowing face of her aunts' house. Amazing. Just as she remembered it. Every Fourth of July, a reunion at the many-colored house, with Grace and Baby like twin, fat Buddhas with their accepting smiles. Lily looked down at Walter, standing open-mouthed and unbelieving at her side. *Please*, she prayed to Buddha, prayed to her aunts. *This has to be the place for us.*

"I told you. Can you believe it, Walter? They did it, your aunts. Do you remember it at all?" Walter shook his head and stared. He felt shrunk, as if he stood before a giant children's picture book, open and beckoning. He could step into the picture and become part of its color. His eyes darted over the face of the house. There was much to see.

The house was painted as a mirror image of the field and hill across the road to the west. It was Grace and Baby's field, edged by woods, the deep greens of the grasses dotted by minute specks of flowers: lupine, dame's rocket, Queen Anne's lace. Off to the left, a tiny group of black and white cows grazed, a few heads lifted and staring. *At me*, thought Walter.

Above the hill, a sunset was painted, a most amazing sunset. Layers of colors arched through the sky and were lost in the eaves. Flocks of miniscule birds sailed across clouds so saturated with pinks and corals, they threatened to sink under their own weight. The more Walter looked, the more he saw. The white patches on the cows reflected the

27

hues of the sky. At the edges of the painted wood, minute faces of animals peeked out at him and seemed almost to whisper. Some of the trees held secrets, too, their dark bark slowly yielding to some jewel-shaded heart.

"Isn't it the coolest thing you ever saw, Critter?" Lily breathed in, as if to pull the picture in through her lungs and hold it there. She smiled. It was like the best high in the world, the one she'd missed. Lily gave a harsh, quick laugh and looked around. "I wonder where Aunt Grace and Baby are?"

Walter turned to the field, a sunny, tepid reflection of the house. Two gray-haired women, fat and wobbling in matching dresses, negotiated its slope, an impatient black dog darting around their ankles. Walter pointed. Lily squinted, took a deep breath, prayed again. Let them be the same, just the same.

Lily is in the doghouse. She is tall for seven and hardly fits. It smells. The dog is old and not making it to the grass in time to do his business. Lily doesn't mind the smell. She is concentrating on the pain. She can feel pinpricks along her cheek and on her bottom, twice. Her mama's slaps, administered in front of everybody at the reunion. Lily picks at the scabs on her knee and suffers.

Aunt Grace squats outside. "You in there?"

"I'm bad."

"You're going to smell bad if you don't come out. What happened? I was in the kitchen."

"I punched Paul in the face."

"Why?"

"He's mean and ugly and gave me an Indian burn on my arm." Lily adds this pain to the others.

"Sounds like he needed to be punched."

"Mama says I'm straight from the devil."

"Hogwash."

"His nose bled."

"Good."

Lily smiles a little in the doghouse but remains.

"*Here comes your Aunt Baby. Let's ask her if you're from the devil. Baby, is Lily from the devil?*"

Aunt Baby laughs her large Christmas laugh and thrusts a fat arm into the doghouse, wagging an orange daylily in Lily's face. The stem is mangled from pulling. "*Lily!*"

Lily takes the flower, giggles, then sobers, remembering the slaps, the humiliation. "*I'll never leave the doghouse.*"

Grace rests back on her haunches. "*You know, I was a terrible trial to my mother. As bad as they come.*" *She can sense Lily's listening.* "*Look at me now. I've got this place and Baby, a stinky old dog, and you to visit me on the Fourth of July.*"

"*Were you from the devil?*" *Lily is skeptical.*

"*Worse, I suspect.*"

"*How?*"

"*I was just myself. That's the worst.*"

Lily's head peeked out the doghouse. "*Me, too.*"

"*Come on, then. I need a Lily-type girl to make lemon frosting for my angel food cake.*"

"*Yellow!*" *Baby crows.*

"*That's right! I dare you to take a big bite, Miss Lily. Only real devils choke on angel's food cake.*"

"*You're on!*" *shouts Lily and bursts from the doghouse.*

Later, full of cake and the glow of fireworks, Lily climbs into her parents' car. Grace and Baby are large, moonlit faces at the window. Lily rolls it down.

"*Wheeuue, you smell like that doghouse.*" *Lily offers a sleepy smile.* "*You coming back next year? I'll clean up the joint a bit for you.*"

"*Will you be here?*" *Lily whispers.*

"*Always.*"

"*Then I'll always come back.*"

SIX

---

*g*race couldn't figure out how Baby knew it was Lily and Walter. She couldn't tell who it was herself until she and Baby were practically standing in front of them. Her own sight wasn't much better than Baby's. It was Lily and Walter, all right, utterly changed. Four years since they last wandered through. Time was obviously harder on some people than on others. One thing, Walter wasn't just a little mite anymore. *He must be at least eight by now,* Grace thought. Grace looked him over. She'd never seen a child so still, so tense and patient at the same time. He was like some forest creature, she thought, waiting in the shadows for danger to pass, ready to melt away.

And then there was Lily. Lily was thin. Grace could almost see the dark blood flowing through her veins, the air that expanded the bones of her chest. Her head had been shaved not so long ago, and if she was lucky, the black stubble might look like a crew cut in a month or so. All they had was a small backpack that Walter still carried and an army surplus duffle bag with the unlikely name PVT. ARNOLD T. McCORKLE stenciled on its faded side. They looked like a couple of concentration camp survivors. Survivors come home.

"Look what the cat dragged in," Grace remarked. Lily was quiet, waiting for Aunt Grace to process all that was in front of her, waiting for the sentence. She had been in this spot before. "The family reunion isn't for almost a month." Grace, standing sturdy in her housedress, had her arms crossed over her chest. She didn't really want any more refugees.

"We wanted..." Lily stumbled. "We hoped maybe you would let us stay. We'll probably be gone before they come."

"Huh," Grace commented, thought: *Can't face them.*

Baby noticed changes, too. On a mission, she stomped indoors. Grace, Lily, and Walter stood quiet and blinking in the sun, the house glowing behind them. Across the road, the cows collected against the fence to watch. They nudged their heads against each other. Baby came back with her sketchpad, came back to show Grace the changes. Where was Lily's hair? Where was Lily's Walter? Agitated, Baby shoved the pad at Grace, pointed with a fat finger at her most recent Lily and Walter, his small, yellow face, hers smoke gray with that yellow question mark bright on her forehead from when Grace had not made eggs. Oatmeal with rainbow sprinkles. Different.

"I know, I know, Baby," Grace soothed. "People change, they grow up. That's all. It's OK." To Lily, she said, "Have you been to your parents'?"

Lily looked away, down the empty road. "They wouldn't...I just thought..."

Grace held her breath and looked down at Walter. She decided. "You look old enough to have your own room," she said. Walter nodded. "You'll have to talk to Baby about colors. Baby, it looks like we got some painting to do."

Baby nodded and thrust her sketchpad at Lily, pointing heavily with her finger. "Lily Walter," she stated with disapproval. She reached out, rubbed Lily's head.

Lily laughed. "Make a wish, Aunt Baby." She took the pad from Baby's hand and cupped her fingers around the sketch of her face, obliterating the black hair, leaving the pale, gray-shaded face with its odd question mark. "See? Still me."

Baby compared. Yes. "Lily," she agreed. She moved on to Walter. The two of them looked at each other, presented with a creature they'd never seen before. But Baby remembered sunshine hair and water eyes and a smile with holes in it. Baby remembered Walter's color. Where had it gone? "Yellow?" she asked.

Walter thought yellow was nice, but if he was going to have his own room at last, he knew what color he wanted. "Blue."

Baby nodded, understanding something had happened. Sad. Walter was blue, *midnight blue*. Baby put her arm around him. Walter stood very still. Baby smiled down at Walter. She would share her yellow days. "Maxwell Smart?" she asked. "Marcia Brady? Andy?"

"Sure," Walter said, and they headed off to the house.

"What's with the hair?" Grace asked.

Lily was stooping to heft their duffle bag. "We were living in the city, and things weren't so hot. I messed up…they said…I wanted to clean up. I went to stay at this Buddhist monastery in the Catskills." Lily smiled. "So quiet there. For a while, I even thought I'd become a nun. I wanted the…" Lily couldn't find the word for what she wanted. She had wanted a different reality, one not needle based, one that you didn't wake up from groggy and crying to dream again. What did you call that? "I shaved my head. But, in the end, I went back to the city. It was all the same, the same people, the same…things. So we came here, Aunt Grace. To you," Lily ended with a coaxing smile, hefted the duffle bag onto her shoulder, let one slender arm hang.

"What about Walter?"

"What?" Lily stood very still.

Ready to run, Grace thought, and knew where Walter had it from. "Where was Walter all through this?"

"With me," Lily began. The weight of the duffle seemed suddenly terrible. Her hands trembled. Her voice dropped to a whisper. "Foster care."

Taken away, Grace thought. Lily hadn't been doing her job.

"I got him back when I said you'd take us in."

Grace stared hard at Lily, at the thinness of her, at the shuddering breath that moved her body like a leaf in the breeze, at her pale, tender inner arm puckered with scars. Wounded, Grace thought, punctured. Lily and Walter were wounded. Baby was wounded. How many ways were there to be wounded? "You're here now." Grace took the duffle from Lily and moved toward the door.

"You look different, too, Aunt Grace," Lily murmured at her side.

What the hell, thought Grace, and said, "I've got cancer. I'm dying."

Lily stopped. She felt some part of her rushing away, heading for the street and the trees on the other side. Run. Hide. Her breath, her voice, fled. Grace watched Lily struggling just inside the front door. From the family room, she heard Baby. "Hoho! Walter! Max, 99." Baby's voice changed, a sliver of bright green jealousy there, "99, Walter. Brown." Grace laughed, a single, soft, accepting humph. Here they were, all the brown things out in the open: Agent 99 and cancer and death and drugs and not doing your job. Foster care in the many-colored house.

"Don't get worked up about it, Lily," she grunted. "Let's just get you settled in. So you're Buddhist?"

Lily suddenly smiled. "Sometimes."

"What for?"

Lily shrugged. "Lots of things. For me, it's letting go of the past and the future, living in this moment…" She wanted the words to impress.

"Has that worked for you?"

Lily hesitated. "It's not easy. You have to practice."

"Hogwash."

"No, Aunt Grace. It's a way to avoid suffering."

Grace wondered, *Can you do that?* She grunted, "Sign me up." She led the way into the kitchen. Past time for Baby's lunch, Baby's insu-lin, Baby's trip to the toilet. Living in this moment, this task. Grace's religion.

"It's all about suffering," Mother says as she dishes out oatmeal. "Life is about suffering and sacrifice. Bearing your cross." The oatmeal is overcooked and drops with singular intent into each of their bowls. In her cage behind them, Baby rubs her head along the wall and hums without tune. Baby doesn't get oatmeal. Baby eats alone in her pen, simple, different foods that don't require a spoon or fork. Baby is a cross.

"Suffering, sacrifice, and just maybe, redemption. Let us pray." Mother sits and grabs Grace's hand on one side, Bill's on the other. Grace sticks a finger out for Ted, in his highchair, to take. Papa, in from the barn and smelling of cows, takes Ted's other hand, then Bill's. Older brother Bud and sister Kate, grown, have escaped the circle of sacrifice and prayer at the kitchen table. Does that mean they are redeemed? Grace wonders and stares down at the hardening mass of breakfast.

"Dear Lord Jesus—" Mother begins. Baby hums and rubs. Mother stiffens. "Dear Lord Jesus," Mother begins again. No redemption for Baby.

As Mother prays, Grace calculates how many Blue Chip Stamp books it will take to get the lamp. Grace saw it at the redemption center. The base is painted "copperesque"; the shade is fuchsia, with silky tassels that hang down all around the rim. Grace imagines how the light will glow through the shade and wash her bedroom with color. She imagines the feel of the tassels on her skin as she runs her fingers through them and watches them sway in the light. Two thousand stamps for a sassy lamp. Two thousand stamps means twenty books. She is halfway to redemption.

"Amen," Mother intones. The family echoes, but not Grace, hovering beneath the hot pink hope of her lamp.

"Grace." Mother's voice is sharp. Grace looks up from oatmeal. "I don't believe you have been praying one bit. Are you to be yet another cross for me, Grace?"

Yes, *thinks Grace. She shakes her head.*

SEVEN

"You might as well come down from there," Grace told the cats. Cat eyes blinked down at them from the moldering hay in the loft. "Come on down now and meet Walter," Grace called and bent over to pour kibble from the box into the big bowl. She felt the thickening inside prevent her middle from bending enough. Pain. A soft sibilant seemed to whisper through the barn, slightly shifting the still hay. *Cancer.* Grace straightened, handed the box to Walter. "You do it."

Walter poured the kibble, and crouching near the bowl, waited.

Stillness in the barn.

"They don't like me."

"They don't know you. Negotiation. That's all we need." Grace fished in the big pocket of her apron and pulled out one of the eggs they had gathered. She handed it down to Walter. "Here, crack that onto their chow and watch what happens."

Walter cracked the egg on the cat food, broke the yolk with his finger, and stirred the egg all through the food. He sat back on his haunches, one hand dripping, the other cupping the fragile shell halves. Cat eyes watched. The hay trembled. A bold-eyed calico emerged, hesitated at the edge of the loft, then launched into the sun-streaked air. Legs splayed and tail up, she landed in loose hay and disappeared. "Wow," Walter whispered.

The calico emerged and slunk halfway to the dish, where she stopped to clean a spot on her leg. All around, cats erupted, slipped

like shadows down the narrow stairs, sailed from the loft into a waiting pile of hay. The calico, faced with competition, hustled to the
bowl. Crouched and still, Walter felt the cats weave around him, the
touch of their fur on his calves and across his knees. He watched as
the cats arranged themselves around the bowl. There was no squab-
bling, no clawing or spitting; just a polite nudge, a delicate step
aside.

The calico was first to finish and approach Walter, stepping up to
sniff the eggshells. Walter held his breath. A raised paw adjusted the
shell. The cat stuck her nose in and began to lick. Walter could hear
a faint echo of rasping tongue. Another joined them, tested Walter's
hand with a touch like the brush of eyelashes, and began to clean his
fingers. The rest of the group swarmed, smelled, rubbed his haunches,
stood on back legs to examine his face. Walter, suspended in joy, felt
the tender press of cool noses, almost weightless paws. He heard Grace
chuckle above him. Without moving an outward muscle, he raised his
eyes. "I did it," Walter breathed.

"Negotiation," Grace confirmed. Watching Walter, she felt a slight
easing inside, an almost infinitesimal shrinking of the mass in her mid-
riff. She wanted to reach down and touch his head. *I wish...*the cat
tongue seemed to say against the fragile, opalescent shell's curve. For
just one moment, Grace held it in her, a sharp, new desire to linger,
to stay. "OK, you fool creatures, that's enough. Walter and I got to
get Baby her breakfast." The cats paused and blinked, continued their
explorations of the boy. Grace stomped her foot lightly. Cats flowed
away, tails high and twitching. "He'll be back," she told them. "Come
on, Walter. Your Aunt Baby's going to be wondering where her eggs
are, and I have a doctor's appointment."

Walter watched the cats' retreat, waited while they chose perfect spots to sit and clean whiskers, ears, the crevices between toes.
He stood reluctantly, then suddenly flung himself at Grace, putting
his arms around her tender middle and hugging hard. Grace didn't
know where to put her hands, settled on tense, thin shoulder blade,
soft, golden head. *I wish...*Dust motes danced in bars of sunshine. The
heavy, warm, wanting smell of hay was everywhere. Grace cherished the

urgent press of the chicken eggs trapped in the apron pocket against her belly as Walter squeezed. Let me in. *I wish...*

"Humph." Grace expelled a long breath, then, her voice firming, "Oh, that old Aunt Baby," she told the top of Walter's head. "She's going to be hollering any minute now, 'Where's my damn eggs!'" Walter lifted his head, raised his eyebrows. "Honest," Grace said.

Walter grinned and took Grace's hand. They walked out of the barn into the yellow day.

"I fed her peanut butter on toast. And milk." Lily stood at the sink in one of Papa's flannel shirts. It just brushed her pale knees. Her feet were bare except for toe rings, two on each foot. She sipped her coffee.

"Baby likes eggs for breakfast," Grace told her. "Breakfast's my job."

Lily, shrugged. "She had peanut butter."

Grace bristled. "Peanut butter doesn't agree with her dentures. Did you put jam on it? She's a diabetic, you know."

"No jam. She liked it," Lily said into her mug.

Spoon suspended over his Cheerios, Walter watched Grace and his mom. They hadn't learned to share the bowl yet, not like the cats. From the front room, he heard Gomer Pyle: "Golleeeeey!" and Aunt Baby's "Hohohohoho."

"It doesn't agree with her dentures," Grace repeated.

Lily was silent.

On the way to the doctor's, Grace stopped off at the village library. She checked out all three of the books on Buddhism and, tucking them under her arm, headed for the hospital.

The clinic waiting room was empty. Grace settled in and opened the books. She didn't know anything about Buddhism except the image it conjured of a statue, cross-legged and straight-backed. Grace wriggled and sat up a little. The Buddha's face was always calm beneath its shaved head, calm and certain, with that soft, bronze glow of some inner knowledge. Grace usually didn't have any truck with religion. Nothing more than empty words for most people. It caused more trouble than it cured; at least, it had in her own house. But now, Lily was a "sometimes" Buddhist, though Grace had seen neither calmness nor certainty in her.

Lily was like some fragile, frantic bird batting itself against its cage, then frightened when it was free. Grace had watched the stubborn, relentless struggle between Lily and her parents, knew where Lily had finally flown. Grace knew about cages, too, seen, unseen. Was something in these books a key to this pale, wild child now grown, still lost? Grace opened the first book.

After twenty minutes, a nurse came out. The doctor had been called up to the ward. Could she wait? Grace nodded and read. Another forty-five minutes, and the nurse collected Grace, put her in an exam room, helped her with the gown and maneuvered her onto the exam table, patted her arm and left. *She thinks I'm feeble,* Grace thought with irritation. "Don't worry. I won't melt away," Grace told the retreating nurse.

Grace blamed it on her pale pink panties. She no longer filled them. Under the open-backed gown, they visibly drooped off her hips and hung down against her thighs in pale pink puddles. Grace hadn't seen any sense in buying new ones. She wouldn't be around to wear them out. As soon as the nurse left, Grace slid down from the table, collected her books, and climbed back up. The room was too cool. She was suddenly grateful for her panties, tugged them up to cover as much of her as they could. She read. After fifteen minutes, Grace was pretty sure she had the gist of it. Patience. Compassion. Giving in. Grace took another two minutes to think it over. "By God," she said and snapped the book shut. The exam room echoed.

The door opened. Doctor and nurse stepped in.

"Hah!" Grace announced to her audience. "I've been doing it for years!" She chuckled, pleased. She was feeling downright holy in her ancient underwear. No, "holy" wasn't the right word…oh, yes…

The doctor and nurse paused, smiled, uncertain. "Come on in. I don't bite. I'm feeling *enlightened.*"

The doctor took Grace's books from her and shuffled through them. "I see you're exploring spirituality, Mrs. Carrier." His eyes were dark and gentle, encouraging. *There he goes again,* Grace thought, *calling me missus.* She stared at him, worked on her compassion. "Exploring

spirituality. You know, finding religion? Many patients do. It's very...
normal."

"Why?"

"Why is it normal? Well..." the young doctor stumbled over his
words a bit. *Poor thing*, Grace thought. "Well, they want to understand
what's happening to them, I...uh...I suppose."

"Bargaining," Grace corrected him. Grace thought of the cats in
the barn, Walter with his fingers in the food. *Come here, let me feed you,
you'll like me, you'll be my friend.* Life wasn't as easy to fool as a barnload
of cats. She could have told this young man that her own mother had
tried striking deals with every religion available in town until, at last,
she had settled for one in a hundred-year-old school house up in the
hills where they rolled in the aisles, immersed themselves in the icy
river—howled at the moon, for all Grace knew. *Please, God. All this for
you. A little for me...please.* "Good luck to them," she told the doctor.

The rest of the exam was conducted in silence. The doctor helped
Grace back up to a sitting position at the edge of the exam table,
checked the whites of her eyes and her fingernails, put her hands back
into her lap. Grace noticed his shirt cuffs were frayed. "It looks as if
there might be some liver involvement starting."

Grace nodded. The doctor and Grace were quiet together for a
moment, each feeling sorry for the other.

"It won't really be necessary to come back here, unless there's a
crisis of some kind," he told her, his voice soft, gentle, a cat-like nudge.
"We'll set up palliative care. Hospice can come in."

"I have someone."

"They may need help."

Grace nodded. Negotiation. Silence settled in the cool room.
"How long?" she asked him, finally.

He hesitated, "It's hard to say..."

She had to help him. "I want to make it through July Fourth. I have
some things to settle."

Three weeks, he calculated silently. "I see no problem with that."

"Good." *Time*, Grace thought, and felt the tug of an icy river. No
bargaining there.

"Good," the doctor echoed. "How are your meds doing, your pain pills?"

Grace opened her mouth. She could feel the words rising from her throat in explanation. She closed her mouth, shook her head. "All out."

The doctor was already writing her another prescription. When Grace left, she forgot the books.

Grace is sitting at the kitchen table in the dark, drinking a long, cold glass of orange juice. She is hoping it will keep her head from spinning. She had been at a kegger, not her first. Grace smiles. She is thinking of Buddy Leitletter's arm. Buddy Leitletter's arm sure has a mind of its own. First Buddy had just stood next to Grace. Then his arm had kind of lifted up and out while Grace and Buddy had stared at the bonfire. Then the arm had draped itself across Grace's shoulders. Grace giggles, thinking of it. Buddy's arm wasn't done yet, though, oh, no. It sort of stretched and stretched. The fingers came down, down, down the front of her sweater, searching, finding, touching. Grace had watched sparks shoot up in billows of smoke into the black, icy night. Thinking of it, Grace feels like she's rising with those sparks right now, right here at the kitchen table. Carry me away, *she thinks. She doesn't hear the pickup pull into the driveway.*

Baby comes slamming through the house, howling. She is dripping wet. Grace is so stunned by the apparition, she nearly falls off her chair. She hadn't even noticed Baby wasn't in her pen. Baby rushes through the kitchen, flings open the door of her pen, throws herself in and pulls the door closed behind her. She stands holding the chicken wire tight with wet, blue fingers. "Hooohooo," through chattering teeth.

"Baby! Shush, now! What's happened?"

But now, Mother is in the kitchen. Her dress is dripping, too. She carries a towel. She clicks on the light. "Oh, Grace, I'm glad you came down. We have to get her dry." Mother tries to pull the pen door open, but Baby is pulling so hard, the tips of her fingers are now white.

Grace is flooded with relief. Mother doesn't know she's been gone, doesn't know about arms and fingers and sparks. She joins Mother at the cage and works to pry Baby fingers from the chicken wire. "Gracie! Gracie! Hoohoohoo," Baby howls and holds on.

"What's happened? Did she run away? Why are you all wet? It's not even raining! Baby, let go!"

"She's saved, Grace!" Mother's voice is ecstatic. She yanks rhythmically at the pen door handle. "She's saved! Open this door!"

Grace is sickened. The floor seems to slide beneath her. She lets go of Baby's fingers. "What did you do? What did you do?"

"I took her to a meeting. We laid her down in the river. We bathed her in the blessed river. Preacher prayed over her and washed her clean! She's saved!"

Grace feels her stomach turn, feels the beer and orange juice rising. A stupid choice, beer and orange juice. She closes her eyes, struggles, feels icy sweat break out on her forehead. "Hooohooo. Gracie…"

Grace opens her eyes. She reaches for the towel draped over her mother's straining arm. "Let me do it. Stop. Stop! I'll dry her." Mother steps back. "It's OK, Baby," Grace soothes. "Let's get you dry."

Baby lets Grace into the cage. Baby is shivering so violently, tiny beads of water fly from her smock and tangled hair. Grace peels clothes up and off Baby's stiff, vibrating body. Baby's arms stay sticking straight up, even after Grace has taken the wet smock and thrown it out of the cage. Grace gently tugs the arms down, then undoes the pins of Baby's diaper. The diaper and its brown, soggy mess drop to the floor.

"Jesus," Grace breathes.

Mother paces the kitchen floor. "Yes! She's saved, Grace. Saved! Everything will be different now. Different…" Her eyes are wild, dancing, green strangers.

"Get dry, Mother. Go to bed," Grace answers.

In the night kitchen, Grace towels Baby's naked body, uses the damp towel to clean her bottom, pins up another diaper, and slips a nightdress on her. Baby, quiet now, throws her arms around Grace and holds on tight. Grace can feel the coolness of Baby's skin through the nightdress, her own sweater and bra, clear through her own skin to the soft tissues of her breasts. Grace closes her eyes, thinks of Buddy Leitletter's arm, a mind of its own, thinks of hands, of fingers. Please, she whispers to the sparks and smoke, carry me away.

EIGHT

ily stood at the back of the wobbling kitchen chair, using all of her weight to anchor it. "If you fall, Aunt Grace will kill me."

Baby looked down at her, brush paused. "Lily. Lily gray. Yellow!" Baby smiled. Baby's dentures were loose, clattering softly when she talked.

Peanut butter, thought Lily. "Just be careful."

Baby chortled, a deep gurgle in her throat. Her head thrown back, body solid with concentration, she added the finishing touches to the star. "Yellow," Baby whispered to the deep blue ceiling. The star winked at her in response. She smiled, satisfied. In a moment, she would point to another spot on the ceiling, Lily would ease her off the chair, and they would move to begin again. While Grace was out doing errands, they were putting the last daubs on Walter's room.

It wasn't what Walter wanted, not exactly. Days ago, at the paint store in the village, he had pointed at the dark blue chip. Baby had pulled out a card and pointed at a glowing yellow. Walter pointed at the blue, Baby the yellow. Grace's and Lily's heads swiveled between the two. Walter pointed; Baby pointed. Walter crossed his arms; Baby crossed her arms.

"My first room."

"Yellow."

"Blue."

"Yellow."

"Won't go in, then."

"Yellow!"

"Blue!"

"Walter." Lily sounded annoyed.

"Baby, it's Walter's room," Grace chimed in. Lily and Grace stared at each other.

"Take the yellow and the blue and something in between, and see what you come up with." The paint lady's voice was squeaky with panic.

"Ha!" Baby exploded, lunging for the paint lady and hugging her fiercely. "Ha!"

After that, it had been easy. "Whatever you want, Aunt Baby," Lily shrugged when it was time to pick the colors for her room. Baby already knew: green and plum and pale, pearly gray.

Baby had started with a sunburst yellow at the baseboards of Walter's room and then began adding white with each trip around the walls. Grace had watched from the bed, shaking her head. "He wanted it blue."

Baby ignored her, worked at blending the lines of color with a dry brush. Lily stepped in to help. When the walls had reached a level of almost white, Baby began adding blue. With exaggerated casualness, Walter wandered in, sat next to Grace, wandered out. By the time the color had reached the ceiling, it was a deep, velvety blue. To Grace on the bed, it felt as if the room was suspended in that moment when morning lifted the blanket of night. But Baby was not finished.

Lily and Baby stood back to admire their work. Baby's arm engulfed Lily's shoulder; Lily stretched an arm behind Baby and gathered to her as much pink-polyestered flesh as she could. Together, they looked up and nodded. Stars sprayed across the dark ceiling, and paler, down the lightening wall. High up in a corner, a moon looked down with Don Knotts's familiar bulging, thyroidal eyes, lumpy nose, and wide smile.

Walter came in, hands deep in pockets filled with cat food. Baby pointed at the moon. "Barney, Walter."

Walter looked and laughed, his fingers running through secret kibble. He nodded. "Good," he pronounced and left.

"Yellow," Baby corrected his retreating figure.

"Blue," Walter's voice echoed from down the hall. Lily grinned and hugged her aunt.

The shading was reversed in Lily's room. Starting with a deep plum at the baseboard, the walls rose and lightened through shades of mauve to an almost translucent gray at the ceiling. Sprouting in great bunches from each corner, Baby had painted long-stemmed lilies with tall, sword-sharp green leaves and blooms the same opalescent shade as the ceiling. Lily swore she could smell them each time she stepped into her room. She loved the room with an intensity she had not felt in a long time.

In the mornings when she woke, she immediately felt the tug of the ceiling, a sensation of rising, rising, her body joining the pearl mists above. She knew this feeling, just after the needle's plunger was depressed, just as the stretched, knotted rubber around her biceps was released, an icy stream tracing the course of her vein. The bones of her head expanding, escaping. That feeling. No, no, she would tell herself. This was better, safer, better. She would let the hands that clutched the sheet and held her to the bed relax, let go. The room carried her.

Painting finished, Lily and Baby were engrossed in *The Brady Bunch*. Standing in the doorway, Walter rolled his eyes. He hated those guys—stupid, smiling kids with their dumb parents and their dumb, stupid, smiley lives. "Can we watch something else?"

"Hey, Critter." Lily smiled at Walter. "What? Not watch the Bradys? You must be crazy! This is a classic."

"Stupid."

"Greg," Baby pointed and leaned a little closer to the TV.

"Stupid."

"Critter, go play or something. Walk Butler. You're interrupting our viewing pleasure here."

"Stupid."

"Marcia!" Baby breathed reverently. She groped for Lily, briefly squeezed her knee. "Marcia, Lily!" Baby reached out, ran her fingers down the screen, along the lines of Marcia Brady's straight, long hair. "Yellow." She turned to Lily. "Yellow."

Lily grinned, "That might be your glasses, Aunt Baby. They're covered with spots. Here, I'll clean them." Lily peeled the thick lenses from Baby and headed for the kitchen.

Walter's head swiveled to follow Lily. "Where are you going?"

"Jesus, Walter!" Lily's voice was sharp. "To the kitchen to wash Aunt Baby's glasses. Where do you think? You need to stop this!"

Walter waited until he heard the water in the sink, and then he walked over to Baby and stood in front of her. She looked different without her thick glasses, her whole body soft and defenseless, her eyes weak and worried, as if she couldn't quite see the edges of the world and she might fall off any second. Walter leaned over and put his nose right to Baby's. "Can you tell who I am?" he whispered.

"Walter." Baby smiled. Her breath was sweet. "Yellow…blue?"

"That's right," Walter told her. "Don't worry. She'll be right back."

Grace came back with two bags of groceries and her weekly magazine. She gathered a well-worn World Weekly News from the pantry on her way to the front room, where a viewing compromise had been reached in the front room. Walter, Lily, Baby, and Butler were all engrossed in *The Road Runner Show*. Butler had managed to insinuate himself into Lily's armchair. He was wedged between the side and Lily's thigh, feet up and splayed, neck stretched, head lolling down over the front of the chair. Lily hummed absently, scratching his neck and chest and the tender crevices under his squat legs. Pleasure-drunk and upside-down, Butler grinned. Every time the coyote went off a cliff or exploded, Baby screamed, "Aaack!" and smashed her hands over her clean glasses.

Walter sat at Baby's feet, smack in front of the TV. "Wile E. Coyote, Aunt Baby," Walter pointed. "Say Wile E. Coyote." Walter peeked around Baby at his mom and Butler. He watched her hand sift through Butler's fur, Butler's chest rise and lower in a long sigh.

"Aaack!"

Walter focused on the TV. "Wile E. Coyote, Aunt Baby. And that's Road Runner. Meepmeep! Road Runner." Grace clumped in, waving her magazines. Butler couldn't even wag his tail. "Aunt Grace! I'm teaching Aunt Baby to say 'Wile E. Coyote' and 'Road Runner!'" Walter piped from the floor. The TV lit up briefly.

"Aaack!" Baby smashed her hands over her glasses.

"Sounds like you're getting somewhere, Walter!" Grace turned to Lily. "I was asked twice in the pharmacy and four times at the market whether you had come to live with me for good. This village is just filled with busybodies! Look at this." Grace thrust the magazines in front of Lily. "Brittany Spears stole some woman's body! A drag queen's! Imagine!"

Lily stopped humming, focused on the *Weekly World News* cover. She grinned. "That explains a lot."

"And see here!" Grace punched the other cover with a finger. "That poor actress got dumped again. Ol' Oprah is binging, too!" Grace shook her head, chuckled.

"What a world," Lily laughed.

Grace looked down at Butler. "Shameless womanizer!"

"He's my boyfriend." Walter looked at his mom. And at Butler.

"Come on, Baby. Let's get some food in you." Grace stomped off to the kitchen.

"Oh, Aunt Grace," Lily called after her. "We ate lunch. Leftover soup from last night." Lily waited, ready to wince.

"Did you take her to the toilet?" Grace hollered from the kitchen.

Lily made a face at Walter. "No," she hollered back.

In the kitchen, Grace nodded, fumed. "What goes in has to come out!" she boomed. "Come on, Baby! Let's pee!" *Oh, well,* Grace thought, giving in. She'd be a sometimes Buddhist, too.

Meepmeep! Crash! Boom!

"Aaack!" Baby hid her eyes.

After dinner that night, they all remained at the kitchen table, illuminated in the circle of light from the fixture above. Walter used

Baby's crayons. Watching Walter made Baby's fingers itch. They mirrored the motions of his hands on the empty tabletop in front of her. Walter frowned. She tried to squish her hands between her thighs, but it was too tight down there. Where? Where could they go? She sat on her hands and sighed and rocked. "Blue. Green. Green. Orange." She recited each color he used.

Walter frowned and chose a different color.

"Pink," Baby mumbled.

"I read about Buddhism while I was waiting for the doctor," Grace told Lily. Lily lifted her eyebrows. "I liked it. No bargaining with God like the others."

Lily nodded, "No, all the bargaining goes on inside." She was drawing a trail of purple spirals across her napkin. "That's where it all takes place, anyway." Lily looked up and smiled. "You know, Aunt Grace? I think you're a little bit Buddhist yourself."

"Sometimes," Grace commented tartly. "So, who won the argument? Inside you?"

Lily shook her head, drew her unraveling spirals. "No one, yet." She looked up. "What did the doctor say?"

"In the liver, now."

Run away, run away, the voices whispered to Lily. She crumpled her napkin, tossed the crayon down. "Come on, Walter. Bed."

After Lily and Walter left, Baby's hands flew out from under her bum. She bent to grope for crayons under the table. "Blue. Blue. Red…"

"Oh, leave it, Baby. I'm tired."

Lily and Walter lay on his bed, looking at the stars on his ceiling. "Aunt Baby sure does love you."

"I like Aunt Grace the best."

"Why?"

Walter considered. "I like the way she talks. She talks to cats. They listen to her."

"She expects it," Lily commented dryly.

"I think you guys need..." Walter groped for the word, "negotiation." Lily laughed. Walter hesitated, then told her, "I like it here." His voice was small in the big room.

Lily, gazing up, noticed how Walter's bedside lamp made the stars overhead shine with an aching brightness. Beyond the circle of light, they dulled and were lost. Only the whites of Don Knotts's nervous eyes, far off in the corner, offered a sight glimmer in the darkness. *Run away*, they said. "Well, Critter," Lily sighed, "just don't get too used to it." Her voice was small, too.

"I don't. I try. I'll go where you go." Lily closed her eyes for a second, then rose to leave. "Mom?"

"Huh?"

"Don't call me Critter anymore, OK?"

"Why?"

"I don't want to be one anymore, not here. I want to be different."

Lily looked down on her son. "Good reason," she whispered, and left.

NINE

*B*aby waited in the blue night, *pacific blue.* She heard Lily go to bed. She heard Grace brush her teeth and flush the toilet. She heard Butler jump onto Grace's bed and sigh and settle. Baby waited. She heard the house make ticking noises, like small, green bugs, *pine green,* with red legs, *wild strawberry,* looking for their homes. Baby waited. Then she creaked out of bed. She shuffled down the hall and peeked at Lily…Walter…Grace. Butler lifted his head, lowered it. Baby went downstairs, hesitating on each step, letting the step complain *red orange* words. In the kitchen, she snapped on the light, blinked. Then she started to work. On her knees, she collected the scattered crayons and put them on the table. She pulled out a chair and sat down.

Grace heard Baby on the stairs, heard the kitchen chair scrape against the wood floor. *No,* she thought and tried to hold the groggy, pill-induced sleep inside her. *I won't get up…I'll wait and see…What's she up to?* Butler jumped from the bed and clicked down the hall. Grace heard the thumpthumpthump of him down the stairs. *Just a few more minutes,* she bargained silently. *Please…*

In the kitchen, Baby surveyed the table. The crayons were a mess. *Unmellow yellow* was next to *orchid*! She fingered the tips. Walter didn't sharpen! Baby shook her head. That was OK. All the colors were Baby's. She could sharpen them. She knew just where they belonged. Butler clicked in and laid down on Baby's feet, sighed hugely, as if saying,

What I do for my ladies! Baby smiled and wiggled her toes under Butler's soft belly, a *periwinkle* tickle. "Blue Butler," Baby mumbled.

Baby sharpened. She sorted. *Neon carrot* next to *wild watermelon*, *mulberry* next to *fuchsia* next to *purple pizzazz*. She knew which colors argued, which ones liked to be near each other. Colors needed to get along. Every crayon in its place. *Don't worry. Baby will do it.* Baby was in charge.

From behind chicken wire, Baby keeps track of Grace's young-girl colors, watches them come like sunlight into the kitchen. They expand. She breathes them in. In the night, she listens. Colors pound at the cage of her chest. Let us out. Let us out. Colors want to be everywhere. Colors are all. Colors are Grace.

TE N

Lily in the garden. Peonies in white, pink, rose; delphiniums in blue and cream; cranesbill geraniums a purple blush below. Lily saw a *becoming* in the flowers. She wanted to roll in them, cover herself with scent, color, possibility. Butler did roll; then, dusted with pollen, he lay on his back in a fit of undignified sneezing, feet twitching from the quakes. Then, up and off, a streak of black and tan trailing yellow and Lily's laughter. "Aunt Grace," Lily called. "Your gardens are amazing!"

"Not mine," Grace told her from the back porch where she sat, feeling the sun along her arms and down her front, searing the polyester paisley.

Lily came up to join her, arms full of peonies. "Somebody took a lot of time, once."

"Not me. Mother." In Grace's voice, the hardness of stone.

Lily did not know what to say. She pressed her face into the peonies. An ant walked from a bud to her cheek. She laughed, let the ant crawl across the bridge of her nose, onto her fingers, and then placed her back on the bouquet. "You should have kept them up, Aunt Grace. They're glorious."

Grace contemplated the memory of her mother, pink gloves and white straw hat, kneeling in her faded housedress among the rich, brown beds. Smiling, singing hymns, talking to her plants. *Nurturing.* How much easier it had been for her to prune and mulch, to train errant tendrils, than face one retarded child, the weed in the family. A sour taste rose in Grace's mouth. She considered another memory: Mother escaped, felled by a heart attack in the rose border, hat askew, a solitary petal on her cheek. *What was the color of that rose?* "Not worth it," she told Lily.

"Well, I will, then." Lily grinned and turned to take the peonies indoors.

Grace watched Lily's retreating form through the screen door. "Just don't get so wrapped up in it you forget about Walter."

Lily paused at the sink, scissors ready to snip stem ends off. "Don't worry," she said from the sink. Her words were for herself.

Grace humphed and let the back porch sun sink into her skin. Cold, always cold these days.

Lily took over the garden. It was better than any drug she had tested, better even than budding Buddhism. She marveled how her fingers knew what to do, which green shoots to encourage, which to rout. Something passed down from her grandmother? Lily was used to accepting people's hand-me-downs. As is. She found tools and an old push lawn mower in the shed, sharpened each with the same careful precision as Baby her crayons. The job before her was enormous, inviting. She remembered Grace's warning and enlisted Walter. Aunt Grace would see.

"What do you do with it," he asked, eyeing the resurrected mower. "You push."

They took turns, first Lily, then Walter, then both together. Their arms pressed against each other, they exchanged sweat. "This is great!" Walter proclaimed, ecstatic with nearness.

"Yep." Lily smiled.

Baby wandered out between *Green Acres* and *Get Smart*. She walked through the new-mown grass, beside the beds, naming colors, watching Lily and Walter separate clumps of iris; thin, golden arms all the same. Walter and Lily wrestled in mauve shade under the oak, Lily holding Walter down, tickling his tummy with her prickly new crop of hair. Grace, sun bleached on the deck. Somewhere, the orange squawk of chased chickens. Butler *hot magenta* today! Baby raised her arms to the bluewhite sky. "Hohoho!" Better than TV.

She rushed indoors for her safety scissors. On the way back out, she clumped on tiptoe past Grace, who might be dozing—*wisteria* dreams. Back in the garden, she massacred the lemon lilies, then clomped over to thrust them at Walter. "Yellow!"

Lily mourned the severed blooms. Walter looked into Lily's deepening eyes, held his breath, felt the weight of the garden resting on frail stems. "First flowers from a girl," he told her, blushed.

Baby pointed at his cheeks. "Pink!"

"I didn't think it would happen for years." *Practice. Let go.* Lily's smile is a sad release.

Lily sold bouquets of flowers and spare eggs at the farmer's market and bought two birdfeeders and a set of large chimes. From beneath the oak, the chimes sent out soft, deep tones that vibrated through the garden and were carried off by the breeze. The days settled into her, the feeling of place, its tastes and smells, its safety. She wanted to stay. This residence of memories. Lily lay under the oak, hearing a familiar call to worship.

Lily lies on the cot listening to the gong call them to zazen. One, two, three distinct waves of sound push through the monastery. A slipping of bare feet passed on the flagstone hallway, the sighing of orange robes, like wind through the trees. Here we go, *Lily thinks. Her feet are already curled and cringing before they reach the icy floor. It is so early, the hills are black, the air blue and thick with dew. Lily breathes in, coating her lungs in cold. Misery.*

They circle the Zendo. Chant. Around and around. Lily has tried to memorize the words. They are thin, like the miso soup served at breakfast, and run through her, leaving her as empty as before. Zendo, zazen, koan. Things to do, places to be. A new language for a new me, *Lily thinks, circling the room, her body warming with movement.* "Each Peach Pear Plum," *her mind chants. Cheeseburger. Double pattie. Walter's face rears before her, stopping her in her tracks. Orange robes slip by, murmur. Walter's grin laced with fast-food cheese, chewed burger visible through the holes.*

The chanting stops, and the others move to their cushions. Lily stands alone, suddenly notices, scuttles to her place on the floor. Meditation. Sit up straight and gather the world's sorrows to you. How? Lily smells cheeseburger and bacon and Walter's sweaty-boy tang as clearly as if he were curled in her crossed legs, tucked beneath her chin. Her stomach growls. Lord, I am so hungry, *Lily grieves in her mind. She breathes in, filling herself with the sharp Walter-smell and sends this prayer out over all the collected suffering in the room, across the hills, down the quiet river, to the city, along dark streets and into a gray, group home bedroom lined with cots, heavy with the breath of sleeping boys:* Wait. Wait. I'll be better. I'll be different. Just wait. Soon it will be you and me and double cheeseburgers. *This will be Lily's chant.*

ELEVEN

The flowerbeds and grass in order, Lily attacked the thick willow bushes at the bottom of the gardens, just beyond the low stone wall. She thinned the dead wood, discovered beyond the masking silver of the tall willows the pond with its water—dark, secret, beckoning. Suddenly, the symmetry of the garden was obvious, the arrangement of beds meant to frame this view of mossy wall and water. Lily headed for the shed and the loppers.

"Leave those willows just where they are!" Grace hollered from the porch, then came jolting down the slope of lawn and gardens toward Lily. Her heart thudded, a great rent had been opened, exposing what had been covered, carefully hidden. "Just stop right there!"

Lily watched Grace's charge, perplexed, willow leaves caught in her spiking hair. She dropped the loppers to catch her aunt. "There's a beautiful pond."

"I know," Grace gasped. "I know it's there. Baby doesn't want to see that pond."

"Why ever not?"

"That water's brown."

"It's clean, you can tell." Lily pushed aside the willows. "Look how it reflects the sky. The spring probably just comes up through peat. It's beautiful, Aunt Grace."

Grace turned her back on the pond, but still its remembered image rose before her: pulling Baby's limp body from the dark, fractured water, the peaty mud sucking at them, the cry for help, no response from the one on the bank. Her new nurse's uniform had been stained the color of strong tea, and that's not all that had been lost. She crossed her arms over her chest, set her face in heavy, disapproving lines. "Dangerous."

"Walter knows how to swim."

"Baby doesn't, and she doesn't want to see that pond, either."

"She will. Everyone will. When they see—"

Grace turned on Lily, her voice acid. "So that's why you're doing all this. They're coming. You think they're going to change their minds about you? Think this'll get you out of the doghouse? Think again, girly." Grace stomped back toward the house.

"That's not why I'm doing it!" Lily yelled. "I don't care what they think! Or you! I'm doing this garden for me...I'm doing it..." her voice trailed off. She felt a withering. Lily grabbed the loppers and began desperate chopping.

"Just don't count on them," Grace muttered, lugging her pain and anger up through Lily's garden. She had sat too long in the sun. The pond, the shock of its reemerging darkness, had reminded her. *Baby*. Something yet to do.

In the hayloft of the barn, Walter, strewn with purring cat bodies, heard the raised voices, buried his head in calico fur. "Moms and aunts are complicated," he told a pair of greengold eyes.

Baby clutched family portraits and crayons to her breast and watched from the window as her sister stomped on green grass through pinkyellowbluewhite flowers. She watched the willows fall, a glimpse of dark water emerge. Brown. Baby turned her back on the day.

They were coming...family...Ted and Fay. Suddenly, Lily's sometimes Buddhism wasn't enough. Flowers were not enough. She needed her music, needed it like a drug. She began to sing. Weeding in the garden, she sang to the tenacious red sorrel that spread through the flowerbeds. She loved almost anything old, the blues of Nina Simone and Billie Holiday, Bing Crosby crooning to the moon, but mostly, Frank Sinatra. Frank had never steered her wrong. Frank was her man, he and the others the only thing she had taken the day she left home for good: all of Ted and Fay's albums.

Among the weeds, her mom's voice rose with hers, unbidden: "It had to be youuu…" *It had to be youuu…* Her mom standing over the stove, singing through cigarette smoke and stirring something tan. Crouched over the flowerbed, Lily sent that voice packing, switched songs, switched singers. "Why don't you do right, like some other men do…" Lily sang off-key and, working her thin fingers through the loamy soil, she eased a mass of roots and tossed whole sheets of sorrel to the side of the bed. The last of the season's blackflies dive-bombed, struggled in the dark, new bristle to reach skin and blood. Lily ignored them and sang, "Get out of here, and get me some money toooo!" Once she let the music out, there was no stopping it.

The closer the family reunion came, the more Lily paced, weeded, sang. Grace's words, *You think they're going to change their minds…*whined, the sound of insect wings inside her head. Baby flipping through her portraits, reciting family names, "KateLarry. PeterKaren. JennyMikey. PaulTina, Tina blue, blue, blue. Rachel…" sent Lily rushing outdoors. She paced in the barn and watched Walter jump from the hayloft into the huge pile of loose hay. She sang beneath her breath, "Folks criticize me anyway…" watching Walter launch himself again and again. He called the game "the Flying Cat." Lily had no idea why. She watched without seeing, paced, broke into full-fledged song. "If I take a notion to jump into the ocean, ain't nobody's business if I do…"

Walking through the woods, she sang to Butler, "You're my thrill…" He loved it. She was driving everyone else crazy. Except Baby. Baby and Butler.

"Does she always do that?" Grace asked Walter, wincing at "Luck Be a Lady Tonight" blown inside by the warm breeze. Grace and Walter, trailing Baby, retreated from the back porch to the kitchen, but it was not far enough. They watched.

Lily among the flowerbeds and tunes.

Baby smiled and patted her tummy in time to Lily's song. *Electric lime* words danced around Lily's head. Beautiful. "Greengreenyellow," Baby explained.

Grace shook her head. "That's no excuse for torturing the flowers."

"She's nervous," Walter whispered, his face tight and frightened. "She sings when she nervous."

"Why's she nervous?"

Walter shrugged, stared out the window. Nervous was not good.

"Why are you nervous?" Grace asked Lily when she came in for lunch.

"Nervous? I'm not nervous."

"Walter says you sing when you're nervous," Grace informed her.

Lily looked at Walter. Walter looked at his plate. "I'm not nervous," Lily told him, then turned to Grace. "I just miss my music, that's all."

"What happened to it?"

"It's back in the city. The box was too big to carry. I was traveling light. It's probably still at my old apartment."

"Maybe you should get it. Anymore caterwauling and the chickens will go off their feed." *CHICKENS MASS MURDERED BY TERRIBLE TUNE!* Grace grinned.

Lily's head shot up, a thought bursting in on her: *Go back. Go back, just for a while. Maybe through the holiday. New York on the Fourth of July. No family reunion. No Ted and Fay.* "I could, just for the music. We can't have those chickens upset." Lily grinned, sensing an easing of dread in her head, a tightening of excitement in her chest, a tingling in her fingers. Weeds lifted from soil, roots and all. "Yes," Lily breathed, nodded.

Walter shook his head at Grace. His shaggy, blond hair flew out, his eyes large, intense, imploring. Grace watched them both, looked over at Baby, who chewed and chewed and leafed through her drawings, reciting family names garbled with chicken salad. With Lily and Walter gone, she could...Grace weighed possibilities. When they came back, if they came back...this could all be theirs...a home for them...Grace's gaze returned to Walter. A spray of new freckles anointed his tanning face, eyes so blue, so...She wanted to be with them. A little longer, just a little longer...

"We'll all go." Grace looked around, caught by her own words. She felt a further relenting. "A day trip!"

"A day? That's all?" Lily's voice wobbled. Grace nodded once. Walter walked out of the kitchen.

Grace stared out the window at the barn. "You better go out there."

"He's fine." Lily hunched over her sandwich, probing the contents for slivers of celery. Her excitement ebbed; disappointment, guilt inched in.

"He is not. And you're not eating that sandwich, so you might as well go."

Lily sighed and stood up. "I'm a vegetarian."

Grace looked Lily in the eye. "You can be all sorts of things when it suits you."

Lily's laugh was sudden, surprised, bright as song in the summer kitchen. "True." She stood. "I'll go." She turned at the door, smiled at Grace. "Even a day is good."

In the barn, Walter climbed into the hayloft and buried himself in the hay. Cats sought him out, pressing themselves between him and his prickly cocoon. They breathed for him. He was still, inside and out, suspended, expecting the worst. Not Walter, but Critter again.

Lily knew he was in there. Somewhere. Despite the barn's dim, forever-waiting air, its spiraling sunlight undisturbed by breath or movement, he was in there. She could feel him. They had that connection. "Walter?"

Stillness.

"Come on, Walter. Let's do something."

Nothing.

"Let's play the Flying Cat. I want to try."

No word, but a relenting in the air. Dust circled, caught in sunslant.

"I don't know how. You'll have to show me."

A stirring of the hay, dust filtered through the boards of the loft; cats stalked off, their tails saying: *Just wait and see if we come to you again.* They would. Walter had already learned that lesson. His mother was different. He never knew for sure. He had to catch each moment, hold it tight. He stood up, looked down at her. "OK."

Lily was up the ladder and next to him in less than a minute. "You know, Walter, you shouldn't worry so much. We're doing OK, so far. Aren't we?" She turned, peeked over the edge. "Aim for that pile?"

Walter nodded, opened his mouth to instruct, to warn.

Too late. Lily, light and spare as a scrap of newspaper tossed by wind, sailed out into the embracing air of the barn, hit, rolled, flung out her arms. She sang, "Come fly with me, let's fly, let's fly away. If you can use some exotic booze, There's a bar in far Bombay. Come fly with me, we'll fly, we'll fly away!"

Walter, caught between forever waiting, forever chasing, took the leap.

From the kitchen, Grace watched bodies flying through bars of sunlight, framed in the barn. A painting. She shook her head, patted Baby on the back. "I'm beginning to feel like somebody's mother." Her tone somewhere between disgusted and pleased.

Baby winced. She didn't like that word. "Mrs. Brady," Baby corrected her. She licked her finger, used it to pick up another crumb from her plate. "Orange. Mrs. Brady."

"I wouldn't go that far."

Baby learns about mothers. Grace sits Baby on a kitchen chair in front of the box and pulls the button. A white hole at the center opens up to light, movement. Sound. TV! Baby gapes, is held from that moment on. Forever. Stay tuned. We'll be right back. These are the first, best mothers. Mothers in shades of gray, mothers in bright colors. Now, Baby knows about mothers, but she won't use that word. When it is a name it is brown. Baby uses names.

Family names: Kate Rachel Rebecca Sissy Fay Susan Not Gail Gail is no more. And Lily. Lily is one too. One is gone. Her. Grace's. Baby's. Gone. Good. Take that name away. More names: June Cleaver in an apron and Harriet Nelson and Lassie and Timmy's Ruth and that Joan from Please Don't Eat the Daisies. *Joan has Ladadog too. Ladadog Lassie Butler! Shirley Partridge and Carol Brady. Alice calls her "Mrs. Brady." Alice in an apron. Opie has*

Aunt Bea. Jethro and Elly May have Granny. Aprons! Those three sons have Uncle Charlie. Uncle Charlie wears a blue apron. Uncle Charlie is a mother.

The best mothers cross their arms across their chests and tap their toes, whose eyes smile. Mothers who ruffle hair and hug. Mothers in aprons.

Grace in an apron, standing by Baby.

TWELVE

ily did chores; she ran Grace's errands. Lily at high speed. She was feeling fine, a pink rubber band ready to fly. They wouldn't be missing the family reunion, the people, the parents. They were hosting, after all. Too important, the event held the weight of history. Habit. Lily pushed it to the back of her mind, vacuumed and dusted and focused on New York City. She sang, "New York, New York, it's a hell of a town, the Bronx is up and the Battery down…" Even one day was good.

Walter hid in the hay with cats, worried. "I don't want to go," he told them. "It's bad there. Bad things happen."

The cats received all of Walter's wishes, most of Walter's words, whole sentences, paragraphs sometimes. They listened, placed soft paws on him, soothed him. Their eyes were wise. They nudged him with noses, groomed him with harsh, pink tongues until his hair stuck out. Be like us, they seemed to urge him, know when to hide, when to pounce. He told them he had been like them, once. Critter. He told them, and they listened.

Critter knows all the places to hide. You can walk along the streets and no one sees you. You are a pigeon, a stray cat, a scurrying subway rat. Wait under the stairs, move along the dark hallway, shadow to shadow.

"Lock the door behind me and don't go out," she always calls, her voice fractured sunshine in the dull room. Then gone.

He doesn't do as she says. Never. She may not come back. He follows her, a nobody stray cat chasing her string of rainbow colors, but her strides are long, purposeful. She unravels in the crowds. Critter slips back home. Home. The back of the couch is slit open. Inside, among springs and stuffing is home and waiting. If she comes back he can hear her, listen to her voice zing through the steel springs. He can gauge her song, low and sad, high and clear with joy. It doesn't matter. He always comes out. When she is not looking. And there he stands.

"Where have you been, Critter." Her words are gathered like separate threads. She picks fuzz from his hair. Her fingers are shaking. Her eyes are deep.

THIRTEEN

The routine was the same, even on this, the morning of New York City. Toilet and eggs and cats and breakfast and insulin shot and crying and soothing and toilet and teeth and last, but best, picking out the dress.

With her back to Baby and the closet, Grace hoped for different dresses. Just today, just for New York. Besides, she was not sure the city was ready for Grace and Baby, the dynamic duo in matching polyester print.

Every Tuesday afternoon for years now, Grace had taken Baby to the village library, set her up at the toddler's table in the children's section with a pile of picture books while Grace read the *New Yorker* and the Sunday *Times* cover to cover. They expected a certain sense of style down there. Grace remembered that, too, from her own brief time in the city. Slick, sleek people on rain-wet streets. Even back then, they wore a lot of black. Smart-looking. Baby would never consent to black.

Grace shook her head and thought, no, black's not our style. Oh, but Grace wanted to wear black, all alone.

Behind her, Baby, with her happy, devious, daily smile, pulled out the aqua housedress sprinkled liberally with large white daisies and their bright pink centers. "Ha!"

Grace turned, sniffed, "That old thing? Don't you want to look pretty for the city? I was thinking about changing mine. How about

64

this orange one?" She rifled through the closet and pulled out the loudest dress she could find.

Baby's face grew blank, dissolved. She hugged the aqua dress to her tummy. She stomped her foot. Her glasses misted over.

"Oh, all right. Don't get your dander up." Grace gave in and pulled the dress over Baby's head. "*ANCIENT ALIENS ARRIVE IN NEW YORK IN MATCHING FLORAL PRINT. CITY EVACUATED! Weekly World News* would love that one, wouldn't they?" Baby chuckled and stood waiting for the next part. "You'll be dressed just like me, Baby. It's like looking in a mirror." Grace's voice hollow. She tugged the dress down over Baby's bulges.

Baby waited.

"Time to get going, Baby. We'll miss our train."

Baby waited.

Grace sighed, eyed Baby, a flowered colossus in the middle of the bedroom, stubbornly immobile. *My God*, she thought suddenly. *We don't look anything alike anymore.* Baby's dress stretched so tightly across her broad breasts and belly that the pink centers of the daisies looked as if they might pop off and fly away. Grace's dress hung in loose folds. She wasn't eating much, but it was more than that. Something was eating up her own curves from inside. She knew what. Something black. Grace was wearing black inside.

Baby had her new Walter and her new Lily and her old Grace to say the right words, to feed her and pat her and put her to bed, to always give in. Baby was expanding, filling up with excellent, yellow life. Grace had let it go too far. Like Baby, she had been enjoying this too-late gift, a house filled with voices, Walter's few words, Lily's many, that damn singing, even Baby, a new volume. Baby booming. Baby blooming. Grace reached out and took Baby's hand, examined the dimples and bracelets of fat. It was good to see, good to really notice, just this once. *I did this*, Grace thought, *and I will end it.* Soon.

Baby waited.

"You look stunning," Grace told Baby. Truth. "Just beautiful. Everyone that sees us is going to say, 'That tall one, she's the pretty sister. She's the looker.'"

Baby smiled, consenting to go.

Downstairs, Lily and Walter stood waiting. Grace inspected their clothing. Lily, humming, wore the only pants she owned and a T-shirt with a silver tiger on it. A black T-shirt, Grace noted, then amended, *with a hole on the shoulder.* Walter wore a pair of brown shorts that hung below his knees and worry between his eyebrows. "Look out, New York City, here we come," Grace said and headed for the car.

Grace argues, "But it's the Junior Class trip!"

"No."

"Mother, everyone is going."

"No."

"Broadway, the Metropolitan Museum of Art, Mother…Saint Patrick's!"

"No."

"I'm going."

"No."

Grace goes. In her smartest dress, gloves, and shoes, she sneaks out the night before. She sleeps in the barn with the cats and her alarm clock so she'll be at school by 5:00 a.m.

Tina Louise Martino, Mabel Parker, and Grace stand at a corner on Fifth Avenue and Eighty-Second and watch the city women. The women wear slim, smooth, dark dresses, gloves and hats, matching purses and pumps. Perfect. Their hair is lacquered, coiffed.

"This is the place for me!" Grace tells her schoolmates. "This is where I'm going to live. Just watch me!" Grace throws out her arms and spins. The future shines like a brand-new pair of pumps with matching purse.

At home, Baby keeps watch from behind the chicken wire, through the blue hours of night and on into the gray day. Grace will come back. Baby knows. Baby waits.

On the train, Grace checked and rechecked her big, white purse: hankie, glucometer, insulin, extra panties for Baby, a pain pill for herself on the ride home, and twenty-dollar bills rolled tight with a red rubber band. Baby checked her big, white purse: crayons, a hankie. Walter watched the countryside's bright green blur changing to gray suburbs, felt the motion of the wheels on the rails beneath him, rushing him forward on a nightmare slide. He patted Baby's knee. Her daisied dress had hiked up. He tugged on the hem for her. "Don't worry," he told her.

Baby wasn't worried. She had colors.

Lily sang, "I'm not much to look at, I'm nothing to see, I'm glad to be living, and I'm lucky to be…"

The other passengers stood and left the carriage by ones and twos.

"Well," Grace commented. "You cleared the joint."

Lily laughed, sang. Walter worried. Grace checked her purse; so did Baby.

A yellow cab was the best thing. "Yellow!" Baby crowed. "Yellowyellowyellowyellow!"

"Yellow!" Lily called out the window to the buildings creeping by.

Traffic was terrible.

"Meepmeep!" Baby hooted. They all stared. A new word. A new world.

"Hey!" Walter said, his face smoothed.

"Yellow!" Baby.

The cab swerved to a stop in front of The Metropolitan Museum of Art. "Wait," Lily commanded the driver as she pulled her aunts and son from the car. Walter didn't want to go.

"No," he said stubbornly and tried to climb back into the cab.

"Two hours, three at the most." Lily held Walter by the shoulders, ran a hand through his hair, picked invisible fluff. "I'll be back. I'll be in the lobby in three hours, Critter." She remembered too late. "Walter. I'll be back." The yellow cab carried her off, leaving Walter, Grace, and Baby on the sidewalk.

Grace clutched her purse, eyed the museum nervously. She was sure it had grown in the years since she had been here. The steps climbed like Everest, crowded with explorers in black. Grace felt suddenly old, small, sick, covered in big white and pink daises. Baby waved and waved at the retreating cab. "Yellow!" she called after it. Once it was lost, she turned and charged up the steps, setting the course.

Walter hesitated, looking out to where the cab had been, up to his aunts. Who should he follow? Who should he watch after? He caught up with Grace, took her hand, led her up the steps. "I've been here," he told her.

"Me, too," she confided. "Once. A long time ago."

There was no stopping Baby through the impossibly tall doors, across the lobby, and straight up the staircase. She could smell the paint, the colors. Stay tuned!

The guard raised his arm as she barged past. "Ma'am, ma'am! You need a..."

Too late. Baby's wide hips were swinging up the marble stairs, cutting a path through appalled museumites, heading straight for colors. "Meepmeep!" she told them, her eyes sparking behind thick glasses. "Meepmeep!"

Walter was at the guard's elbow, tugging. "It's OK. My Aunt Grace is buying buttons. Aunt Baby is..." Walter couldn't think of a word to explain Baby. "She's special," Walter finally told him. He remembered something about that from school: special kids. Aunt Baby was special.

The guard looked down at Walter, over at the line of people waiting to buy tickets and tin buttons. He recognized the matching dress handing a wad of greenbacks to the counter girl, looked back down at Walter. "You better catch up with her, then. Hard to tell what she'll do like that."

"Aunt Baby's OK. She's special."

Grace hurried, jamming twenties into her purse. The guard pointed up the staircase. Grace took time to stick a red button to the collar of Walter's T-shirt, grabbed his hand. They were off after Baby. People still stood riveted to the staircase. They eyed Grace and Walter as they passed. "Well, we won't have trouble finding her," Grace puffed.

"Nope," agreed Walter. "Meepmeep," he laughed, allowing himself to enjoy this adventure.

Baby rushed up a hallway, photographs and drawings in black and white on either side. No color. She turned a corner at the end of the hall and entered a large gallery filled with bronze statues and large canvasses. She didn't like the statues; they looked uncomfortable, their brown muscles strained as if to escape. She wouldn't look at them. At the end of the gallery, a painting stopped her. "Grace!" she said, her voice surprised. Walter and Grace found her there, staring up at the glowing painting, laughing. "Grace! Hohoho! Grace!"

"Here we are, Baby. You led us on a chase! Don't go running off again!"

Baby pointed. "Grace!"

They all stared at the painting. The girl was ample, wearing a pooling, golden skirt, a head of tumbling black curls. She looked out at the world with amused, provoking eyes that seemed to say, *Well, just what are you going to do about it?*

"Saucy," Grace commented.

"Grace," Baby nodded.

"I think she thinks that's you, Aunt Grace." Walter's voice bubbled with trapped laughter.

"Humph."

Baby nodded. "Grace," she said happily, hugged her sister, and was off.

"Hold on, Aunt Baby." Walter rushed after her.

Grace didn't rush. She stood still a long moment in front of the painting of the black-haired girl, remembering.

Yellow cab, now this everywhere color, Baby gathered it in. Still, ripe fruit laced with permanent moisture, greenredwhite. Old men looked down from velvet blackness. She put her nose so close to Rembrandt, alarms shrieked orange. Guards rushed from archways. Walter stepped forward, pulled her back. "She's special," he tried to explain.

Baby was off again, a comet with this tail: first, Walter; then agitated men in blue blazers; a growing, amused crowd; finally Grace, thinking: *We're an exhibit; they should stand us up against a wall. NEW ACQUISITION, "GRACE AND BABY," TAKES ART WORLD BY STORM!* Grace paused, smiled, followed. Not *Weekly World News;* definitely the *New Yorker.* Good for Baby.

The Impressionists stopped Baby in her tracks. She was caught where purple-green lily pads floated red flowers. A midnight castle hovered in red orange fog; a peacock stiff with cerulean pride ruled a scarlet world. Color. Points of color, splashes, dots: Baby leaned close to see them. *Orchid* next to *tangerine* next to *olive*. Alarms sounded. Walter urged Baby on. Blue blue irises in a white white vase. White clouds combed blue-green sky, swept above green-gold wheat. Baby could see the wind, reached to touch it. The room hushed. Walter was there, this time; Grace, too. "Baby!" they said together.

A man all in slick, gray leather; a pointed, gray beard; long, pale hands moved forward. "May I take your picture?"

No, thought Grace. Then, *Why Not? Put us on a wall*. "You may."

"Can I be in it, too?" Walter asked.

"Sure."

Walter stood between his aunts, holding their hands, Van Gogh's shoes overhead. "You can't do that!" three guards chorused.

Too late.

Then, wandering downstairs, Baby found the choir screen: famous, ancient bars stretching up to the tall, tall ceiling, reaching wide, blocking progress. A dark, unwanted familiarity tugged in the dim, vaulted room. Through the cage she could see a world of madonnas, on the walls in gilt frames, on pedestals around the room, each carrying their precious charge, some gold, some rich hues of earth and wood, some pale stone. Mothers. Baby blinked. She saw a deep blue flame in each of them, burning clear and true, in the babies an answering glow. Baby knew that color. *Midnight blue*. Alone. Mothers with round, soft faces looked down at their babies or out into the day with gentle, sad eyes. Babies reached for cheeks or breasts.

Baby felt colors ebb away from her, the wind white and pale-wheat gold. Brown rushed in. In a different world, midnight-blue madonnas held their knowing babies and watched. Alone together. Not Baby. Baby saw it all through bars. Mothers. She grabbed the choir screen, shook it, and howled.

Other Sister Kate sits at the kitchen table with a baby in her arms nosing her breast. Chirping noises like the birds at the window. Let me in, let me in. *Other Sister Kate is not pink, but the baby is, all in pink. That other mother, Her, Kate's mother, Grace's mother, is there, too. Grace's mother wears an apron. She sticks out her arms to hold the baby. Other Sister Kate hands the baby over when the chirping stops. "Angel," Her says.*

"She's a lot of work." Other Sister Kate smiles, buttoning her blouse.

Baby wants to hold the baby, wants to be held. She wiggles her fingers through the chicken wire, grasps and rattles it. On the other side of the screen, they do not notice her. They are not real. They are a picture: mothers and pink baby. Baby watches.

"Mother," Other Sister Kate says. "You look good like that, holding her."

That other one, Grace's mother, looks down at the bundle, smiles, says, "Oh, everyone loves a baby."

The cage rattles. Let me in, let me in.

71

FOURTEEN

*L*ily was on her way back, down Broadway, then cutting across the
park. Next to her on the black seat of the cab was the cardboard
box filled with her albums. They had been right where she had left
them, at the back of the closet of the one-bedroom apartment she had
shared with six other people. She still had her key.

Lily draped her arm across the box, sang, "Blue skies smilin' at
me..." The driver glanced over his shoulder, grimaced, pressed his
foot to the gas.

It had been a quick in and out. Clean. She had paced the streets for an
hour and a half, watched the apartment's windows for movement. Finally
sure, she had gone in, padded through the rooms, checking for stoned
bodies. Relief flooded her, no one in the apartment, no explanations to
make, no offers to turn down. But the stale air of the apartment still held
a sharp hint of incitement, want. She had clutched the box to her chest
and fled. All the way down from 135th, Lily could have picked out the
places, the faces. Stop here for a second, she could have said to the driver.
She could have pulled out ten bucks, had a fix in five minutes flat. Her
mouth was dry at the thought. She shuddered in the hot, vinyl backseat
of the cab. She tried to remember what she had learned at the monastery.
The practice: create space around the need, examine it, acknowledge it,
breathe in, breathe out. Move on. It was hard, constant work.

Instead, Lily sang, "Nothing but blue skies from now on. Blue
days..." She loved that song; loved it slow, soft, sad, the way Billie

Holiday had sung it, off-key, bittersweet. Never trust happiness. Too much had happened. Too much still could happen. Move on.

"Open invitation," her roommates laugh to her as she clears out, heading for the monastery.

"You'll be back!"

"Screw Buddha. Here's peace, right here," one says, holding up the syringe, tapping it, watching the bubble rise.

"Yah, baby," another croons.

Scott, always the first to trip, slips his long fingers over Lily's already-shaved head, then down, touching closed eyes, lips, neck, breast. "You'll be able to find veins real easy. Stay," he whispered. "One for the road."

Lily's body sways toward him. Desire still there, hunger. But Walter's blue eyes stare back at her behind her closed lids. She cannot look away. Walter, taken, waiting. She steps back from Scott, turns with a rag-doll movement. Her legs are weak, shaky, but they carry her through the door. Time to move on.

At the museum, Lily checked the box in the cloakroom, moved out into the lobby. Commotion there, alarms, a distant wailing. She followed. Nearing, she knew it had to be Baby. Only one human she knew could make that sound. Baby cried like that every time she felt the needle's prick. Lily ran. "I'm back. I'm back. I'm here!" she started calling before she even saw them.

Walter heard the voice, turned, pushed through the phalanx of blue blazers, plowed into his mother, his head finding the hollow beneath the peak of her ribs.

"Walter! Walter, what's wrong? What happened?" Walter shook his head, tried to burrow deeper into his mother.

Baby continued to wail. Amid the noise, Lily could hear Grace, her voice strained, frightened. "What is it? Baby, stop that. Let go now. Don't touch her. Baby, stop. What is it?"

Lily moved forward, Walter still clinging. The gathering crowd made way. Lily muscled through the tight knot of guards around Grace and Baby, turned to face them, herself a cornered street cat.

"Get away!" she spat. Her short hair stood out in electric, dark spikes; her eyes were fearless, mean. "You're making it worse!"

The guards blinked, backed off. Lily turned to Baby, saw Grace trembling next to her, so small. Baby had her hands wrapped around the choir screen, her fat knuckles white, sweaty, her face pushed into the bars. There were red marks along her arms where the guards had tried to pull her loose, but Baby had been invincible in sorrow. Lily glared over her shoulder at the men. "What happened, Aunt Grace?"

Grace shook her head. "I don't know. Something. She was so... then...I don't know. I don't know what..." Her voice was thin. Everything had been going so well, Baby so happy, running through the rooms of paintings. Free. Now this.

Lily put her arms around Baby, hugged her broad, heaving back, Walter pinned between them, legs dangling. "Shhh, Aunt Baby, shhh. It's OK."

Baby felt the arms around her holding tight, felt a small form pressed against her rump, squirming. She pulled her face back from the bars, saw Lily looking up, Walter sandwiched, his feet reaching for ground. Lily gray Walter yellow...Baby brown. "Hoooo," Baby cried. "Lily. Lily. June Cleaver," Baby explained. "Hoohoohoo."

"I know, Aunt Baby," Lily soothed. "I know." Lily stroked Baby's knuckles, hummed, loosened Baby's grip. Baby cried; Grace stood mumbling; the guards shifted from foot to foot; Walter held on. Lily's movements were slow and soft, her humming off-key, her eyes sad. Her heart wide open. She had a lifetime to do just this one thing. Here was a lesson; here was the practice. "I know, Aunt Baby. I know."

When she had Baby free and turned around, she took her hand and Grace's and, with Walter still stuck to her side, she led them out. Tears streamed down Baby's face, "Hoohoohoo."

Lily collected her box, led them out the doors and down the steps toward the rows of idling taxis at the curb. City people stepped aside for the two old ladies in matching flowers, one damp with tears, one shaking, confused. "Hoohoohoo." Baby clutched her big purse with its remnants of colors to her chest. Tears slid down the vinyl surface, dripped, enlarged the circle of wet on her tummy.

"What was it?" Grace asked over and over. She couldn't understand it. She held fast to Baby's elbow, wondering how a room full of damn madonnas could set Baby off. What was it? Maybe something was wrong with her sugar level. Check it on the train. "What?" grumbled Grace.

Walter trailed along behind, hollow with wonder: *She came back. She came back. My mom.* Still halfway down the steps, he watched Aunt Grace and Lily put Aunt Baby in the back of the cab.

Then it happened. He watched it all. It took less than a minute.

Lily leaned in the open front window, telling the driver to take them to Penn Station. Aunt Grace had one hand on the open back door, one foot up, ready to step in next to Aunt Baby. A dark blur exploded past, blocking Walter's view for an instant; then it was gone, along with Aunt Grace's purse. Walter's jaw dropped open. Below him, Aunt Grace spun like a patterned top on the sidewalk, her dress ballooning. She fell, the back door of the cab slamming closed. Lily turned her head, dropped her box of albums, shot off after the kid under the ski mask with the purse. Walter watched her weaving through the crowd, raised a hand, let it drop.

The taxi driver glanced over his shoulder, saw the passenger in the center of the back seat. *Jesus,* he thought, *hellofa big, old blubbering broad.* He looked around. The door was closed, the girl disappeared, the other old lady, too. "Penn Station?"

"Hoohoohoohoo."

The driver pulled into traffic. The taxi merged into the flow of yellow rushing south.

Walter raised a hand, let it drop. There was Aunt Grace laid out on the curb. Walter ran down the steps.

Lily could barely feel her sneakers on the pavement. She was fleet-footed. She had done a lot of running. Just in front of her, the kid and the purse took a sharp right into the park. Lily cut the corner, grazing an arm on the fence without noticing. She was gaining. A launch into the air. The Flying Cat. She landed squarely in the center of the boy's back. The air left him in a huge "Humph!" The purse flew into the bushes. Lily didn't care; she had her man. The purse wasn't going anywhere. She wrenched off the sweaty ski mask and flung it to the side, flipped the kid over and sat on his chest, held him by the back of his ears, pulling, pulling, leaned close to his face. "If you ever steal my aunt's purse again, I'll kill you."

The boy, pinned, couldn't shake his head. He tried. He won't steal her aunt's purse ever again. "Crazy," he whined.

"Yes." Lily sprang off his chest. "Run away."

The boy, up and gone, left the crazy woman, the purse, and the staring crowd. A man in a dark, striped suit and a bow tie gingerly handed Lily the purse. Lily's knee was bleeding, and so was a long scrape on her left arm. She did not notice. She was reborn. She flung her arms up in triumph, headed back to the front of the Met, belting out, "Fly me to the moon, let me play among the stars. Let me know what spring is like on Jupiter and Mars! In other words..." Her first song of triumph.

As Lily pursued her perpetrator, Walter pried Grace off the sidewalk. Grace was stunned, wobbly. "Where's Lily? Where's the cab? Where's Baby?"

Walter pointed first north along the park, then south toward the sea of taxis. They watched the yellow flow in silence.

"Oh." Grace watched the yellow sea ebb beyond a far traffic light. A tiny thought sprang before her eyes, hovered there, lowered her voice, rasped her brain like sandpaper. "Gone," she whispered, almost a question. She put her hand to her head. Baby belonged to the yellow cab company now. Everything solved.

Lily danced up, arms still outstretched. "In other words, darling, kiss me...Purse!" Lily handed it over, stooped to pick up her albums. "Where's the cab? Where's Aunt Baby?"

Walter pointed. Grace shook her head. "Gone," they said.

"Shit!" Lily roared, reared.

FIFTEEN

The fat old woman in the cab was still blubbering. Tears pooled along the bottom of her glasses and cascaded down her moon face. The taxi driver had never seen so much water come out of one human being. "Jesus!" he muttered, sifting in his seat, glancing forward, glancing back.

"Hoohoohoo."

"Heading home?" The driver raised his voice, waited for a response.

"Hoohoo."

"Always hard to leave the kids," the driver hollered over the awful racket. "Tough to be a mom!"

"Brown!" Baby wailed.

"Brown? Your name's Brown? Well, that's easy!" The driver tried to lighten the mood. "Mrs. Brown from out'a town," he sang and tapped the steering wheel with nervous fingers. "Mrs. Brown from out'a town!"

"Hoohoohoohoohoo!"

The driver was glad for the open windows. The blubbering streamed out onto Seventh Avenue. Heads turned. "Jesus." The driver stepped on the gas.

Baby slapped around the back of the cab, big, wet, soft, absorbing impacts.

At Penn Station, the driver yanked the taxi to the curb. The old woman in the back seat didn't seem to notice. She was caved over to the side, still blubbering. Tears streamed. "Penn Station. Eight-fifty."

"Hoohoohoohoo."

"Come on, Mrs. Brown. Penn Station. Eight-fifty."

"Brown. Brown. Hoohoohoo."

The driver peeled himself from his cab, flung open the back door, and hauled Baby out. He pointed. "Penn Station! Eight-fifty!"

Baby didn't respond. The tears slid down her face, her purse, watering her daisied dress. The driver eyed the purse still clutched to Baby's chest, reached out, tugged gently, gently. Nothing doing. "Jesus. Come on, lady. Eight-fifty."

"Hoohoohoohoo."

The driver looked around, fiddled with the metal clasp of the purse, inched close to Baby. He could feel the heat of her tears as he peeked inside. A box of crayons and a hankie. No money. He took the hankie out and offered it to Baby. She wouldn't take it. "Jesus."

"Hoohoohoohoo."

The driver hesitated. He didn't know what to do with the hankie. He mopped Baby's face, cleaned her glasses, looked around nervously. *Somebody might see.* He stuffed the wet hankie back in Baby's purse, fastened the clasp, turned and dove into his waiting cab. "Jesus." *This town!* The driver shook his head and pulled out into traffic.

Baby was no longer the responsibility of the yellow cab company. The crowds gathered her through the station doors and placed her out in the wide, gray terminal. Everywhere people, noise, movement, but Baby's glasses were filling up with tears again. She cried for the madonnas, for the mothers and babies. There was a lot to cry for. She let go, felt warm urine run down her legs.

Baby knew Grace would be brown. She knew Grace would cross her arms across her chest and tap her foot. Grace would say, "Oh, Beaver." Grace in a blue apron like Uncle Charlie. Madonna blue. Grace. Baby stood in a pool of pee and wept.

"Brown!" She wailed at the gray heaven above her.

No one noticed. Baby was in Penn Station. She was one of many. She was part of the scenery. She was not special.

Lily, Walter, and Grace careened around the back of the cab. The box of albums produced bruises, threatened death. Hindi music screamed from the front seat. "Faster!" Lily hollered through the plexiglass.

"Gone now." Grace calm, disbelieving. *So simple.*

Walter prayed to private gods. He prayed to cats: *I'll never leave you. I'll feed you every day. She's special. Help us find Aunt Baby.*

And so they did.

On the train, Lily checked her war wounds. One knee was bleeding, one album was chipped, one cracked clean through. She mourned minimal casualties, her only pair of pants, her "White Christmas." Walter sat staring out the window at the passing green, torn between thankfulness and worry. They were all together on the train, going home. *Home-for-now,* Walter amended. Had he wasted a wish? Aunt Baby had been pretty easy to spot. Walter knew there were only so many wishes, so many prayers. He was afraid he'd need them all.

Grace took Baby to the toilet and, in the rocking, cramped space, changed Baby's panties, washed her legs, wrung out her bobby socks and flushed them down the toilet. "What the hell. Easy come, easy go." Grace checked Baby's blood sugar level and gave her a shot. Baby was too tired to cry. Grace promised her something to eat from the dining car. "How about a treat. Maybe they have ice cream." Grace watched Baby brighten. "What do you know? You're not gone, not gone at all," Grace told Baby. She gave Baby a small smile.

Grace didn't cross her arms on her chest; she didn't tap her foot. She didn't ruffle hair or hug. Here was Grace, plain Grace, no apron, no deep blue flame of sadness igniting her heart. Just Baby's Grace. "Yellow," Baby sniffed.

Grace pictured Baby flowing forever away in sun-hued traffic. She let the vision go. "Not anymore." Grace shook her head at Baby. "You're mine again. Next time you run away, you better take me."

This nightly ritual. Grace is chasing Baby along the path and through the midnight trees. Grace is thirteen, Baby nineteen. The pen door is wide open in the dark kitchen. The house is asleep, little Bill and Ted, Mother and Papa, asleep. Grace's feet have whispered down the stairs and into the still kitchen where Baby waits. Grace has untied the twine and lifted the latch with infinite patience, infinite quiet.

Grace's white nightgown glows among the trees; Baby, naked, glows too. Above, the pale moon treading across the sky slips in and out of branches and watches. They are three wild things set loose. Grace takes off her nightgown, chooses a low branch, and leaves the nightgown to hang limp and still in shadow, a husk, an empty ghost of daytime. Grace sees Baby darting away into black trunks, then out onto the sloping, starlit field, hears the muffled clatter of startled cows. She calls to Baby softly, runs to catch up. There is time. The moon and Grace and Baby have all night.

SIXTEEN

*B*aby was busy, hunched at the kitchen table, nose to paper, arms blocking her drawing tablet from view. She looked up and around, squinting with suspicion. Bold strokes left the crayons in need of sharpening. The table was covered with discarded crayons she has not bothered to put back into the box. *Burnt sienna* rubbed against *purple mountain's majesty.*

"You're slipping, Baby." Grace, coming in, noted the mess, reached for the stack of papers lying facedown at Baby's elbow. She could detect hints of color from the other side. "What are you up to?"

Baby slapped both hands on the pile, scowled. "Gah!" She wouldn't remove her hands until Grace backed away.

"Fine, you old coot. I know what it is, anyway." Baby sniffed at Grace, searched the tabletop for *midnight blue*, proceeded. "More of those damn family pictures. That's what. Like you can conjure them just by drawing them. Like they'll be just the way you want them. Orange faces and blue hair. Well, they won't. Believe me." Grace, testy with pain, shifted in her seat, stared at the kitchen wall and thought: *Like they'd be of any use.*

Outside, the crunch of wheels on gravel, then car doors slammed, one...two. Laughter. "Lily," Baby mumbled to her picture. "Walter." Baby raised her head, peered through glasses at the door. Her nose was smudged green. "Yellow."

"Humph," Grace commented.

81

Lily and Walter burst through the door laden with bags. Sunlight and air eddied around them. "We're home!"

"See that. You're letting flies in."

Lily turned to Walter, grinned, "Why is it that as people get older, they become obsessed with flies?"

"Humph," Grace answered for Walter.

Walter came to stand by Grace, checking her over carefully with solemn eyes. "You're not getting older, Aunt Grace, are you?"

"By the minute, Walter. Old and sickly. One of these days, some fat, nasty fly is going to land on my food and give me germs, and I'm going to die of it." Grace scowled at Lily.

Walter turned to his mother, his forehead wrinkling, but Lily was laughing, laughing so hard the bags she carried shivered and chattered as if they were laughing, too. Walter smiled and turned back to a frowning Grace. His smile slipped.

"Don't you worry, Walter," Grace told him, her voice crab-apple tart. "It will give your mom a chance to dance on my grave…and sing!" Grace executed an exaggerated shiver. "They call that adding insult to injury, Walter."

"Well," Lily countered, "to hear you talk, that would just raise you right back up!" She turned to Walter. "Then she'd have to thank me. Now, that might really kill her."

Grace opened her mouth, snapped it shut. Somewhere down in her belly, among the pain and mess of the thing that would really kill her, there was a loosening, a chuckle forming, expanding, rising. Grace couldn't hold it down. Her shoulders began to jiggle, her eyes to water. "Thank you!" she managed between gasps. Lily smiled from sunlight and air, then reached back to close the door. "No, no, girl," Grace sighed, wiping her eyes. "Leave it open."

Walter, watching, was relieved. He could never tell whether his mother and Aunt Grace were teasing for fun or for something else, something mean. Sometimes the two of them reminded Walter of the chickens out in the yard, pecking at each other, aiming for a tender spot. Working out who was in charge. Sometimes Aunt Grace was the big, white hen, sometimes Lily. It seemed like Lily was the big, white hen more and more lately, ever since the city. Sometimes Aunt Grace cared. It made Walter nervous. Those were the times he escaped to the barn and told the cats all about it. This time, no one was the big, white hen. Walter smiled, checked the clock. "Come on, Aunt Baby. It's almost time for *Get Smart.*"

Baby's head popped up from her drawing, eyes wide, jaws working with excitement. "Max!" She smacked her latest drawing facedown on the pile, peered suspiciously at Grace, gathered her drawings to her chest, heaved up to standing, and lumbered from the room. "Meepmeep!"

Walter followed, grinning back at Grace and his mom. "I taught her that...Did anybody notice her nose is green?" Grace and Lily nodded in unison. Passing through the doorway to the living room, Walter grabbed the fly swatter from its hook. Just in case. He would kill every fly he came across.

Lily dropped her bags on the counter, began rummaging. "We found some great stuff. Organic everything. This is going to be the best Fourth of July picnic ever. Arugula!"

Grace grimaced. "Don't be trying to impress those people with arugula, and no tofu hot dogs, either. They'll put you on a spit instead."

"No." Lily shook her head. "Not this time." Grace watched Lily examining peaches with silent intensity, her long, thin fingers probing for bruises. She knew they were talking about different things. *Be tough,* Grace silently urged her. *Fight, or move on. Just leave us all in your dust.*

"Did you find anything for you and Walter to wear?"

"A pair of nice jeans and a collar shirt at the SPCA thrift store for Walter. Nothing for me. I'll just wear these." Lily's fingers brushed her painter's pants. "They're my armor." Armor protected; it hid what was underneath. She had set the bloodstain at the knee with salt water so it would never wash out. Ever. That marked the beginning of courage. She could face *them* in these pants. In these pants, she was the Flying Cat. *Don't mess with me!*

Grace didn't see the Flying Cat. She saw a torn leg in front, and in back a seat so worn, Lily's panties with their pattern of tiny telephones were clearly visible. "Their eyes are pretty sharp, girl. I better take you up to the attic. I promised you that record player, anyway."

The attic stairs pulled down from the hallway. Grace and Lily peered up through the hole in the ceiling to the dim space above. Grace thought she might hear a scrabbling. "You better go first. It's going to take me a while to negotiate this contraption. Watch out for spiders."

Lily, nimble as a monkey, skipped up the steps and found herself in a huge, open space roughly the size of the floor below. The roof peaked above her, and two deep dormer windows were cut into each sloping side. A pale green light leaked through dark tarp coverings. Walking across the floor toward the windows, Lily startled up clouds of dust around her feet and legs. Behind her, Grace struggled through the opening and sneezed. "Old and sickly. Just like I said. See any spiders?"

Lily laughed and tugged at a tarp. "Aunt Grace, are you afraid of spiders?"

"I hate a spider. Nasty."

"Spiders, flies. Don't worry; I'll protect you. I've faced worse." Tugging at the window covering, Lily thought about some of the places she had lived, cockroaches and rats big enough to carry baby Walter away, and those other places she'd lived, in her mind, where the creatures were darker, hungrier. Lily yanked hard, and the tarp came down in a shower of dust and floating cobwebs. Light flooded the attic. Aside from the dust, it was utterly neat and organized, nearly empty. Labeled boxes were stacked along one wall, a chest of drawers against another. Four extra dining room chairs lined a third wall in a precise, waiting row.

Brewing thunderheads with her feet, Grace clumped across the floor, sat down heavily in one of the chairs, sneezed at the rise of dust. "Clothes in that chest, record player over there, next to those boxes."

Lily moved around the attic, yanking down window coverings, pounding casements, pulling up sashes. She could smell the green of the trees easing into the open spaces of the attic. "This is a great space, Aunt Grace. It has possibilities."

Grace laughed. "Oh, yes. That's what this whole attic is filled with. Possibilities."

Lily ran her fingers over the boxes, read titles: Drawings '62–68. Drawings '69–75. Birth Trauma-Mental Retardation-Autism-Developmental Disorders. Drawings 76–85. Life for Baby. STUFF. "Is that what's wrong with Aunt Baby?" Lily ran her finger along the long label.

"Doctors said probably something like it. By the time I got her in, it didn't matter anyway. She wouldn't be tested. You know how she is." Lily smiled. Grace continued, "For years, I collected every article I could find on all that. I kept thinking there might be something. Something. She doesn't want that kind of help. She needs someone to give her a shot, to climb into the shower with her and wash her hair, someone to take her dentures out and tuck her into bed. That's Baby."

"She's perfect."

"You try taking care of her."

Lily was quiet, listening for that small voice. *Run away.* The attic was still with waiting. The air hung with the smell of green leaves, dust, and new sunshine, on the floor a pattern of footprints, their steps like an intricate dance. And, near the windows, the spattered spill of shade from the oaks outside. No spiders, no voice. "I want to try." She paused. "What's 'Stuff'?"

Grace smiled. "Oh, that. I used to steal everything Baby liked and squirrel it away up here. My sister Kate's favorite pink angora sweater went missing the day after she turned seventeen and was never found… my papa's navy blue dress suspenders gone right from his drawer…a little, red hat and mittens from when I was just tiny, nabbed from my mother's hope chest…your own dad's marbles, just the puries, a blue one and a green one." Grace grinned at the memory. "It was a house of mysteries. No one could figure it out."

"Why did you do it?"

"I was the only one who noticed."

"Noticed?"

"Noticed that she saw things; that she wanted." Lily nodded. She was thinking of the eyes that looked past her, through her, eyes that didn't notice on purpose. Strangers' eyes, parents' eyes. "Well."

Grace's voice was gruff. "Once you start, you can't stop. Even if you want to."

Lily moved from the boxes and kneeled in front of a squat, leatherette box, lifted the lid. "Yes! The phonograph!" She tested the needle with a finger, leaned close to read the label on the LP still on the turntable. "Souza?"

Grace chuckled. "We went through a marching phase about ten years back. I read an article on how march music stimulated the brain. Poor, old Baby. I had her marching around the house like she was training for war. Souza at ten decibels. Up the stairs, down the stairs, through the living room, through the kitchen, out the door, through the yard, around the barn, chickens scattering for their lives!" Grace chuckled again, remembering. "Never did a damn thing. Made her eat more, and she already did too much of that. Article's probably still in that box somewhere."

Lily closed the phonograph, dusted its top with gentle fingers. "Aunt Grace, you are truly amazing."

"Desperate, more like."

"I don't think you've had a desperate day in your life."

Then watch me, Grace thought, remembering the sloping hillside, the urge to push...She acknowledged the pain that revolved in her and marked the shortness of time, the job undone. "Look over in that chest of drawers. There might be something you could wear if you're not too picky."

Lily tugged open the top drawer; the sharp scent of mothballs rose to greet her. Each piece of clothing had been carefully folded in pale pink tissue, lightly packed. Lily turned to Grace, raised her eyebrows.

"Go on. Just some old things."

In the top drawer, a white cotton blouse with a round eyelet collar, a black silk blouse, low cut, a navy blue pillbox hat. Lily put it on her head, where it perched on bristle. Lily turned to grin at Grace.

"I thought I was the bee's knees in that."

"You probably were."

"Well…"

Lily pulled out a pair of chartreuse capri pants. Tissue floated to the floor. "Wow! These are great!" Lily held them to her waist, looked down. "You were so slender!"

Grace looked down at her lap, nodded. *Once and again,* she thought. "Back in style," she told Lily.

Lily was deep into the second drawer. A navy blue woman's suit, the jacket fitted to the waist, then flaring dramatically, the skirt narrow and smooth. White gloves. Navy pumps, two-inch heels, the toes cut open just enough to show a bit of cleavage. Lily lifted them up, wiggled them at Grace. "Hotsy totsy!"

Grace grinned, pleased.

The third drawer. A bright pink sweater. Blue capris and matching polka-dot blouse. A small, white cap with black piping. A nurse's dress. Lily held it up. It unfolded reluctantly, revealing its bottom half stained a murky brown. "You were a nurse."

"For a while." Grace watched Lily cradle the dress against her chest, examine the line of demarcation, white to brown.

"Wouldn't it come out? Couldn't you have…?"

"No need." Grace looked away.

Lily folded the dress, careful to match its creases. She wrapped it in its tissue, placed it back in its drawer with the white cap sitting on top. The cap's black piping marked a short, dark underline across the center of the package. Lily closed the drawer. Whatever was in the bottom drawer pressed to be let loose. The tissue sighed against the drawer's upper casing as Lily pulled it out. Beneath the pale paper, a throbbing red. "What is it?" Lily whispered.

Grace leaned forward on her chair, felt an instance of floating, sat back. "Prom dress."

Lily squealed, released the dress. Tissue flew. A cascade of screaming-red slipper satin. Lily jumped up, clutching the dress to her, twirled around. Mothballs dropped from the loosening folds and careened around the attic floor, tracing spirals through the dust. "Oh my God!" Lily laughed, ecstatic. "Strapless!"

Grace nodded with a wide, satisfied smile. "I sold about a million eggs to get that dress."

Lily and the dress danced around the room, pirouetted in a shaft of speckled sun. Lily sang, "Would you like to swing on a star? Carry moonbeams home in a jar?"

"Mrs. Mildred O'Dell sewed it. Took forever."

Lily twirled past Grace's chair. A shiver of satin slipped across Grace's lap, was gone, leaving in its wake the scent of mothball and something else. *Brylcreem,* Grace remembered. "I lost my virginity in that dress."

Lily caught midspin, one arm flung out, the other holding red satin to her waist. Stopped. Her eyes, her grin widened.

"Graduation night." Grace gestured with her head. "Out there. Barn."

"No!" Lily crowed.

"Mortimer Mott. Class treasurer. 'Course, I let him chase me around the circumference a time or two first…Morty Mott." She tasted the words.

"*Yes!*" Lily erupted. "Hooray!" She tossed the red dress toward the rafters. It arched, spread its skirts, almost floated. Grace watched its reluctant descent. *A great, red parachute,* Grace thought…*almost carried me away.* At last, it landed with a sigh, draping over Lily's head and shoulders. A girl lost in red.

"Not much to choose from, here." Grace raised her voice to be heard by the someone beneath the dress. "I guess one of the capris might work for the Fourth."

Lily pulled the red satin from her head, hugged it to her. Better than armor. Diversion. Spectacle. "This."

Grace laughed. "You might be a bit overdressed for the occasion."

"No." Lily smiled. "It's perfect."

Grace nodded. It was.

JULY

SEVENTEEN

*B*aby sat on the porch. Watching Grace. Waiting for Grace. Grace beside her, sleeping again. Grace in *apricot* dreams under *unmellow yellow* sun. Baby sweated and waited, listening to Grace exhale *apricot* dreams, listening to Lily and Walter shout *electric lime* laughter down below. Baby had plans today. She sighed loudly, peered at Grace. Nothing. Baby shifted, annoyed, felt sweat slide down her forehead off her nose; she stuck out her tongue to catch it. Where was lunch?

At the bottom of the garden, Lily and Walter were swimming in the pond. First Walter, then Lily, struggled from knees to standing on a large, black inner tube. They clutched at each other, laughing, the inner tube quaking beneath them. Butler barked hysterically from the shore, rushed at the water, rushed back, barked a further complaint. Too much fun going on without him; it needed to stop. Baby agreed. She had plans today. Backside to the garden and pond, she wouldn't watch. Lily and Walter in the brown water. Skin *sepia* like Grace's special, white dress. *What do you think of me now, Baby?* Baby remembered Grace's voice in the white dress. *Wild watermelon* voice. Soap won't wash. Brown water changed everything. Baby stuck her nose up to Grace's, called out, "Grace! Lily Walter, Grace! Butler!"

Grace surfaced through currents of dream-drenched sleep, slit open her eyes, saw Baby's glasses impossibly huge before her, closed her eyes again.

"Grace! Lily Walter, Grace!"

91

Grace worked her mouth, managed, "Leave 'em be, Baby." Grace willed herself to sink again, to find the stream of forgetting, to float away.

Nothing doing. Baby stomped her foot. "Grace!" The porch shuddered.

"OK, OK," Grace said, eyes still closed. "Get away from my face now, so I can see what I'm doing." Baby backed off, smiling. No more *apricot* dreams. Lunch. Baby headed for the kitchen, the screen door smacking the frame behind her.

Grace opened her eyes at the sound, grunted, sat up, contemplated stretching. Her body felt like a rusted hinge too long submerged. She warned herself, *Don't move too fast. Something might snap.* She focused on Lily and Walter, both giggling, tipsy on the skittish inner tube. Lily in her once-white bra and a pair of men's boxers, Walter in his brand-new, red bathing trunks, steeped now a deep mahogany. A squawk of alarm from Lily, a squeal from Walter, the inner tube shot out from beneath them. Their bodies arced out and back and down. The dark water swallowed them. Butler went silent. The tube spun alone. They surfaced at the same time. Grace let her breath out, ragged.

"Fourteen!" Walter shouted. "Mom! We were up for fourteen!" Lily backstroked toward the escaping tube. Walter treaded, waiting. "Let's do it again! Twenty this time."

Lily maneuvered the tube before her, dipped beneath the surface, came up butting the tube with her head. "Simple," she said, pushing the tube the last few feet to Walter. She executed a backward roll, her head emerging as her toes disappeared.

A mermaid in the pond, Grace thought, watching. *Changes every-thing.* Grace could not figure out how Lily managed to wade through Grace's familiar places, her memories, her truths, tinting them different shades, smoothing wrinkles…making her want to remain.

Baby banged flat-palmed at the window. Butler commenced his barking. Grace felt the lateness in her bones. Too late. She braced her feet, pushed with arms, urged herself to standing, gathered breath. "Lunch!" she bellowed out over the garden.

Chicken noodle soup from a red-and-white can. Yellow. Noodles to slide down her chin and escape back into the bowl like slippery minnows. Baby fished. "Aaugh," she commented, chasing noodles around her blue bowl. Grace reached over, speared noodles for Baby, and crammed them in her waiting mouth, her other hand cupped below Baby's chin to catch runoff. Baby gave Grace a big, wide-open grin. Noodles escaped. "Baby! You could help a bit!" Grace dumped a palmful of noodles, broth, and saliva back into the bowl, smeared her hand across her apron. "You can feed yourself, you silly old thing."

Baby fished. "Hah!" She trapped a noodle against the side of the bowl, eased it up to the rim until it draped over. She hunched, stretched her lips down, vacuumed the noodle in. The bowl tipped and righted itself, juice sloshed onto the table, dribbled to the floor. Baby chewed, swallowed, felt excellent yellow noodle make its way to her tummy. "Hah!" she said to Grace's back at the kitchen sink.

"Have it your way," Grace retorted.

Outside, Butler launched himself at the screen door, black eyes intent on the growing puddle of chicken broth beneath Baby. It might be mopped up at any moment. He made another assault on the door. Behind him, Lily struggled to open it between his charges. "Butler! Butler, we'll all starve at this rate!" She laughed.

Grace came over to the door. "Shoo, now!"

Butler fell back a few paces, plopped down on his bottom. The tips of his ears quivered. Lily eased Walter through the door, followed him, then held the door open eight inches and gave Butler a significant look. He hesitated, watching Grace's back retreat to the table, then streaked through the opening and beelined for the puddle of chicken broth. Baby, intent on noodles, felt Butler's fur tickle her calves, felt Butler's tongue, decisive and friendly, on her spattered ankles. Yellow yellow yellow. Walter sat down next to her with a big bowl of soup. "Swimming," he informed Baby, "is hungry work."

Baby dropped her spoon and captured Walter's hands, examined them minutely for traces of brown. The palms were wrinkled and white, slippery as noodles. She sniffed them. She could smell it. Not noodles, brown water. Baby snorted, dropped the hands.

"I washed in the hose," Walter said defensively.

"He'll shower after lunch," Lily added.

Baby turned away, rediscovered lunch, yellow in a bowl, silver circles of cooling grease shimmering the surface, noodles settling in the deep spots, waiting. Better.

"Told you Baby doesn't like that pond." Grace's comment was punctuated by her heavy drop into the chair across from Lily.

"Chicken noodle." Lily's voice was mild. "My favorite." She wolfed the soup. To the side of her bowl, a small pile of stringy chicken meat collected.

Grace wasn't eating. She watched, nodded at the pile. "There's still chicken in there, bits, broth. You're eating chicken." Grace shook her head in mock disgust. "Sinful."

Lily's eyes sparkled at Grace. In her stained bra and boxers, she felt strong, clean, baptized. Inside her, she nursed an easing, a shifting of rules. The Flying Cat could risk it. *Let them come.* "No," she answered her aunt. "Modified." She smiled down at the pile of nasty, canned chicken, considered scooping it up, swallowing it whole in front of Grace. Instead, she dropped her spoon. It landed with the clear, bright note of a bell in the bottom of the empty bowl.

Baby stood up. "Andy," she informed them, hesitated, considered Walter. Brown smell. Not invited. She shuffled from the room.

"Whoa, there, Baby." Grace stood. "Let's take you up to the toilet, first. Then Andy."

Lily, Walter, and Butler sat in the auntless kitchen, held by the quiet. Butler cleaned the floor where Baby's shoes had been. Lily smiled at her son, reached out, and took his hand. "Well. I guess we better get you cleaned up."

Brown water changes everything. Baby knows. Baby remembers. Before brown water, after. Grace's color changes after brown water. She is not the Grace who runs through midnight trees. Then, yellow, lighting the trees, answering the moon. After brown water, Grace is dark blue.

After brown water, Grace is in charge. That one, Grace's mother, is gone. Long time gone. Dead in flowers. Good. Now the other one, the man is going, too. Upstairs, slipping away into his silence. Baby can hear his breathing, slow, gray, louder than his voice ever was. He is slipping into brown water. Good. Grace is the one now.

No more cage. Baby watches, chewing her fingers as Grace rips and tugs at the cage. The noises are huge, mean, bright red. Baby plasters her hands to her ears.

No more diaper. Stairs and toilet. Stairs and toilet. All day long. Grace with a frown. In the kitchen, Baby still sits against her wall, rubs her head. Hard to give up. Grace with a frown.

These good things. Outside in sunshine. Chickens. Cows. Rides in a car. People. Crayons in a Big Box! Yellow everything. Except Grace. Grace is dark blue. She has lost something. She has lost yellow. Lost in brown water. Brown water changes everything.

Grace has Baby. Baby will wear the panties and climb the stairs, will pick the dresses and not rub her head. Baby will fade the dark blue, slowly, slowly. Baby will give her Grace back the yellow. That's what Baby will do. Baby has the colors.

EIGHTEEN

*W*alter's feet squeaked on the stairs. His hair was spiky, his skin pink from a long soak in the tub. He stood in the archway to the living room and watched Baby. He waited for Baby's OK. Baby looked over at him, back at the TV. Barney Fife was locking up Otis. Drunk again. "Hoho!" Baby barked at the screen. She knew what was coming next. Barney would end up inside the jail cell, Otis outside with the keys. Drunk Otis with the keys, sleeping in Barney's chair. Snoring. Barney in jail. Walter in the doorway, wet again.

Walter inched into the room, stood next to Baby's chair. She could smell him. Pink and sweet as snitched candy. Baby left Barney in jail and turned to Walter. She gathered his hands and examined them, soft and clean. Sniffed. Raised his arms, lowered them, raised his shirt, pressed her nose to his ribs. Walter giggled. Baby's nose was round and wet like Butler's. Baby stared hard at Walter, looking for the change, looking for dark blue. Walter put his hands on Baby's shoulders. "It's me, Aunt Baby."

Yes. Baby's Walter. Yellow. They watched the credits together.

Next was Baby's plan. She had been waiting all day for Andy and After Andy. Yellow Walter, not changed by brown water, would help. Perfect.

Baby shut off the TV and took Walter by the hand. In the kitchen, Baby stopped first, looking for Lily. The sound of her singing "Mack the Knife" drifted through the screen door. Baby dragged Walter over to the kitchen window and pressed her nose to the pane. Yes. Lily

96

deep in flowers. "Hah!" Baby commented and pulled Walter over to the "everything" drawer next to the refrigerator. She yanked open the drawer and rifled through it with thick, searching fingers. Band-Aids, pencil stubs, stamps, tape measure, used batteries shifted and spilled noisily to the floor. Upstairs on Grace's bed, Butler barked twice. Baby froze, waited for Grace's call.

Walter caught himself holding his breath, feeling a slight knot of guilt forming in his stomach. "What are we doing?" he whispered.

"June Cleaver..." Baby mumbled, deep again in the everything drawer. "Hah!" she erupted, at last finding what she wanted—a clear plastic box filled with brightly colored tacks. Grabbing Walter's hand again, she plowed from the kitchen, leaving the everything drawer hanging on its back edge, the contents scattered across the room. Walter bumped off Baby's behind as she dragged him up the stairs. She paused at the top, hugging him close, peering down the hall toward Grace's room. On the bed, Butler raised his head from Grace's bare feet, one ear inclined to investigate, the other at half-mast, inclined toward napping. Horizontal pursuits won out. He sighed, dropped his head back onto Grace's feet. Grace didn't move. Asleep, asleep. Baby shook her head, tugged Walter toward her room at the other end of the hall, pulled him in and shut the door.

Once inside, Baby shoved the tacks at Walter and flopped down on her hands and knees. Walter watched the pattern of blue flowers stretch and contract across Baby's bum, and she reached and reached under her bed, her hands searching, smacking the floorboards. He breathed in the closed smell of Baby's room, pee and polyester sweat, a bouquet of Lily's late peonies, and Baby's own sweet exhalations. Walter held the tacks and a wild curiosity, as if both were wrapped presents that might explode. Gifts from Baby.

Baby surfaced. She had found them, her stash of secret drawings. She placed them on her bed and then, using Walter, struggled to her feet. Walter was almost floored by the weight of her. Dust bunnies clung to her forearms and knees. Walter grinned and brushed her off.

Baby laid the drawings out, side by side, on the bed. There were too many to fit. She plowed the spare blanket off the top of her hope chest and laid them there, too. She was about to swipe the contents off the top of her bedside table when Walter finally jumped to help her. He steadied the wobbling lamp and caught a framed photo of her and Grace an inch from the floor. Too close. Walter's reflexes were slowed. He felt glued where he stood. He had never seen anything like the drawings. Aunt Baby was special.

Baby took a drawing from the middle of the bed, looked around the room, considering, and stuck out a hand for a tack.

By the time Lily came in from the garden, Baby was enthroned in front of *The Partridge Family*. Walter, reading a book on the couch, listened to Lily wash her hands, open the fridge door, and then chop something on the wooden cutting board.

Lily came in with a plate of orange wedges, grinned a wide smile of orange peel at Walter and then at Baby, offering the plate. "Agh!" Baby roared at Lily's orange smile, scooped up two fistfuls of fruit, and returned to her show. Shirley Partridge was going on a date! Lily flopped down next to Walter.

Walter eyed Baby, leaned over, whispered to Lily, "Mom, I have to show you something." He eyed Baby again. "Meet me upstairs in a few minutes." Walter stood up, stretched. "Got to go to the bathroom," he announced to the room.

Baby hunched toward the TV. Shirley was nervous!

Walter waited for Lily at the top of the stairs, hopping from foot to foot in excitement. Lily joined him after a few minutes. "Bad date," she told him. "Poor Shirley." She noticed his hopping. "Haven't you gone yet? Is there something wrong with the toilet?"

"Oh, Mom!" Walter tugged Lily toward Baby's room.

Lily had to touch them, had to run her fingers over the sharp, catching dots and along the soft sweeps of color. She recognized each style, though she could only put a name to a few: Seurat's million points of light...Van Gogh's heavy strokes...some ancient master, perhaps Rembrandt, smooth and dark...stark, angular Picasso...the fullness of Gaugin...Lily let her breath out in a long, slow escape. She wanted to place her cheek against them, absorb them. "No, *look* at them, Mom," Walter urged.

Lily stepped back, blinked. More than the styles were familiar. The faces. All around the room, they looked down at her: Grace and Baby, Baby and Grace, Grace and Walter, Lily and Walter, Baby and Lily, Lily and Grace, Baby and Walter, over and over. "My God," Lily whispered. Walter nodded. "Aunt Grace has to see this." Lily turned to the door.

"She's tired," Walter warned.

"She has to see this."

Butler's stub of a tail trembled when Lily entered Grace's room. Lily hesitated over Grace. Sleeping, she seemed a painting of suffering, her mobile face stilled, caught in deep lines, grayed and thin in the late-afternoon light. A fluttering pulse in her crêpey neck. The skin of her arms, hanging vacated. Aunt Grace. Lily's heart constricted. "No. Stay. I'm not ready yet," she whispered, then leaned over, gently shook a bony shoulder. "Wake up, Aunt Grace. You have to come."

Grace sat on the edge of Baby's bed, Walter on one side, Lily on the other, Butler between. They stared at the walls. Canned laughter drifted up from downstairs, Baby answering, "Hohohoho!" Grace couldn't quite take it in. She rubbed her face, scratched her chin.

"What does it mean?" Lily asked.

"Aunt Baby's special," Walter told them.

Grace grunted.

"Well," Lily said after a minute, "she obviously got more out of that New York trip than we knew."

"I thought she hated those things, kicking up a great fuss like that." Grace stared.

"They're not the same, though." Lily's voice was soft, at the edge of understanding. It was more than the multitude of styles. It was more than the faces, their faces, reinvented, made new in this different context. She struggled to grasp it. "What does the blue mean? They all have it. At the center of each of them."

Grace shrugged her weary shoulders, looked into the knowing eyes that lined the wall, and wondered: who knew what Baby saw, what Baby meant? *MYSTERIOUS MESSAGE! MUUMUUED MADWOMAN MIMICS MASTERS!* Grace shook her head. What was it?

Madonnas gazed down on them, madonnas with their holy charges, each with a face of Grace, Lily, Walter, or Baby. Each sheltered a secret, offered a gift of truth. The deep blue interiors of their hearts. Each drawing a family, complete, alone.

Walter waited. Grace shook her head again. Lily stood so close to the pictures, they dissolved into separate hues before her eyes. Lily ran her fingers over them, feeling their ridges. She sought a way in, ached for it. "Tell me," she whispered.

Lily stands in the Department of Social Services office hallway. She can't let go of Walter's brown paper bag of clothes. She clutches it so tightly to her chest that her arms go numb. She fights for breath. One pair of jeans, four shirts, seven boxers, three socks. Why only three?

"I got him calmed down. He's coloring." The social worker's hair is dyed the bitter red of pomegranate rind. "This is the way it's got to be." She tugs at the bag of clothes.

Lily won't let go. Behind the woman, Lily can see Walter sitting at a desk at the back of the office. He holds a fat, dark crayon in his hand suspended over a blank, white page. Lily can see a round cheek, a crest of sweaty hair. No tears mar the page. He won't look up. I'm already gone, *Lily thinks. She opens her arms, lets the bag drop. One pair of jeans, four shirts, seven boxers, three socks abandoned to the hallway floor. Lily turns and runs.*

The social worker scoops up the paper bag, holds it in a fist, a bar of gold rings across her fingers. Her voice unravels behind Lily's back. "Do what you have to do. Come back, talk to the judge."

Lily runs with her arms wide open. She feels blue blood rush down her arms to fill the vacuum in her veins. She feels needle pricks advance. She knows it won't help. Nothing can fill this space.

NINETEEN

When the menu was first discussed, Lily had wanted to make curried chicken salad with slivered almonds and white raisins. "It's completely amazing!" she had promised.

"You don't even eat chicken."

"I could make an exception. I'm telling you, Aunt Grace, it's a sure winner."

Grace shook her head. "Macaroni salad, potato salad, bean salad, deviled eggs, ambrosia."

"But—"

"Macaroni salad, potato salad, bean salad, deviled eggs, ambrosia."

In response, Lily had performed a manic dance around the kitchen table, undulating, waving her arms, chanting, "Macaroni salad, potato salad, bean salad, deviled eggs, ambrosia, hey!" Walter joined her.

"They're crazy," Grace told Baby, who watched gape-jawed. Mashed potatoes adhered to her big spoon, caught midjourney from plate to mouth. "They just don't understand about family reunions. Do they, Baby? They just don't know about the Fourth of July."

Lily switched to a Souza piece she remembered from the cache of attic albums, fitting the litany of menu offerings into the melody, swinging her arms and marching, head high as a majorette. Walter struggled to follow, stumbling and giggling until caught in the rhythm. Baby jumped up to join the line, the spoon of mashed potatoes still clutched in one big fist. Her face was fierce with concentration. Her arms pumped; her feet pounded the floorboards. Crockery rattled in the cupboards. "Grace!" Baby called out as she marched by, her eyes wide with surprise.

Grace chuckled despite herself. "So, you remember all that forced marching way back, eh? Never did a lick of good."

"Grace! Hah!"

"Look what you can do, Baby. That's just fine!"

"Join us, Aunt Grace!"

Grace shook her head. "No thank you, Walter. I've already danced to that tune too long."

The fifth time around the table, Baby's mashed potatoes loosed their hold on the spoon, arced through the air to land with a soft splat on Grace's plate. Most of the marching band disintegrated into help-less laughter. Baby continued to march in place, the giggling mass of Lily and Walter at her feet. Her fists punched the air. She called out, "Yellow Yellow Yellow Yellow...Yellow Yellow Yellow!" Perhaps a hint of Souza tripped through the words.

It hurt to laugh so hard, made her insides feel like they were rip-ping apart. Grace didn't care. She wrapped her arms around her mid-dle and let it come, the laugh, the pain, the bright, sharp, shouting yellow moment. She held on tight.

Lily was at her side, kneeling, touching her back hesitantly. "Aunt Grace. Aunt Grace, are you OK?"

Grace gasped, "Good! I'm good."

"Macaroni salad, potato salad, bean salad, deviled eggs, ambrosia." Lily's voice gentle, her face a promise.

Ambrosia had been the hardest part of the promise. "Nothing edible is this color."

"Sure, there is. Lots of things." Grace was providing moral support from the kitchen table, where she nursed a cup of mint tea.

"Name six."

Grace couldn't think of one. "You used to love that stuff. Every Fourth of July. 'Is there ambrosia? I want ambrosia!'"

"Well, I've certainly obliterated *that* from my memory. It's probably why I turned out the way I did." From an arm's length, Lily dropped tiny, pastel marshmallows into the quivering mass. She pulled the glass bottle of maraschino cherries out of the fridge, opened it. Next, canned fruit cocktail. Lily shivered extravagantly.

"It probably is, because you turned out just fine." Grace's voice was tart and crisp as new apples.

"Well then, remind me to stuff some of it into Walter when the time comes."

"I'd rather eat worms," Walter informed them through the porch door screen.

"Poppycock," Grace told him.

"No, Aunt Grace. I really would." Walter's eyes were solemn, darkened by the mesh of the screen. His nose pressed a dent.

"Oh, that's it!" Grace said, smacking her palms down on the table. She pushed her body up to standing. "I'll finish it up myself. You shoo."

"Aunt Grace, I'm sorry." Lily was repentant. "I'll stop teasing. It's just...have you ever actually looked at this stuff?"

Grace eased back into her seat. She grimaced and took up her mint tea. "It turns out in the end."

Lily's head was in the freezer hunting the bag of chopped walnuts. She came out with a heavily frosted dish of lemon pudding. "Look at this. We could chop it up and add it. Visual interest."

"No!" Grace gasped. How could she have forgotten? "No!" Her voice was choked by tepid mint tea. "Stuff was terrible. I tried a new recipe. Throw it away!" In her mind, a headline formed. *AMBROSIA KILLS ENTIRE FAMILY!* A somehow satisfying thought. Grace smiled slightly.

"It's a shame. I didn't even know you could make pudding that didn't come from a box. It's such a lovely color, too. How bad could it be?" Lily scraped through the protective frost with a fingernail.

Baby came in from the back porch. Chicken feed speckled her green Keds. She spied the bowl of pudding and thumped over. "Yellow!" She reached out her hand for a taste. Her fingers stopped, suspended above the bowl, memory dawning. She looked at Grace, her face drawn down. "Brown," she growled, snatched her hand away, and stomped toward the TV room.

Grace checked the clock. "Time to test you, Baby! Time for a shot!" she called and rose gingerly. "See?" she said to Lily. "Trust Baby. No good. You go on. Put it in the garbage now." She waited. Once the sleeping, pain-killer-laced mess was in the trash, she took the glucometer and headed for the TV room. "Where are you, you old thing. I'm coming for you."

Walter banged through the screen door with Butler, seed in both their pelts. "That's done! We fed 'em, then Aunt Baby and Butler gave 'em some exercise. Chickens are fast, but so is Butler. Right, Butler?" Butler responded with his sharp-toothed grin, tongue lolling. He gave a great shake, and chicken feed flew from his coat. A few seeds landed in the soft-gelled ambrosia and sank before Lily could retrieve them. She shrugged and looked at Butler, who had plopped down, panting for reward.

"Too bad for you, Butler. You just missed some very pretty leftovers." Lily offered him the spoon, still laced with the yellow pudding scraped into the trash. Butler sniffed, closed his eyes, and turned away as if the spoon and offering hand didn't exist. "Boy. It must have been bad," Lily admitted. "Butler, sometimes you remind me of Aunt Baby." She tossed the spoon into the sink. "How about cheese?" Butler's tail stub trembled.

In the pale, blue light before dawn, everything was almost ready. In the newly cleaned fridge, a big bowl of bean salad had marinated for three days. Next to it, the Pepto-Bismol-pink lump of ambrosia vibrated to the hum of the old GE. On the shelf below, macaroni salad settled under plastic wrap. An open spot waited.

Lily, scrubbed to a raw, glowing cleanliness, wore only a strapless bra and panties that stated a bold, orange *Thursday* on this Tuesday morning. She stood at the sink and sliced red potatoes. Next to her, three dozen eggs chattered in boiling water. Against strict instructions, she left the skin on the potatoes for the salad. She planned on cutting way down on the mayonnaise, too. She sang to the empty kitchen, "I've traveled each and every highway, and more, much more than this…" Lily grinned at the potatoes and kissed one that was especially dimpled and cleaned to a sheen. She felt kinship, a shared future. *Today is the day.* Finishing her song with a soaring "I did it my way!" she hacked the potato into small cubes. It was the only Sinatra song she hated.

Lily had to admit, the ambrosia turned out fine: a scalloped mountain of pink, nuts and maraschino cherries peppering its slopes. She had had to suppress a desire, for drama's sake, to throw herself against the fridge door, arms splayed, and to cry in her best horror-film-goddess voice, "Don't go in there! It's alive!" Wanted to, but hadn't. Instead, she had added black beans to the other beans in the bean salad, a clear departure from the rules. It smelled lovely, scenting the fridge with its vinegar tang. Scenting the ambrosia? Lily winced at the thought. *Uh oh…*

At least Aunt Grace had said nothing. Well, an Aunt Grace humph, maybe. These last days had been days of small relentings. Lily hoped that today, this culmination of salads and nerves would be a day of relenting, too. In her mind a running commentary: *You talk to me, I'll talk to you. We'll all behave.* Could it happen? Lily chopped the last potato, hitched up her sinking bra, switched the gas flame off beneath the kettle of eggs, and began dumping in the remaining ingredients. *What is it with this family and mayonnaise?* Family…the word echoed in her head. She searched for a song, something, anything. Nothing came. *Frankie boy, don't desert me now!*

The light changed in the kitchen, from dim blue to watery gold. Walter and Grace, holding hands, groped into the dense air of the kitchen. "Already hot," Grace grumbled. "Scorcher today. Figures. Those potatoes have their skins on. Thin on the mayo, too." She inched into her seat. "They won't like it."

Lily pulled in a breath, let it out slowly, put a cup of coffee in front of her aunt, ruffled her son's hair. "Cheerios?"

"Can't," Walter mumbled, rubbing his stomach.

"A knot?" Lily asked. He nodded. "Buck up, you two." Lily's voice was overly bright, sharp, slicing the thick, moist air of the kitchen. She swallowed, her head jerking with the effort. "Look what I found. Look what I found!" A flurry of arms and legs, she rushed to the everything drawer and pulled out a pair of enormous, round, pitch-black sunglasses. She put them on and posed. "I'm wearing them today."

Grace took her time, blinking, the smile coming with the headline. "*JACKIE O. ALIVE!*" she drawled. "*SPOTTED IN STRAPLESS BRA AND WRONG-DAY PANTIES ON UPSTATE FARM!* Well, they sure aren't going to recognize you in those."

"That's what I'm hoping." Spectacle…diversion…

Grace pointed lower down. "You're escaping the barn there, a bit. That might cause a stir. What would your Buddha say?"

Lily tugged at the bra. "Buddha would smile. But don't worry. I've got it covered."

Baby stomped in, blessing Lily Walter Grace with a denture-free smile. "Meepmeep!" she crowed. The kitchen filled with *dandelion* light. Baby ignored the jagged, *atomic tangerine* feelings coming from Lily and Walter and Grace. The color of the light told the truth. It told her *today is the day*! Family-colors day. All of them here, and pink pink pink ambrosia, too. "Yellow!" Baby proclaimed.

Grace stood wearily. "Come on, Baby. Let's get you to a toilet, quick. You'll have yellow running down your legs any minute."

Lily, suddenly galvanized, issued orders. "I can do that. You guys have got to eat something. Now. After, Walter, you take Aunt Baby out to do the chickens. Feed them and then try to get them into the barn. I'll help later if you can't. I need to devil the eggs and then scrub the kitchen floor. Walter, while I wax, you'll need to keep Aunt Baby in front of the TV." Walter nodded.

"Andy?" Baby asked. She shuffled from foot to foot, holding her crotch.

Lily rushed to her. "No, Aunt Baby. *Green Acres* on Tuesdays. Come on. Let's get you to the bathroom."

"Green! Green, Grace!" Baby called breathlessly from the hallway.

Grace looked at Walter. "Sometimes *Green Acres* is orange," she told him. Walter nodded, his forehead scrunched with worry. Grace sighed,

"Well, today's the day. I think I'll go rest in my room 'til it's time for Baby's shot."

Walter watched Grace's back, considered going with her. *Let's hide,* cat voices whispered in his head. From the bathroom, his mother's voice sounded like chalk on the blackboard when you were standing there in front of the class and didn't know the answer to the problem. *Forty-five times nineteen. How do you carry?* Tiny, desperate screeches. She sang. "You're the top! You're the Eiffel Tower!" Walter nodded. *Today is the day.* He'd stay. He reached for the Cheerios.

Lily waxes the wooden floor of the sanctuary on her hands and knees. With a soft, flannel cloth, she rubs small circles that bloom to a diameter of twelve inches before she hobbles on. She makes sure she can see her face in each circle before she starts the next. The dark grain streaks her reflection. I know you, *each polished circle says.* Soon they will blend into one vast, shining surface. The sanctuary is huge, seeming to stretch away to infinity down here at eye level. Buddha watches Lily, smiling his serene, stone smile. This is how you get back, *she tells herself, rubbing, rubbing, rubbing.* This is how you get better.

In the twelve-inch circle beneath the gong, Lily has an epiphany. Right there on the floor, midwipe. She is not an addict. Her reflection tells her this. It's all in your head, *it says, sounding remarkably like her mother. Lily knows why. It's her mother's stock phrase. All the confessed fears and hurts, all the longings of childhood.* You don't really want that. It's all in your head. *So Lily stops confessing.*

Lily consults her reflection again. Really? Not an addict? *She sits back on the floor, puts a corner of the waxy rag in her mouth, chews, and thinks. Not a bad flavor. Lemony.* But would it go with bean sprouts? *Lily smiles. Not an addict? She chews and, in her mind, inches over the interiors of her body. A soft probing, probing, probing. She knows what it looks like, trying to come off heroin. She has been there with friends. The shakes, the sweats, the terrible pains, the craving, begging, for something, anything sweet. She pulls the rag from her mouth. Considers. Nothing there. Normal insides, rose-pink, quivering and thumping, contracting, expanding, breath and blood and whole grains moving on their way. Just in her head. That memory of sweet giving over, that sharp-edged desire, that longing. In her head.* Shhh. *Lily stills it. Nothing. Nirvana. She turns to Buddha for confirmation.*

"Really?" her voice whispers through the room.

Buddha smiles.

"Thank you."

Buddha smiles.

Lily pulls back the big wooden clapper, lets its lightly muffled head crash against the gong. Sound echoes down the corridors. She can hear running feet slapping stone. Students, monks, visitors burst through the doors and crowd the room. She is standing, waiting for them. "It's all in my head," Lily announces. Her voice is her own, clear and ringing in the sanctuary.

Buddha is the only one smiling.

TWENTY

*B*y afternoon the air was thick, the sky heavy with humidity. On the hill across the road, rainbow cows floated remote and dreamlike in the haze. In contrast, the painted house glowed vivid and real, a window cut through gauze. Grace, Baby, Walter, and Lily stood in front and waited, each thinking: *Any minute now.*

The sun shimmered off Grace and Baby in decades-old red, white, and blue polyester muumuus, worn this one day a year. Walter, in his thrift-store jeans and itchy, collared shirt, listened to the siren song of cats echoing in his head. Lily, in black sunglasses and the red, red dress kept up by hidden rolls of duct tape, needed to run, to fly. She held herself on earth with bare, clenched toes deep in grass. "They come all together," Grace warned, watching the lifting curve of the road. "The whole passel of them, their own little parade. Remember?"

Lily nodded. "We used to meet in front of the paint store. Why?"

"That's them. A herd."

Lily grinned, "A gaggle."

"A pack."

"A swarm."

Grace nodded.

"Too late to hide?" Lily whispered.

"Too late," Grace said. The first car came over the rise.

Five minivans followed three pickups. In the back of the first pickup, precarious stacks of molded plastic chairs and folding tables;

in the backs of following pickups, large gas grills swayed, demanding care and a reduction of speed. Behind the closed windows of the procession, the vehicles were stuffed with bodies.

"They look like they've been canned." Grace's voice was grim. She felt the knife- edge of pain. *Is it cancer, or family?*

Lily tried some mental math, but she could not remember who had had whom and how many. It had been fifteen years since she'd faced any of them...since she'd run. *Run.* She felt rising panic. "Do they always *all* come?"

"Oh, yes," Grace confirmed. "Every one of them. Wouldn't miss it."

The vehicles made slow, inevitable progress down the road to the house. Faces pressed to windows. Lily, Grace, and Walter gazed back and listened to the tires popping the hot tar bubbles, a cracking, encroaching sound. Walter broke ranks and ran for the barn. Lily and Grace clasped hands, each feeling the other's fragile bones and thin skin. "Meepmeep!" Baby proclaimed and waved both arms about her head. *Family colors!*

"Well." Lily smiled. "At least someone is looking forward to this. It's the family, Aunt Baby! Finally!" Lily's words hung in the air, then sank with the weight of their brittle heartiness.

Baby arms flopped through the wet, sticky air. She called joyously, "OrangePaulGreenGreenSissyKateNotPinkPaulBillBlue!"

Grace shook her head at Lily. "It's hard on her."

Lily looked at Grace. "I don't remember."

"You'll see."

"Are they mean?" Lily began to bristle, to find purpose.

Grace shook her head. "No, no. Not like that. They're just—" Grace closed her lips and stepped forward, dragging Lily, as the minivans unsealed in the driveway and bodies spilled out.

Baby wanted to hug them all, big open-armed hugs that gathered them into jiggling, waterbed tummy and soft, moist breasts. She wanted to pat their heads and touch their faces, check for changes, and give them their colors. They didn't hug back. Some were wood stiff, and then they patted her on the back or shoulder, arm's length. "How are you there, Baby." Hearty pats. Baby was big; she could take it. Others melted away in her arms like slivers of chocolate on her tongue, promising sweet, then gone. The little ones struggled, active resistance, like Butler or the chickens when cornered for a friendly snuggle. Baby's smile slipped. She tried harder. She flapped her arms and ho-hoed and offered all her colors. She thumped after them, blocked their way, a wall of Baby, but they swarmed around her with their bags of buns, hot dogs, preformed hamburger patties, sliced tomatoes, jars of pickles and bottles of catsup, chairs, and folding tables. They had a job. They were busy. Too busy to hug.

Lily felt as if she had been masticated, swallowed, moved along by the juices of their will and the force of their efficiency. The Relatives had her. They didn't mention the near-shaved head, the '70s sunglasses or the strapless dress, the bare feet, the years of absence, Walter. She felt absorbed, washed down, a bacterium lodged in some unfortunate place inside them, quickly sealed off by protective coating. They didn't quite look at her. "Oh, Lily," they said. They handed her things. Lily looked down. Her arms were filled with mayonnaise. When she looked up, her parents were standing there: Ted and Fay.

"Cut your hair." Fay.

Lily nodded, hugging the mayonnaise jars. She swallowed. "How've you been?"

"Same. Bronchitis last winter." Fay again.

Ted nodded. He couldn't take his eyes off the dress. Lily thought he might be squinting, leaning away. "It's Aunt Grace's old prom dress." It was suddenly important to explain. "It's red." Lily's teeth clicked shut.

"You're going someplace." In Fay's voice a blank certainty. Ted looked away. Lily hoped it was question, wanted it to be one, and opened her mouth to explain, really explain. She was staying. But Fay had turned to Ted. "They'll be wanting these burgers down by the grill soon."

"Probably so. I better get going on those chairs."

"Don't be trying to carry too many. Let the younger ones help."

"Don't fuss."

Ted and Fay. Lily opened her mouth. "Walter's…" Too late. Ted and Fay had moved on, Fay toward the house, Ted back toward a faded blue pickup and its stacks of white chairs. Lily watched them and felt her duct tape easing, sliding, letting her down. "Oh. Walter," Lily whispered and headed for the barn, still toting mayonnaise.

Grace was herded to the back porch. Every single one of them wanted to say something nice to her, kiss her cheek, give her just a little squeeze. Bright, chirpy voices, secure in the knowledge she was so happy to see them.

"I hope you made that ambrosia!"

"Hello, Aunt Grace. You look great!"

"Umm, umm! That's my favorite, too!"

"I just look forward to it!"

"Well, here we are! Another year!"

"Grace, you're looking so slim!"

"Girlish!"

"I've always liked that dress!"

"I wish I could lose some weight."

"It's the cutest material."

"I tried that grapefruit-and-garlic diet. Nasty!"

"Festive!"

"What's your secret, Grace?"

They reached the back of the house.

"Oh, my! Look what you've done with Mother's gardens!" Grace's sister, Kate, pressed her hands to her heart.

"Lily—" Grace tried.

"No wonder you've lost so much weight."

"Gardening's wonderful for that!"

"Look at the colors!"

"I wish I could lose some weight."

"I think I'll sit down," Grace told them and aimed for the nearest chair.

Lily heard Butler's repeated assaults on the inside of the huge barn door: *Thump! Scrabble scrabble scrabble. Thump! Scrabble scrabble.* Lily smiled, turned to the small side door, set down her mayonnaise jars, and let herself in. The interior of the barn felt crowded. A trapped, distressed feeling hung in the dusty air. All the chickens had been herded in before the relatives arrived. They roosted nervously, complaining each time Butler thudded against the door. The cats were hiding, sulking. Lily could feel their displeasure, sharp and strong. Walter was nowhere. "I know you're in here."

Thump! Scrabble scrabble scrabble.

"You have to come out and try."

"Butler wants to go instead."

Lily turned. She could just make out a small face in the shadows. "He can't, Walter. One of the cousins is very allergic."

"I'm allergic."

"To what?" Lily asked.

"To cousins."

Lily laughed. Walter couldn't help it. He had to come out of hiding then, had to come to her. She always did that to him, her laugh, her smile, her standing there maybe waiting.

Lily picked hay from his hair. "We have to try."

Walter held out his hand. "One of the cats scratched me."

Lily took his hand in hers, traced the two red tracks. "They're nervous. Too many visitors."

Walter shrugged. Still holding his hand, Lily drew him through the side door. Butler noticed at the last minute and charged. Too late. The door shut in his face. *Thwap! Scrabble scrabble. Thwap!* The thin wood of the side door shook. Lily grinned and picked up her jars of mayonnaise. "We could try this on those scratches."

"You hate mayonnaise."

"It's got to be good for something."

With arms around each other, Lily and Walter headed for the reunion.

Grace was surrounded. They settled around her like a flock of birds: the women in chairs under the shade trees; the children splayed restless in the grass near them, impatient for food then release; the men standing in the hot sun around the grills, shifting foot to foot, sweating, nursing beers. Smoke from sizzling meat rose and dissipated, leaving its taste in the humid air. The sound of chunking ice in glasses, of desultory talk, was held down, heavy in heat. Everything was an effort. Above the hills to the west, storm clouds built, dark and necessary.

The call came: burgers and dogs were almost ready. The women rose. Grace didn't make a move to help. She sat in her chair, hands in her lap, and watched them. Something unfamiliar was building inside her, tightening her guts, filling her chest. She wondered: *What is this? What does it serve?* She watched the efficient activity, plastic bags of plates and forks, chips and buns ripped open and stacked on the long, folding table. Lily fluttered by, an exotic butterfly, balancing bowls of potato salad and macaroni salad, a look of concentration. Sweat sheened her shoulders. Pies were produced. Two young nephews fussed with the ice cream maker.

In the west, the clouds reached the sun, swallowing it. Everyone paused, testing the air for a temperature change, returned to duties.

Platters of meat were set at the table. A line formed. Grace's nephew, Nick, came up, asking if she wanted him to get her a plate of food. Grace shook her head; she was glued to her chair, watching, watching. Walter inched by carrying ambrosia stacked on bean salad. He sighed as he set it down, wiped his forehead with a palm. His bangs stayed where they had been plastered by his hand, upright, alert for trouble. Walter took his place at the end of the line, a bumper of air between him and his great-uncle, Larry.

Not one of them, Grace thought, different, like Lily. Grace savored for a moment the memory of Lily in the old doghouse. Before Lily, me. Before me, Baby. Who made these decisions? *Will it ever end?* At that instant, Grace knew what it was inside of her, the thing growing, taking hold, darkening the day. *Truth.* From the west, a low muttering of thunder. Storm warnings.

Lily tried to coax Baby from the TV. "They're all here to see you, Aunt Baby." Baby hunched her shoulders and brought her face closer to the screen. She was watching an infomercial on facial hair. Where was Marcia Brady? Baby held her pile of family drawings pressed to her tummy. She had them all right here with her, in her arms—Kate and

Larry and Little Bud; Adrianne, whose hair was orange and heart was bright green; Teddy Nick Charlene. She pressed down hard on the papers against her tummy. She had them just the way they were meant to be, like crayons in her box. There was an order. "You could show them your drawings. They'd love them," Lily tried again.

Baby frowned and leaned closer to the TV. The kitchen chair creaked ominously. Her nose so close to the screen, the facial-hair woman disappeared. The picture gave way to dots, tiny rows of dots, colored dots floating in blackness. Baby blinked, stared again. "Hah!" She pressed her hands against the screen. The stack of drawings slid from her belly and scattered at her feet. She had known it all along. There was nothing in the world. Nothing but color.

Lily put her arms around her aunt, pressed a cheek to the soft, gray curls on top of her head. "I'll leave a plate for you on the kitchen table. You'll be able to see us all from the kitchen window. A big helping of ambrosia. Don't tell Aunt Grace." Lily gave Baby an extra squeeze.

Baby was busy, too busy to hug. The harder she stared, the closer she came, the more it seemed possible: she could be one of those dots. Find the right row, fit into the pattern. Redredredgreengreenblue. No more watching from the other side of the screen.

Walter sat down with his plate near a sprawling patch of cousins. The space of grass around him felt like a boundary until an older girl moved aside, saying, "Come on. I remember you." Walter inched over, his plate tipping precariously. The hot dog rolled, lodging against the potato salad, distributing catsup. Beans slid into his lap. Walter looked down, miserable. The big girl, who turned out to be cousin Adrianne, took his plate and organized it, handed it back, and wiped the beans from his lap. "You're Walter," she told him.

Walter nodded. "That's like an old man's name," a kid across the clump of bodies said. Twitters from the clump. Walter shrugged.

"Shut up." Adrianne's eyes promised pain. The clump grew quiet and stared at Walter.

"My mom made the salads," Walter offered, his voice a whisper. A look ran through the clump. They burst into laughter, even Adrianne, then began talking among themselves. Walter felt a loosening in his chest.

"I like the ambrosia!" a boy hollered at Walter. He was tanned and fat, the stripes on his shirt expanding over his belly.

Adrianne leaned over. "That's Paul. Frankly, he'll eat anything." Paul grinned, worms of ambrosia squeezed in his smile. "So, you came from New York?" Adrianne asked. Walter nodded. "That's where I want to live. I bet you can hardly wait to get out of this hellhole and go back." She looked around, her gaze bored and grown-up.

"No." Walter shook his head. His plate trembled. "I'm staying." Cousin Adrianne didn't know hellholes.

Jamal is caramel, his eyes, his skin, his dreadlocks. He holds the washcloth to Walter's nose. "Keep your head back. Keep it back," Jamal advises.

Jamal knows everything. He is a head taller than Walter and the longest in this place. Jamal is king. Walter can look up into Jamal's eyes with his head tilted back. Blood escapes from the edge of the washcloth, slides down Walter's cheek, drops to his T-shirt, where it spreads.

"Man, you a mess." Jamal shakes his head. "You got to stand up. You got to use these." Jamal lifts a fist above Walter's tilted head, brings it down slowly to between his eyes. Walter blinks, winces; blood flows. "Man, they gonna eat you alive." Jamal shakes his dreads, grins down at Walter.

Jamal is missing his four front teeth, top and bottom. His mom's boyfriend did that. "She told him not to hit me no more. He didn't listen," Jamal explained. "She shot that fucker. That's why I'm here."

The hole in Jamal's mouth is dark plum, making his smile seem wider, his remaining teeth whiter, his skin and eyes more deeply gold. He peeks beneath the washcloth, declares Walter cured, and mops his face of spattered blood with gentle, long fingers. "Remember, man. You got to stand up!"

Walter shakes his head. "My mom is coming to get me," he tells Jamal.

Jamal shakes his head, disgusted now. "Man, you a sorry little white boy, you know that? You gonna die here." Walter shakes his head fiercely, holds his nose. He will not die. He will hide. He will wait for Lily. Like always. Jamal relents, drapes an arm across Walter's shoulders. "That's OK, man. You OK. I got you covered."

At night, Walter climbs into his bunk and wishes for something small and softly furred to hold on to. His nose is swollen and throbbing, his right eye blackened. Wishes for something warm and quietly breathing against him, something he could whisper his words to, he could convince. In the dark room, there are coughs and whimpers, mutters and snores. Walter listens, tries to distinguish Jamal's breathing from that of the eight other boys in the room. Jamal, who has Walter covered. Jamal, whose mother has killed for him. Jamal, who also waits.

TWENTY-ONE

*L*ily was having a marvelous time. She felt she had sipped from some elixir that had made her both invisible and hyperaware. Perhaps it was the ambrosia. She had tried it. Not bad, though its tooth-aching sweetness made one taste enough. Now she circulated, sashaying in her red dress, urging food, humming, freed from answering questions by everyone else's inability to ask. They didn't want to know the nasty details of her life; they wanted to imagine. Fifteen years provided quite a pile of fodder for thought. *Let them.* She smiled at the thought. She flitted among them, feeling long looks cool on her bare back, answering tight smiles with her own toothy grin, even with her brothers and sisters decked out in matching disdain. She hugged them, kissed each glowering face. "Darlings! How are you?" She thought she heard a hint of Myrna Loy in her voice, grinned at their dumbstruck responses. It had to be the red dress. Everything bounced off it. She had been right; it was perfect. Spectacle worked. She was invincible…almost.

She avoided her parents.

Conversation eddied in her flow. She caught snatches. It seemed old Uncle Larry has discovered alternative medicine, was drinking a quart of aloe vera juice a week. Little Paulie was flunking eighth grade. Teddie might be moving out of the state for his job. A pair of matched giggles, an answering male chuckle, drew her. Callie and Sissy with her own brother, Nick, huddled on the grass near the spirea. "A tart and two old nuns."

118

"She could probably teach them a thing or two."

"You don't know…Aunt Grace was young, once. She may have…"

"Oh, Nick! Yuck!"

Lily swept over, leaning down, her rolls of duct tape visible on either side of the shallow valley of her cleavage. She offered her platter one-handed. "She did. In *this* dress." Lily smoothed a length of skirt with her free hand, then pointed. "In the barn. She says it was *incredible*. Deviled egg?"

Grace sat in her chair, the clouds congregating above, the freshening wind slicing through barbecue smoke and bringing with it promise of rain. She sat in her chair with a piece of untouched peach pie in her lap and listened. They came to her. She was Grace, and this was what they offered her: thin slices of pie, snippets of gossip, small encouragements like chucks under a baby's chin, and their jolly, jolly presence, this one day of the year. Hands open, eyes closed, gone before the fireworks. *Well*, thought Grace, *this is the last time I'll need to do this*.

"Where is that Baby?" Kate asked. "She never wants to come out and visit!"

Grace humphed.

"You're so good with her, Grace. Such patience!" Fay admired.

"She always was." Kate looked around for confirmation, a nod from the gathered gray and dyed hairdos. "Even when she was a bitty thing."

Grace humphed.

"That's how she stays so young." This from Kate's Jenny. "Keeping up with Baby keeps her young."

"You're just as slim as a girl, Grace!" Brother Bud's Doris piped up. "I don't know how you do it."

"I'm dying," Grace told them.

"Oh, pooh, Grace!" Kate with her older sister's voice, wobbly with age. "You're always so gloomy. I wish I had half your health. I thought I'd never make it through this last winter. And sciatica! You have no idea!"

"Sciatica is nothing, sister," Doris countered. "Flat on my back with some bug, I was. Months!"

"Bronchitis," offered Fay, then turned to Grace. "Why, Grace, if I had half your energy, my garden would look this good. But I have to watch myself. Doctor says. And I so miss my garden."

"Lily did it," Grace told them, raising her voice to be heard over their litany. "And the salads."

There was a short, tight pause. Leaves, restless in the rising wind, chattered. Thunder. "You shouldn't let her impose on you, Grace." Kate's voice was stern again. She gave Fay a sidelong glance. "Her *and* the boy. It's too much for you."

"You have your hands full with Baby." Doris frowned. "You need to think of yourself."

"She's way past old enough to take care of herself."

Doris nodded to Kate in confirmation, then with a slow sneer. "Well, she'll be gone soon. She's always running off."

Grace stared hard at Fay. *Say something,* she urged her sister-in-law in her head, *say one good thing. Your own daughter.* Fay's mouth was a thin, hard line.

"Well, enough of that." Kate turned the discussion. "We all have our trials with kids. Oh, I remember Mother struggled so with Baby." Kate smiled amid her reminiscence.

There it was, the thing inside Grace, full beyond bursting, rushing out, hot beyond belief. Grace 's voice matched the lashing wind. "She put her in a cage."

Kate's head whipped back as if slapped. Lily picked this moment to glide up, drawn by the words. "She did what?" Lily's voice was empty, her face stunned like a struck child.

Kate ignored her. "How can you say that, Grace!"

"I can say it because it's true," Grace spat back at her sister.

"Mother did her best. She did her best! I won't have you running down Mother!"

Lily's head swiveled. "Oh dear," said Doris.

"We all do our best," Fay murmured.

Grace turned on Fay. "She put her in a cage."

Kate pressed her hands to her ears. "I won't hear this!"

"Ignorance!" Grace's voice was hoarse, painful from this load of last, shared words. "She put her in a cage, and none of us did anything to stop it."

"No," Lily whispered, shaking her head at Grace. "No." Grace nodded, turned her head to look over the dark, wind-combed pond.

Walter charged into the tense group, burying a tear-stained face into the red dress, clutching tightly, nearly releasing the dress from its taped grip, heaving sobs. His cousin Christopher came fast on his heels, eyes scrunched, bawling, bleeding from his nose. "Grandma! He punched me!" Christopher managed between gasps.

"Oh, there, my baby," crooned Fay, dabbing Christopher's nose. "What did he do?" Fay's voice was fierce as she rounded on Lily. "What did that boy do?"

Lily held her son tight. "Walter wouldn't hit someone without a reason."

"He's just like you! You always had a reason. No reason. That's your reason!"

Lily put her back between Fay and her son, bent down to Walter, felt the first stinging drops of rain on her bare back. She wiped his hot cheeks, looked into his red eyes. "I bet those cats are missing you. You better check on them." She watched Walter run to the barn before she turned back to Fay. Lily took a breath, felt rain catch in her hair, run down her face. "He has a name, and this is not about him, is it?"

"He's just like you! Wild! Vicious!"

"You don't know him. You don't even know me."

"Always hitting out. Always in trouble. Something wrong with you from the first day!" Fay clutched Christopher to her chest, rocked him in time to her angry words.

Lightning cracked, the rain came in sheets. Groups of family broke for the house. Kate hesitated, wanting to see Lily's long-due comeuppance, but Doris dragged her toward the back porch, gestured to Grace. "You'll catch your death!" Grace stood her ground. This was why she was here, to witness.

"Selfish! Running off! Crawling back, wanting something. From us! From us! Expecting us—expecting us to—I don't know what! Men and drugs and God knows what else! Fifteen years since you been to one of these things, and here you are, in that dress!"

"No!" Now Lily had found the voice, the words to match Fay's. "Not fifteen. I came back eleven years ago. I called. I begged! You never came." Lily turned her back. "His name is Walter, Mother." She headed up the yard toward the house.

Fay wasn't finished. "Run away! Run away! What will you steal this time?" she screeched at Lily's retreating form. Lily hesitated, thought of all those Frank Sinatra albums. Yes, she had stolen them, but she had come back, had offered something else in return, the most precious thing she had. They had not wanted her; they had not wanted him.

"Well," said Grace to no one. "I'm soaked. Think I'll check on the chickens." She headed toward the barn and Walter, leaving Fay standing in the wind-whipped rain, holding her grandchild of choice.

Teenagers invaded the living room. Baby could not keep their colors in order. They took over the TV, changed the channel. MTV. Baby changed it back, put her nose right to the screen. The teenagers turned it back to MTV, turned up the volume. "You'll like this, Aunt Baby," one of them shouted, laughing. "Everything looks the same that close."

"Make her move, Adrianne," another hollered.

Adrianne didn't need to make Baby move. She moved on her own, holding her ears, backing up. "Ack!" Baby closed her eyes. The dots of color throbbed, ready to attack. In the dark, she was nudged; her chair tipped. She took her hands from her ears to hold her chair seat down, but the music was too loud, screaming. Not music. Not Lily singing limeyellow words. In the dark before Baby's eyes, the dots in their sea of black faded; the black faded, too, until there was only one color. All around her, bodies, more bodies, all the family colors. They were wet. They were colliding, melting into each other, mixing. Too noisy! Baby could not keep the colors in their pattern. "Brown!" she wailed and fled.

In the kitchen, she pulled the chairs toward the wall, crouched down behind them. "Hoohoohoo," she moaned, rubbing her head against the wall. She was back where she belonged. That's where Lily found her.

Grace unlatched and slid open the huge barn doors. Their rumble matched the thunder moving off to the east. A cool, rain-scented breeze filled the barn. The chickens complained at the change of temperature, the additional light, then, realizing freedom, made a break for it. Chickens flowed around and through Grace's legs. She chuckled. "You can come out, too."

No answer, so Grace came in. The cacophony of raindrops on the corrugated roof filled the barn with noise. Feathers floated, no other movement. Grace found Walter in the pile of hay in the center of the barn floor. Butler lay draped across him, belly exposed, intoxicated with scratchings. Walter's eyes were still puffy and red.

"You used your dukes on him, did ya?"

Walter blinked, nodded, buried guilty fingers deep into Butler's fur.

"Said something about us?"

Walter looked down, "I was nervous. Too many visitors."

"Doesn't matter. You did right." Grace studied the pile of hay, Walter, and Butler at her feet. It was a long way down. She negotiated with her body: *Just let me get down there. I won't ask another thing of you today.* Grace eased herself onto the pile. "I'm going to need some help here, Walter, when it's time to get up."

Walter smiled. "OK."

Grace sighed and settled, seeking slight comfort in the hay. "You know, Walter. Your mamma always ended up poking some cousin or another every Fourth of July. She'd crawl into the old doghouse. Baby and I were always coaxing her out of there." Grace smiled.

"She said I was just like her."

"Your grandma."

"Fay."

"Well, being like your mamma is a good thing, isn't it?" Walter couldn't answer, the stew of feeling inside him too mixed, fears and wants and needs. He scratched Butler, listened closely to his contented, rumbled sigh. "Butler knows just what he wants," Grace observed. Walter nodded, scratched gently. "Rain's letting up." Outside the barn doors, the evening sky was lightening. "We'll have to go out pretty soon."

"Can't we just stay here until they go?" There was an edge of desperation in Walter's voice.

"They'll be back, Walter. You have to face them. You can't let things go on."

"Why not."

"Clear the air."

"They don't like me."

Grace sighed, "Remember the cats. Give 'em a chance."

Walter knew the difference between cats and cousins. "Maybe they won't come back next year." Walter's voice was hopeful.

"They'll be back," Grace told him. "Next year." *Sooner,* she reminded herself. A month? Less? More? For the funeral. Hers...and Baby's. "Well, Walter, come on and help an old bird to her feet. At least we can say good-bye."

Lily was stuffing Baby's wide rump up through the opening into the attic. She prayed the ladder wouldn't give way. She didn't want to contemplate how she was ever going to get her aunt back down again. All she knew was that they needed to be up here, in this clean, empty space with its safe, ordered memories. Above, a giant sneeze nearly sent Baby back down the ladder, but Lily stiffened and braced herself, then pushed. The muscles on her neck, shoulders, and arms strained, stood out like cables. With a final heave, they were through the opening.

They lay in a heap on the floor of the attic, Lily panting, Baby amazed, delighted. "Hah!" Green and sun-gold reached in through all the rain-spattered windows, patterns of light moved on the floor. Brown sank from Baby and slipped down the ladder, forgotten in discovery. Up here, each raindrop, pink pink pink, tapped on the roof, blue-green wind whispered. Baby sighed. A good place. Lily's and Walter's and Grace's and Baby's. Good. Yellow in a brown day.

Lily wandered to a window and watched the activity below. The relatives had started cleaning up. The chickens were helping. Down on the pond, red, white, and blue paper plates coasted on dark water. Baby clomped over to see. "Hah!" Kate chased white chickens. Susan stomped on a blue garbage bag. Bud and Bill and Ted stacked chairs. Family. "Red green orange blue purple blue! Hah!" Baby knocked at the windowpane and waved, knocked again harder.

"Come see, Aunt Baby." Lily coaxed Baby from the window. "Come see. This is your stuff. All about you." Lily led Baby to the boxes, pointed to the words. "See. It says 'Baby.'" She pulled down a box. "*Drawings '62–68*. Let's see what's in here." With a gentle tug, the flap came up, tape and all. Lily stepped back to watch.

Baby flopped to the floor and began to dig. Drawings erupted. "Hoho!" Baby exclaimed over and over, punctuated by an occasional, raucous "Ack!" as a drawing would be sent sliding across the floor, rejected, not up to current standards.

From over her shoulder, Lily saw an evolving talent in the drawings: first, crude lines and heavy-handed scribbles, but soon, more discernible shapes, gentler shades. Baby pointed. She wanted another box. Lily opened the next one for her, then wandered over to the window. Below, activity continued. Fay folded a blue-and-white gingham tablecloth; Ted bent and hoisted a stack of chairs, laughing at some comment from Uncle Bill. Wind ruffled his hair. Fay passed by, raising a hand to smooth it. Lily slid her fingers down the glass, wanting a way through. They were the same; she was the same.

Lily sweeps the flagstones. From inside the monastery office, raised voices she can't help but hear. Yoshi, Robert, and Carol are arguing about the failing septic system. Robert accuses Carol of flushing toilet paper. Carol says Robert should be the monastery's septic system, he's so full of crap. Yoshi is master, in charge, his voice beyond the locked door serene. "We have a rule here. There is no flushing of paper."

"*You're siding with him! You always side with him!*" *Carol bangs from the door, pushes past Lily, knocking the broom across the floor. Lily bends to retrieve it.*

From inside the office: "*She's a wacko,*" *says Robert.*

"*PMS,*" *Yoshi laughs.*

Later, in her narrow bed, Lily listens in the dark to the couple next door perform their tired, nightly litany. Hannah and Steven are troubled.

"*You don't touch me anymore. Why don't you touch me?*"

Silence.

"*I see you look at her.*"

"*Who?*"

Lily puts her pillow over her head. She doesn't want to know. In the rushing silence in her head, she has already figured it out. It doesn't matter. It will be someone or no one. It is all the same. In the monastery, in the cramped apartment of addicts, on the street, at home. We are all the same.

The next morning, Lily hitchhikes into town and calls her caseworker. It is time to move on. Walter. A week later, she stands before him. He has grown in six months. She reaches out and takes his paper bag of clothes. "*I came back,*" *she says.*

He nods as if he has always known this. But in his solemn eyes, she sees these questions: Are you better? Are you the same?

TWENTY-TWO

*L*ily turned from the window and watched Baby as she chuckled and hooted and worked her way through her drawings. Something happened here, Lily thought to herself. Something huge and ugly. *"None of us did anything to stop it."* Lily shook her head. Aunt Grace was wrong. She did something. She did this. She changed a world.

Lily joined Baby on the floor, opened the box marked *STUFF* for Baby, the box *LIFE FOR BABY* for herself. Every issue of *Life* magazine, sixty years saved, waiting for Baby. Some photos had notations: *"I remember this as if it were yesterday!"*

Baby sorted through her *STUFF.* Kate's soft, pink sweater, still smelling of powder and young girl; two marbles, green and blue; a jay feather; a golden rock; a tiny red hat and mitten; a pressed flower. Baby examined each item, held them close to her nose and her eyes, rubbing them over her cheek. She laid them out on the attic floor in neat rows, each offering a color, a memory. She was restoring the pattern.

Grace, Baby, Lily, Walter, and Butler stood in the front yard, sunset transferring its glow to the painted house, to the white stars and stripes of Grace's and Baby's dresses, to Butler's creamy ruff. Lily's red dress burned with brilliance, her skin a burnished copper. Across the road, pink mist collected in the hollow at the bottom of the hill. The rainbow cows turned as one and headed home for milking. Five minivans and three pickups filed past, from their windows smiles, waves, mouths open with laughter and talk. Walter raised a tentative hand and waved back. He was the first.

"Well, that didn't go so badly." Lily's quick grin flashed in the sunset. Walter stared. Grace snorted. Lily put an arm around each of them. "At least they liked the salads."

"They always do," Grace admitted. "They try."

"We tried, too, Aunt Grace," Lily said.

"I guess we did. It never gets finished, though."

The last of the sun's rays lifted from the face of the painted house. Baby began to blubber, a low, mournful hooing. Walter touched her hand. "What's wrong?"

"She's missing them already, Walter," Grace told him.

"Don't worry, Aunt Baby," Walter soothed. "They'll be back."

Grace nodded. Next year. Sooner. When she and Baby were gone, who would offer them that sweet taste of ambrosia, that yearly absolution?

That night, Grace couldn't sleep. Exhaustion, as well as Butler's head and one forepaw, pinned her to the mattress. She lay in bed staring upward, waited for her pills to kick in. She conjured a vision of Baby, Lily, and Walter in the swimming darkness above her eyes. Grace imagined them where she knew they were at that moment: on the blue plaid blanket in the middle of the golf course's eighteenth green. The lake lapped near their feet. They were prone like her, eyes skyward, waiting. Baby's fat hands smashed her fuzzy, leopard-print earmuffs to her ears. Grace placed Walter's head in the hollow of Lily's shoulder. Their bodies fused in the darkness. Perhaps Walter had a hand on the round swell of Baby's tummy. Yes. That was good. Grace had seen Walter do that before. Grace filled the air around them with scattered laughter of children, the low murmur of adults, the intense, momentary fizz and luminescence of sparklers. Crowds stirred the mist around them. Yes, mist was important, always ground fog on the Fourth, fog to catch the sifted sparks of color that dropped from the sky. Grace created mist and the bobbing lights of boats cradled between the dark, hunched hills, red and blue running lights of invisible boats slipping in and out of the drifting fog, agitating the still, black lake and the moon silver that rested there. Sky, hills, lake, and crowd, all were ready for the show. In the center of the vision, Baby, Lily, and Walter, joined in their waiting, still as a painting, Grace's trinity. Ready.

At the first pop far over the western hill, Butler raised his head, growled deep in his throat. A distant boom, the screen at the open window flashed cool silver and subsided. Another pop, an answering growl, a boom, and glowing screen. Butler checked his Grace, but she was unmoving, staring at the ceiling, her breathing even, unworried. He lowered his head to her shoulder again. His cheeks puffed with a sigh, and winking with sleep, he watched the show.

Grace concentrated. She wanted to be there, but didn't know where to place herself in the picture. Between Walter and Baby, a hand for each? On Lily's other side, their shoulders touching, the length of their arms a mingled warmth? Perhaps just looking over them, watching the light of the fireworks fracture in Walter's moist, tangled hair and spark off Baby's glasses and dentures, Baby with eyes and mouth wide, drinking the colors that splashed and dripped from the dark sky.

Grace closed her eyes. She could almost feel the painful thump of the fireworks in her chest, almost hear the rolling echo down the lake. Like life leaving with a bang and a holler. Life. If she could look down, there would be Lily, grinning her devil's-child grin, and Walter, at her side, amazed at his first fireworks, exploding right over his head, loud and brilliant and perfect, drifting down to him with a whiff of sulfur. The slight curve of a smile eased through Grace's lips. She knew what Walter would do. He would raise his arms, reaching, reaching, until his fingertips touched the light.

Something to see. A sharp spark of longing arced through Grace, leaving her aching to be with them. Her last fireworks, Walter's first. She felt Butler's chin pressed to her shoulder, his whiskers tickling a patch above her collarbone. She felt the bed cupping her, keeping her. She had seen her share of fireworks, but God, how she loved the show.

Grace is grounded. In bed since 4:23 p.m., she lies with her arms crossed, raising first one and then the other leg, letting them drop like dead things and bounce to stillness on the hard mattress. No dinner. That's OK. She can still taste Cousin George's blood in her mouth. Meal enough. She would bite him again if she ever had the chance, the dirty cheat. Ten-year-olds don't bite? Hah! Watch me, *Grace thinks.*

Downstairs, the front door closes, and she can hear excited chatter and the crunch of gravel beneath her window. Car doors slam. They are going to the fireworks. They will have an ice-cream soda at the drugstore afterward, but Grace is in purgatory. She is exiled to her room, banished to her bed. Cousins, aunts and uncles, Grandpa Harv, all the world of her family knows the truth. Grace is a biter. Outside, the Plymouth starts, stalls, and starts. Leaves Grace behind. Grace can feel a white-hot charge explode in her chest. She wants to see those fireworks.

Darkness slips in through the window. The pale walls of her room, pinked from sunset, fade. She could turn her head on her pillow, watch the fireworks, tiny and far through the square of window, but that is nowhere near enough. Grace lifts her legs, lets them drop one more time. She listens to the still, heavy waiting held captive in her house. Then she is up, off the bed, out the door.

In the kitchen, Grace pauses, hand hovering over the cookie jar. Does her mother count the cookies? Grace backs away from the loaded jar. Behind her, Baby sticks her fingers through the chicken wire. "Grah."

Grace turns, considers. Yes. She will open the pen, open the back door, leave it wide on its hinges, let out all the pent-up waiting in the house, let it explode into the night. "Come on, Baby." Grace holds out her hand.

They take the trail through the woods, the moon floating above them through tall, black trees, leading the way upward. Cool mist stirs around their knees, flows down the trail past them. Again and again, Baby must stop and reach down, comb her fingers through soft, escaping gray. Grace tugs and coaxes and finally pulls Baby through the break in the trees and out into the field at the crest of the hill. Below, behind, fog pools around their dark house. At their feet, the land sweeps away to the village lights, fuzzy and shapeless in dark and mist. Up here it is clear, sharp, stars only inches away.

"Watch there, Baby." Grace points, and they watch.

A pop, a thin streamer of smoke, a low, pleasing thump. The sky ignites. A fiery red orchid blooms in front of them. Baby gapes. Grace is suddenly bounding, leaping, whooping, dancing on fireworks. "Dance with me, Baby!"

Baby can't. She is rooted. Saliva runs from her open mouth, sparks blue and white as it drips off her chin.

"It's fireworks!" Grace laughs, spins away.

Fireworks. Baby reaches out to touch them, to gather them, to breathe them in. "Grah…"

Tears on Baby's cheeks. Grace stills, watches them paint sparkling streaks down Baby's face. Grace reaches out, reaches out to Baby. Arms around each other, they watch the show. Baby is laughing; Grace is grinning. She gulps in the tang of sulfur. She will have to remember to bite someone next Fourth of July.

TWENTY-THREE

*G*race rested. Days inched by. Midsummer limbo, fevered and dry, settled over the painted house. Lily wandered the gardens, hoping for the green prick of weeds through dirt, anxious for something to rout. She carried buckets of water up from the pond and watered plants by hand. She worried about the state of the well. She worried about the chickens, who had stopped laying and turned querulous. She worried about Butler, watchful and unmoving at Grace's side. She worried about Walter, solitary in the barn with his cats or in an inner tube on the dark face of the pond, adrift like a dropped leaf.

She worried about Baby. Baby, sweating and sullen in front of the TV, Baby scowling at every food offered, unwilling to change from her week-old, crusty nightgown, Baby wanting whatever program wasn't on just then, asking for Walter, wanting Grace. Lily couldn't coax Baby outdoors. She wouldn't walk on crisped grass. It made her plug her ears and curl her toes. "Brown," she'd whisper, shivering, and wobble back into the house. Lily could find no comfort in Frank Sinatra. She hummed anxious snatches of tunes, then forgot them midmeasure. Walter, Baby…Grace. Grace, at the vortex of Lily's worry, lay in her room, rousing herself only for Baby's shots.

"I can do that," Lily had offered. "I know about needles."

"Then better not to be around them." Grace had shaken her head, unwilling to give up this last vestige of her life's work. Maybe she would need to use it on Baby in the end…still, her mind veered away.

Lily had stepped back, stung and angry. Then her eyes caught the tremor along Grace's jaw, in her thin, speckled hands. Grace, weary of being careful of feelings. "Let me try," Lily offered again.

"Not yet. My job," Grace had said and then proceeded to take the blood, to measure the insulin, to give the shot, afterward holding her trembling hand to Baby's bruised haunch as she always had, willing the pain to leave her whimpering sister.

Not yet. The words echoed in Lily's head. But when? When would Grace leave them? Tomorrow? A week? A month? On the fifth morning of Grace's retirement, Lily decided. *Not yet.*

Grace and Butler woke simultaneously to bacon, the aroma lifting noses to the air, teasing eyes open, pulling heads up. Grace thought she might be hungry; Butler was sure. Grace creaked down the stairs and showed up in the kitchen in her pink nightgown. Butler beat her there by long minutes.

Grace cleared her throat. "Country-smoked bacon can raise the dead and start them drooling." Her voice was hoarse.

"I thought so," Lily said.

Lily, Walter, and Baby were beaming; Grace nearly had to squint in the gleam. *I might have missed this,* she thought. "I thought I'd eat," she told them.

Walter pulled out a chair and helped Grace into it, feeling thin bones beneath his fingers. *Cat bones.* He didn't want to let go, but had to because Baby was there. Baby had to touch Grace, had to rake her fingers through Grace's pillow-mashed hair, had to hold her cheeks and squeeze her arms. Not enough Grace. Where had the rest of Grace gone? Baby searched the spaces inside the billowing, pink nightgown for her sister. Pink! Baby suddenly realized her own nightgown was blue. "Pink!" she roared and began undressing on the spot. Walter smacked his hands over his eyes, and Lily laughed out loud. Grace smiled, first time in days. She felt she might float right off her hard, wooden seat. All this thanks to bacon.

Grace ate one piece and a quarter of a scrambled egg, sipped a glass of milk. The unfamiliar food churned in her stomach, seeking a way out. *Stay with me,* Grace counseled it. Watching Lily gobble piece after piece of bacon provided distraction. "What happened? Became a carnivore while I was resting?"

Lily grinned, her lips a smooth, greased curve. "I'm still a vegetarian...except for bacon. Besides, bacon isn't meat." Lily searched for the perfect term, found it. Her words bubbled with laughter, "It's...ambrosia!" Grace laughed; the contents of her stomach sloshed and settled.

"Believe me, Mom." Walter waved a strip at her. "It's better."

Lily was giddy with victory and bacon. She had the day planned. She wanted to take Grace outside, set her down in the middle of green summer day and white-gold sunshine. She wanted to feed her. They would have a picnic at the top of the hill across the road. Bacon, lettuce, and tomato sandwiches, peaches and cold apple cider. Walter danced with excitement; Baby in knickers and nothing else, pendulous bosom swinging, declared, "Meep! Meep!" Butler's toenails skittered around the kitchen floor, ever ready. Best of all, Grace was willing. "I think I could just manage that," she told them and headed upstairs to get dressed. From her bedroom, she went into Baby's to dress her. Rows of madonnas with child watched with gentle, knowing eyes, awaited the ritual. "What're you going to wear today, Baby? You can't go around naked all day. I'll just sit here and mind my own business while you decide." Grace eased down onto Baby's bed and closed her eyes. The floorboards creaked as Baby sneaked toward the bed and leaned down. Grace could suddenly taste Baby's bacon-and-eggs breath at the back of her throat, feel its moist heat against her cheek. "I'm not peeking. Go on ahead. Pick something out before I expire here." Grace listened as Baby clumped toward the closet, counted in her head the sliding hangers, heard Baby's grunt of satisfaction, and knew it was time to open her eyes.

"My gosh!" Grace summoned just the right tone. "You'll be dressed just like me! People'll say those two must be twins!" Baby chuckled and hugged the orange-and-gold dress to her chest. Grace struggled to sitting, then to standing, swayed with a bout of dizziness. She continued. "They'll say, 'That tall one, though, she's the looker. She's the beauty in the family.'" Grace collected one of Baby's bras and a pair of pink panties, held them up. "By golly, Baby, these days, you could fit a whole herd of me in a pair of these. How did that happen, huh?"

Grace helped Baby into her underwear, then sat and rested before she stood again to pull the dress over Baby's head. Swirls of orange and gold like breaking waves caught midcrash swept over Baby's tummy and down to a ruffle at the hem. Grace tied the bow at the scooped and gathered neck. Grace stepped back to survey the end product. "My God, Baby. This is about the ugliest dress we've ever had. What possessed us?"

Baby's attention was caught in the dress, her fingers tracing the swirling patterns of color. Orange flowed into gold; gold swept up into orange; orange crashed down, exploded into gold. She looked up at Grace, her smiling face a map of mounds and crescents. Treasure. "Yellow," she breathed, ecstatic, her fingers still moving along the ceaseless confluence of color.

Grace nodded, "Oh, yes."

Lily, Walter, and Butler met them outside with a blanket and a basket filled with sandwiches and drinks. "Holy cow," Lily commented on the dresses.

Grace shook her head. "Fashion suicide. Baby likes it. Don't you, Baby?"

"Yellow." Baby was guiding Walter's fingers over the waves of changing gold and orange across her tummy.

Grace gathered two handfuls of sugar cubes for the cows. "Let's get this show on the road," she told them and headed for the trail across the road.

It took forever. Lily had to restrain the muscles in her legs from taking longer, stronger steps. They ached from the effort, the need to move. Grace shuffled on; stopped often; pushed damp hair from her brow; slid down a tree trunk to squat and breathe; accepted a hand only back to standing before trudging on. She felt the sugar cubes moistening in her pockets, melting from sweat. She knew if she could make it to the top, the cows would take it any way it was offered.

Ahead, Baby, with Walter and Butler in tow, announced her trees. "Purple!" she hollered back, hugging the oak, pressing her cheek tightly to its rough bark.

Walter gave it a try, feeling the tough, craggy bark resistant in his arms but like a cool, rough kiss at his cheek. He liked it. "Purple!" he called down the path to his mom and Aunt Grace.

At the top of the hill, Grace gave the cows their sugar cubes and set Butler after them. They scattered like wishes. Lily watched from the blanket, smiling. "You have it down to a science," Lily commented.

"Practice. It has to be done just so," Grace told her, collapsing onto the blanket next to her. "Just the way everyone expects it." Grace lay flat on her back, winking in the sun. "Otherwise it's a mess of barking, nipping, kicking cows. Terrible. Life's that way."

"I'm beginning to see that," Lily told her. "I never lived that way before."

"Takes some getting used to. Took me years."

Lily lay back and began to sing, "Summertime...and the livin' is easy..."

Grace closed her eyes. "I don't recall Frank Sinatra ever singing that one. Nervous?"

Lily smiled. "No. Sometimes there are other reasons to sing... sometimes. I'm trying to branch out...Fish are jumpin'...and the cotton is high..." *Practice.*

The hard walk up through the woods, the sun's warmth, Lily's soft, off-key singing worked on Grace. She drifted where she lay, the smell of green fields teasing a memory from her: Baby smelling the sun and grass in Grace's summer clothes, wondering, rubbing at Grace's young, brown arm...

"It's a tan, Baby, just a tan. The sun does that. It's good."
Baby rubs. The sun is beyond the cage, beyond the window, beyond reach.

Lily's voice pulled Grace to consciousness. "You're goin' to rise up singing...Then you'll spread your wings, and you'll take to the sky."

Grace felt the heat lick her flesh in great, curling waves. Orange and gold. She thought: *No sunscreen. Doesn't matter. Too late. Could lie here all day and fry, could drink to excess every short day the rest of my life, could eat those artery-clogging foods. Bacon, bring me bacon! Doesn't matter. Gone before they caught me. Could commit murder...*She let the heat sink into her, felt it reach her bones, the back of her eyes, her brain, the jumble of ruined tissues inside her gut. She looked around for Walter and Baby, saw them safely away. She turned to Lily. "This is my last trip up here."

Lily felt a clamping down, an answering pain from her constricted chest. She sat up and hugged her knees. "I'm glad we came. It's beautiful up here."

"It's a good place," Grace told her. "For me and Baby, a good place. This is where I want the ashes scattered."

Lily couldn't look at Grace. "I love the way the house looks from up here. It's like looking into a mirror, a magic mirror. If we could just walk into that picture, everything would be..."

"You should leave here."

"I thought I might dig up the land behind the barn this fall, work some good manure into it. I want to plant vegetables and flowers to sell at the farmer's market next summer."

"I have things to get on with. Baby and I."

"A few more chickens, and we'd have enough eggs to make some real money."

"It's time for you and Walter to go."

"We could even sell the manure." Lily's voice was tight, desperate.

"You don't want to let that boy of yours watch me die."

"Flowers and organic vegetables and organic eggs..."

"Go someplace else."

"Where?" It was almost a sob. "Where? *Please.* This is it for me. There's no place else." The words were hard and bitter in Lily's mouth. She pinched each of her toes in turn, hard, to feel the pain. "That's saying a lot, believe me." Lily looked over and searched Grace's closed face. "And Walter's strong, Aunt Grace. He is. Stronger than me, I know that. For him, this place is so..." Lily's rushing voice trailed off. "Do you want us to leave?" she whispered finally.

"I want you to be free."

Lily's voice was grim. "It's not all it's cracked up to be. It's not a garden and chickens and a pond. It's not you and Aunt Baby."

"You can't have that."

"I can try."

Grace lay still, felt the weight of the sky, its gold heat, its endless width and height, felt herself make way for it. *Right here on this spot is where I want it done*, she thought, *the place where my ashes will fly...our ashes*. She smiled and nodded. She told Lily, "I'll visit the lawyer."

"I don't need anything, Aunt Grace. We don't need anything. Just to stay."

"You need a garden."

Lily smiled.

"I'm here." Lily hates the sound of her own voice on the telephone, can hear panic and need carried along the cord and over the wires, amplified on the journey to her parents' living room. The silence from that end is booming. Lily holds the receiver away from her ears, the emptiness too much for her.

"Why?" The word is distant and hard when it comes.

"I—"

It is at this instant that Lily's body gives her a full explanation. A cramp sweeps through her belly. She feels a sharp ripping, thinks she hears a pop. The town's only phone booth is awash in amniotic fluid. Her skirt drips; her Keds fill. Lily looks at the phone as if she had never seen it before. Why has it done this to her? A tightening begins at the top of her belly and rolls through her. Lily curves her arms protectively around her huge stomach, bends with pain. Something in there is trying to get out.

"Lily. Answer me." A tinny, far away voice demands.

More fluid. She will drown if she doesn't escape this phone booth. Lily struggles with the door. It is only when the smell of fresh air hits her sweating face that she drops the receiver and waddles, dripping and scared, into the square.

From the hospital, she calls again. "I'm here at the hospital. I'm having a baby." Lily feels a contraction starting and braces herself.

Through a narrowing tunnel of pain, she hears, "Whose?"

She knows not to say. "Does it matter?" and can't answer anyway. Her words have been stolen, and she is caught. By the time she can say, "Mine," the phone's response is a low buzz.

She tries again from her bed in the ward. Her baby lies in her lap, wrapped up like a cocktail sausage. His eyes, clear and dark, watch her with a look that says, "I know you."

"Fourth floor maternity ward, room four-sixteen," Lily tells the answering machine and hangs up. "Don't worry," she whispers. "They'll come."

Lily stays on the ward seven days. There is excess bleeding, then a slight uterine infection. Her breasts grow painful and hard but then learn to do their work. She is outside her body, observing hers and the baby's progress, observing the parking lot below the window. Her parents have a blue Ford with a long dent running down one side. When the baby nuzzles her breast, her belly cramps. Some days, there are twenty blue cars in the parking lot, none of them the Ford.

When the baby is taken away to sleep, Lily feels a cold, moaning rush through the hollow of her body. "Why is the baby so quiet?" Lily asks the nurse.

The nurse smiles, "He's just fine. We know he can hear. Count it as a blessing, believe me!" On the way out, she turns, adds, "He's listening for you."

She tries one last time.

"I'm checking out today. We can come home..." she tells the answering machine.

She sits on her bed fully dressed until four in the afternoon. No blue Fords with dents enter the parking lot. The lady in the bed next to her is having a celebration. A man with a party hat and a clumsily wrapped package appears. He cries when he holds the lady's baby girl.

After they all leave, Lily asks, "Was that your father in the hat?"

The girl laughs. "Oh, no. That's my Uncle Walter. My dad died years ago."

"He loved your baby."

"Uncle Walter loves everything. My mom calls him a born blessing."

Watching the parking lot, Lily knows her parents won't come. There will be no welcoming, there will be no home. Walter, *she decides. She picks up her baby and walks out of the ward, through the hall, down the elevator, and out the great sliding doors of the hospital. She heads across the crowded parking lot with five blue cars and turns toward the phone booth and the bus stop. She will not use the phone. She still aches from the hole it has put in her. She will climb onto a bus heading south to the city. She will go back to the city, she and Walter.*

TWENTY-FOUR

*g*race's snores were shallow, soft huffs, the quiet sounds of an animal nosing its way in the dark. Two monarch butterflies landed on the swirling pattern of her dress without disturbing her. They rose and fell with Grace's chest and, seemingly mesmerized, clung there, a new-sprung breeze tipping their wings sideways. Their long, black tongues unfurled and searched for the hidden nectar of polyester. Two more monarchs joined them. Lily, watching at Grace's side, smiled. *Aunt Grace.* Another monarch fought the freshening breeze and settled on the ruffle at Grace's hem. Lily thought to wake her, show her, but the gentle, patient snoring stopped her. *Let her rest.* Instead, Lily rose carefully and wandered off to join Baby and Walter, gathering flowers far down in the corner of the field. She would bring them back to see... Grace among the butterflies.

By the time Lily and Walter trudged up the hill with their offerings of color, Grace had acquired a flock of monarchs, a congregation with wings nodding in unison to the east. There were three in her hair, perhaps twelve on her chest and belly, another two clinging to her left knee. Grace snored on, her mouth open. A fly tested the sheen of sweat. Grace's forehead wrinkled in response. The fly teetered, then escaped. The butterflies remained.

Walter, clinging to Lily's free arm, whispered, "They won't bite Aunt Grace, will they?"

141

"No." Lily smiled. "I don't think they have teeth. They just want to be near her. Maybe it's the dress, the colors, or the way it sparkles in the sun."

"I think it's just Aunt Grace," Walter said.

The wings opened and closed.

"I think you're right, Walter."

Baby finally achieved the top of the hill with her load of flowers. She saw Grace bedecked with butterflies, the backsides of their wings quaking brown in the sun, and squawked in alarm. Her arms opened. She bellowed a warning that changed to a deep bark of delight as flowers cascaded and butterflies unfurled and rose. "Hah! Orange!"

Grace opened her eyes to the sight of pinks, whites, reds, purples, and golds falling; flames of orange swirling, rising. "My God," she gasped, blinking.

"Orange! Orange!" Baby pointed to the sky and then collapsed to the ground, crushing flowers and hugging Grace. "Orange!"

"By golly, yes, Baby," Grace soothed, patting Baby's back. "Monarch butterflies. A cloud of them! Orange and black. *OLD WOMAN CARRIED OFF BY BUTTERFLIES!* eh, Baby?" Grace chuckled, "Beautiful things."

"Orange," Baby echoed, now distracted. She released Grace and rooted beneath her haunches for the dropped flowers. They came out crushed and broken, some just stems, flowers lost in the tugging. Her bottom lip trembled; her eyes began to blink.

Lily rescued her before the wail, gathering Baby's flowers, surrounding them with her own and Walter's bouquets, handing them back to Baby. "The butterflies were amazing, Aunt Grace. You were covered." Lily grinned.

"You were the queen!" Walter told her.

"Queen for a day. About time. Though, could be like my mother always said: 'Butterflies like a good mess.'"

Lily laughed. "Well, you must be doing something right, because even we brought an offering to the queen. Didn't we, Aunt Baby?"

Baby thrust the flowers at Grace.

"Look at this! My! Did you pick these, Baby?"

Baby chuckled, crowed, sobered instantly. "Walter," she told Grace.

"Walter, too?"

Walter blushed. "Mom, too."

"My!" Grace glowed in the warmth of the sun and attention. "I better see what we have here." She laid the flowers in her lap and struggled to sitting. She picked through the blooms with shaking fingers. "We got some oxeye daisy, I see."

"White," Baby corrected.

Grace nodded. "And some wild marjoram, that's in the mint family, and this is too—dittany."

"Purple purple."

"Yes, they are," Grace agreed. "Bedstraw, birdsfoot trefoil, crown vetch, bush clover." The names came to her easily, teasing her memory. Baby provided the colors. "Why, look! You even found some lobelia. Cardinal flower."

"Aunt Grace, you know all their names!"

Grace nodded, ran her fingers over a cluster of pale pink. "Learned them…this is…is…bouncing Bet…" The colors in her lap blurred. She heard Walter's distant giggle, Baby's declaratory *Whitepink*. She couldn't respond; she was caught, plucked from the present, held…

"Bouncing Bet."

Grace giggles. Her mother smiles back at her. It is deep summer. The grass where the cows have not been is as tall as Grace's ten year-old waist. Grace and her mother are on their hands and knees. They are hunting flowers.

"Yes, I suppose it's a silly name. It's also called soapwort, from the saponaria family. It's good to know the names of things. They're yours, then, forever. And look…" Grace's mother's slender fingers expertly pluck a stem of blossoms. Grace can see the sun shimmering off the hairs of her mother's extended arm, can read the constellation of summer freckles across her mother's nose. There are tiny flecks of brown in her green eyes.

Grace's mother reaches out. Grace sucks her breath in as her mother slips the flower into Grace's crown of black curls. "Beautiful." Mother smiles. Her fingers linger.

Grace cannot breathe out. She doesn't want to. For this one, crystal moment, there is just Grace and Mother, deep in tall grass. Baby recedes, a nameless one. Just Grace and Mother and this flower, bouncing Bet, its gentle weight at Grace's temple, an unexpected gift.

"Aunt Grace?" Grace felt Lily's breath at her ear. "Bouncing Bet?"

"Yes." Grace focused, pushed this divergent vision away. "Saponaria family. Wilts too fast to keep."

"You haven't named these." Walter pointed.

"Oh, those." Grace smiled. "Those are special, Walter. This one here's a day lily."

"I knew that one!" Walter piped.

"Lily orange!" Baby chortled and pointed to the sky. Lily grinned.

"This one's the last of this year's dame's rocket. It's in the mustard family. And this one here's my favorite—everlasting pea."

"Whitepurplepink."

"That right, Baby. They're not true wildflowers, Walter."

"Huh?"

Grace winked at Walter. "Well, these three flowers are like your mom and me. They escaped cultivation." Walter stared. Lily laughed. Grace explained, "That's what it's called. See, Walter, someone planted them in a nice garden, but they escaped. Escaped to fields and roadsides!"

"Why?" Grace shrugged. "Did they try first?" Walter wanted to know.

Grace eyed Lily. "Maybe they did, maybe not. Doesn't matter. The garden didn't suit them."

"I want to escape cultivation," Walter announced.

"You're on your way, boy," Grace told him.

"What about Aunt Baby? Can she escape, too?" Walter's face was suddenly serious.

"Oh, Baby." Grace told him, "Doesn't need to. She's an exotic." Grace warmed to her story. "One of a kind. A seed dropped by some traveling bird. Don't know where she came from, don't know her name. She's rare. You have to take special care of the rare ones, Walter. They're finicky." Lily smiled and reached over absently to pluck pink petals from Baby's mouth. Grace nodded, her face solemn. "Take special care, loads of attention. Otherwise they sicken. Can't pick them either, no matter how pretty they are. Once you do, they're gone for good."

Walter looked at Baby. "I knew it," he breathed. "You're rare."

"Gah!" Baby stuck out her tongue, displaying specks of wet pink and purple.

"Well, Dame's Rocket," Lily laughed. "We'd better get Miss Everlasting Pea down the hill. She's about to wilt."

Grace wanted to avoid the cool dark of the woods, wanted to walk down through the steep field, through tall grass and flowers and floating orange and black butterflies. She wanted to gather this day to her like a bouquet, keep it from dying, wanted to wear it like a crown. Walter and Baby plowed forward, hand in hand, running headlong. Butler barked and leaped at them, his black head intermittently visible just above the wind-bent grass.

"Watch—" Grace caught herself in midyell, remembered in a sharp flash that other time...how long ago...six weeks? A bit more...She had almost, almost...pushed...then called out a warning and chased Baby down the hill. She had almost ended it then, snipped the bloom, quit the long habit of care. Lily and Walter came that day. Escaped from cultivation to Grace and Baby.

"They'll be fine." Lily smiled and put her arm around her aunt, taking some of her weight.

Grace drew in the scent of her flowers, held it in until there was no place left to put it, then let it go, a slow, unwanted release. "Lily," Grace said, letting her niece and gravity ease her down the hill toward all that still needed to be done. "I want to thank you for this day. I didn't expect it."

AUGUST

TWENTY-FIVE

*B*aby watched Andy Griffith. Lily and Walter and Butler were out for a walk. Grace was resting upstairs. Baby sighed. Andy was no good today, a more modern Andy in colors not of Baby's choosing. Barney Fife was not there. Where was Barney? Out for a walk, or resting.

Baby sighed. She could feel the weight of Grace on the bed in the room above, heavy and gray-brown. Andy was in color, and Grace was not. No Barney Fife. No Lily or Walter. Baby lifted her chair and turned it so that her back was to the TV. She crossed her arms and sighed. She could feel the colors seep around her from Andy, smudged and pale. Grace was smudged and faded too. Baby had watched the colors leaching from Grace for days. Too fast to catch and put back. Where did the colors go? Baby closed her eyes. "Redyellowbluegreen. Redyellowbluegreen."

Those were the first colors. Whenever she closed her eyes, there they were, the first colors. Baby remembered when they came, when Grace gave Redyellowbluegreen. In a thin, paper box, white. She still had the box, scratchings of color along the inside. Redyellowbluegreen. Somewhere. Baby had to show Grace she still had them, still remembered. Time to give colors back.

She clumped upstairs and scuttled down the hall to her room. Somewhere. In her room, she searched. House dresses erupted from the closet, a bright, slick, polyester flow to the floor. Caught by the

149

cascade of color, Baby paused, smiled, moved on. Outsized bras and panties, white, white, pink, white, whisked from gaping drawers, floated. Sweaters plopped like splashes of bright paint around her. On the walls, the madonnas swung on their tacks, rustled in the stirring air, lending a sound of soft, pink applause. Baby laughed and pushed the mattress off her bed to check if the thin, white box was on the springs. No.

Baby suddenly smiled, and thrusting her hand into a slit in the mattress, she pulled out great handfuls of white batting and tossed them behind her until her hand found what it was seeking. Yes. "Redyellowbluegreen." Baby remembered.

Lying on her bed, Grace could hear the commotion, thumps and steps, mutterings. Her body felt weighted, sunk deep, held down by traitorous memories. A mother smiling like a bright blossom, naming each flower; a father laughing at the kitchen table, relating cow anecdotes, each animal known by sight, name, personality quirk. No. Grace refused them, these treacherous spots of soft color, fleeting joy. Unbidden. Unwelcome. Outside of the selected pattern of her past. *No.* Grace almost whispered it, wondering why now, and receiving her answer in pain. From the end of the hall, more thumpings and a delighted crow. "Hohohoho!"

Grace struggled up through the layers of tiredness and doubt, sat at the edge of the bed, pulled air into her compressed lungs. "Grace! Grace! Redyellowbluegreen!" Baby called from her room.

Grace sighed and rose. "All right, Baby," she said, more to herself. "I thought I left you downstairs, watching Andy." Grace's voice grew in volume and irritation as she stumped down the hall. "All right, All right! I admit it! I admit it! I wasn't watching you! Five minutes, that's all. What's all the hubbub? Where's Lily and Walt—" Grace stopped in the doorway, clutching the frame. "What?"

Baby stood in the center of monumental disaster. Above her, a light green sweater and two pink bras rotated slowly on the ceiling fan. Grace was stunned, speechless. "Redyellowbluegreen." Baby smiled and showed Grace the thin, cardboard box, filthy and mangled.

Grace stared at the unrecognizable scrap and shook her head. She could feel herself begin to tremble, her heart pound. "Why?" she gasped at Baby.

"Redyellowbluegreen." Baby worked to reshape the box. She stuck her fat index finger inside, wiggled it. She nodded. "Redyellowbluegreen." She offered Grace a peek.

Grace looked at the little box. A crayon box, she guessed. Grace, a veteran of a thousand crayon boxes, thought: *So what?* What was it supposed to mean? All of this mess for one of those cheap boxes they handed out at restaurants to entertain the kids? To entertain Baby. Important to Baby. Grace shook her head. Baby Baby Baby. Always Baby. Feed Baby, interpret Baby, keep Baby living. Kill Baby.

All Grace had wanted to do was rest, *just rest*. But Baby. *Always Baby*. Grace felt the tears well in her eyes. Something she hadn't done in years and years and years. They came from some disused place inside her chest. It hurt. "Crybaby," she said at herself, annoyed, and lifted her eyes. All around her, the madonnas looked down from skewed angles, their eyes blue with wisdom, their smiles soft with secrets. In their arms, their little charges sat impassive, separate.

Baby nodded, took Grace's hand, put the broken box in it. "Redyellowbluegreen."

Grace clutched the stupid, empty box and let the tears run. Baby turned from Grace to her room, pushed up her glasses, threw up her arms to the palette of color and texture around her, and proclaimed, "Hah!" Grace had them now, the first colors, the most important. They would fill her up.

From below, the door banged, Butler scrabbled across the floor and up the stairs, shooting into the room, a dark torpedo. Lily and Walter followed. The smell of sun-imbibed bodies filled the room. Grace cried.

"Holy God!" whistled Lily. Walter just blinked in astonishment. Both felt like they stood at the edge of a charmed circle filled with chaos and two old women. Baby stood with her arms thrown to the heavens. Aunt Grace's face was wet with tears, streams of tears, like rivers from a great, glacial thaw.

"Redyellowbluegreen!" Baby crowed.

"Everywhere," Lily commented and turned to Walter. "We better get started." They eased past Grace and into the room. Baby greeted them with bear hugs.

Holding Walter, Baby's face emptied. She gasped, "Greg! Marcia Brady!" and rushed from the room.

"It's not so bad, Aunt Grace." Lily's voice was gentle. She reached out, almost touching her aunt. "What was it all about?"

Grace sobbed and held out the mangled, dirty cardboard. "This."

"What is it?"

"She never gave me anything." Grace hiccupped. Her voice shuddered. "Not once that I can remember. Never. Then she gives me this. This."

"It's important." Walter, peeking into Grace's hand, spoke at last, his voice quiet, reverential. Grace nodded and scrubbed at the tears on her face. *WOMAN FINDS ANSWER TO LIFE IN SISTER'S MESSY ROOM!* Grace sniffed and rubbed her nose. *What was it?* She closed her fingers around the damp crayon box and held on, mourning all the lost memories, clues to the pattern of truth.

The kitchen is all white. Mother likes white. She says it's a godly color. Even the wood chairs and kitchen table, even the wood-planked floor is painted white. Every speck and crumb is scrubbed away like sin. When the morning sun comes over the far hill and through the picture window, the kitchen glows like a spotless, stripped refrigerator with the door suddenly flung open. Mother says, like heaven.

Baby provides the color, a deep, organic brown. In her pen, along her wall, a stripe runs the perimeter, three feet up, a palm's width, brown, joined, and imbedded. Persistent in the face of all Mother's scrubbings. Baby rubs her head along the stripe. There are two bald spots, one on each side of her head, that fit the brown stripe perfectly. Father puts the salve he uses on the cows' sore udders on the spots. Watching from her cornflakes, Grace can tell it must burn. Baby cries quietly, "Hoo, hoo, hoo," sounding like an owl far off in the woods.

Baby must touch her stripe. If her head is too sore, she runs her hands over it, left hand to the left, right hand to the right, watching closely, never straying. Mother says Baby mines her diaper and paints the stripe with the contents. Sick, Mother says, inhuman. Grace is not so sure Mother is right about Baby and the diaper and the stripe. Wouldn't the kitchen smell of it? Grace knows all the kitchen smells: cooking, cleaning, and, in between, a flat, waiting nothingness. No, Baby's brown is not from a filled diaper. It is something cleaner, some little bits of herself, like tears or sweat, something from inside that comes out to help her mark and find her way around this world.

Mother hates seeing Baby follow the stripe. She bangs on the chicken wire with the ladle. But she can't stop Baby. Sometimes, Mother flings the cage door wide and rushes in to slap Baby. Again. And again. Baby hides on her mattress, whimpering like a puppy. Mother comes out, not feeling one bit better. "She is my cross," Mother says.

Grace can see behind Mother where Baby's arm, released from the tight ball of her body, strays upward along the wall, seeking the stripe. The cross is made from wood, Grace remembers from Sunday school. It is brown and heavy and hard to carry. Perhaps that is it. Baby is the cross.

Father takes the family out to dinner for Mother's birthday. They go to the B&J Diner on Route 28. Grace, at seven, is the only one young enough to receive a special menu and a surprise: a small, white box with four crayons, red, yellow, blue, green. When they return to the house, they hear Baby hoo-hooing all the way from the driveway. They have forgotten to leave a light on for her. Grace runs ahead. In the dark kitchen, she can see the whites of Baby's eyes reflecting the moonlight through the picture window.

"Shh, Baby, shh." Grace tries to quiet Baby before Mother comes. She shows her the special menu she has colored and been allowed to keep. She pulls the crayons out of the pocket of her yellow dress, taking out a red crayon and drawing a line on the back of the menu. "See? For you. Red, yellow, blue, and green." Grace slides the box of crayons beneath the cage door and turns quickly as she hears Mother's steps.

The next morning, stirring her oatmeal, Grace notices a patch of yellow in Baby's cage. Still holding her spoon, she gets up and walks over. Over the stripe of brown, a yellow ball is peeking up, tinged with red around its edges. Grace looks at Baby, but she is moving along her stripe, left to right, right to left. Grace turns and looks out the picture window, sees just where the sun is inching up beyond the hill. Grace's spoon clatters to the white floor. "Hey! Baby drew the sun!"

Everyone, Grace's brothers and sister, looks and laughs, except for Mother, who is outraged about her walls. She gets out the Clorox and a stiff brush. The sun is scrubbed away, and Baby is searched, but the crayons aren't found. This time, Grace is slapped. Later, when the coast is clear, the others ask Grace how she got in and drew the sun, and why. Grace tells them. They don't believe her.

The next morning, the sun is back in Baby's pen, and there is grass, too, lush and hopeful along the top of the brown stripe. Farther up, blue marks the sky. This, too, is scrubbed away. Baby is persistent. Each day the scene grows darker, more exact, a precise mirror of the world marked by the edges of the window frame. Mother is persistent, too, but now the marks will not yield so easily. They are heavy and sure; like the brown, they cling. Mother scrubs and scrubs, but they are always there, that shadow of the world above the brown.

One day, a small figure appears above the rising green, beneath the sun. Grace coils her fingers through the chicken wire and looks closely. A red sweater, hat, and mittens above a blue skirt. Me, *Grace thinks. Baby scrabbles back and forth in front of the picture, her head sliding along the stripe. "Me?" Grace whispers to Baby, but Baby takes no notice. She is in a groove, creating the rich, brown base beneath the picture. Suddenly, Grace knows. Baby is not the cross. She is the earth: dark, silent, and waiting beneath the bright world.*

TWENTY-SIX

*g*race was filling up. She imagined a sea, dark, thick, noxious, rising up inside her. Within the course of a few days, the roundness of her belly returned, though her arms and legs remained stick-thin. She walked carefully, tried not to slosh. Baby was encouraged by the roundness. Grace was coming back to her, filling with color. She patted Grace's belly. "Yellow," she proclaimed, her voice a happy crow.

Grace pulled Baby's hand away, held it, said nothing. Her thoughts whispered: *Brown water.*

A final trip to the doctor confirmed it. Lily drove her; then, as Grace waddled off with the nurse, she sat in the waiting room with all the others who would sink or swim. At home, Walter hid with barn cats, whispering his worries; Baby hooted at *Green Acres,* happy. This new development had scattered them like leaves across a pond.

The young doctor's eyes were still tired and kind, the probing fingers still gentle. Only the words seemed harsh. Liver. Shutdown. Fluid. Last things. Had they called hospice yet? He would let them know she would be in contact. Grace shook her head. He would do it anyway. He wanted her to think about it. He held her hand, offering his earnest, sad smile, a prescription for stronger pain pills. His words floated in the exam room, eddied around them. "I'll go home now," Grace dismissed him.

Treading back into the waiting room, Grace saw Lily, saw fear in her eyes, saw lips silently moving to some interior song. *Nervous,* thought Grace. She stopped and turned, feeling a wave in her belly. At the nurse's station, Grace asked for the hospice number, tucked the card into her purse.

Lily stopped at the drugstore to fill the prescription. She was helped by *Hi! I'm Amy*, who wanted to chat. Lily couldn't. Frank Sinatra crooned in her head, "Come fly with me. Let's fly, let's fly away," his voice deafening. Grace waited in the car. Baby and Walter at home. Home? Lily snatched the bag of pills and almost ran from the building. *Hi! I'm Amy* watched, open-mouthed.

They drove up Pioneer Street. Above them, the trees tossed in the wind, a liquid movement. Grace watched as if from a distant shore. "We like to walk here. Baby, Butler, and me," she told Lily.

Lily could barely hear her for the din in her head. "I think the weather's changing," she hollered. "Look at that bank of clouds."

Grace didn't respond. She had turned inward again. She listened to the lapping of approaching seas.

The afternoon turned cool and rainy. Grace dozed on the couch, occasionally startled awake by Baby's chortle. *Get Smart* followed by *The Partridge Family* followed by *My Three Sons* followed by *The Andy Griffith Show* followed by *Please Don't Eat the Daisies*. Hours of yesteryear's favorites. Laugh tracks wove in and out of Grace's dreams. In the attic, Lily rooted through boxes, trying to glue herself to an activity, to a place. She organized Baby pictures, picking the best to bring downstairs and hang. Frank Sinatra fought for her attention. "Let's take a boat to Bermuda, let's take a plane to Saint Paul. Let's take a kayak to Quincy or Nyack, let's get away from it all!"

Walter, wandering the house, mourned the loss of his afternoon swim and settled for a soak in Grace's claw-foot tub. In the kitchen he gathered a ladle and anything that looked like it might float and headed upstairs. Water roared from the faucet, covering the sound of his mother's mumbled, worrisome singing coming from a spot directly above him. *Nervous*, Walter thought. Steam rose in the cool bathroom. Walter filled the tub all the way to the overflow drain. It was practically a lake. Walter stepped in, then eased down inch by inch, his skin turning instantly rosy in the hot water. Water slipped down the over-flow drain with a satisfying gurgle. Overhead, the intermittent singing stopped. Walter sighed. Perfection.

Walter was deep into a battle between Tupperware containers when Baby joined him. She stood in the door, listening to the high whine of missiles and the deep boom of explosions echo off the tile walls and floor. Tupperware sank. Baby watched the tub water splash and slosh. Deep water. She stepped back.

Walter declared victory. "The Allies have won! Hurray!" He raised his pink arms in triumph, suddenly dropped them. "Oh no! A huge tidal wave!" The remaining fleet of pale green Tupperware contain-ers was wiped out. More water cascaded to the floor. "Hi, Aunt Baby!" Walter's pink, wet face was joyous.

"Walter," Baby said.

"Yep."

"Yellow?" Baby wanted to know.

"Yep." Walter searched the bottom of the tub for his vessels, pull-ing them up one by one and emptying each over his head.

"Hohohoho!" Baby beamed and, deciding the water was fine, splashed over to settle on the toilet seat next to the tub. The toilet groaned beneath her.

"Aunt Baby!" Walter was scandalized. "I'm naked here!"

"Pinkyellow." Baby told him, grinning. Her glasses steamed over.

Walter stared at his aunt a long time. "OK," he relented. "This time."

The battle recommenced. This time the green fleet was destined to lose. After another fifteen minutes, Walter pulled the plug and let half the water drain out before he replaced it. He turned on the hot tap and sank back, letting the newly heated water creep up his body. Baby watched the procedure through mist and running drops. "Garg," she commented.

"It's so the water stays hot, and I can be in here forever," Walter explained. He stuck his big toe in the running spigot. Water shot across the bathroom, pattering against the door of the shower stall, spotting Baby's pink daisy dress. As the dots of water soaked in, Baby's daisies turned lurid red. She squawked and rubbed. Walter laughed. "It's only water."

Walter sank to the bottom of the tub. Sea-grass hair. He blew bubbles that parted his floating hair and surfaced with a gurgle. Baby forgot her dress and watched, enchanted. Walter surfaced. "See. Just water."

"Walter!" Baby beamed.

Lily was at the door. "Walter, I need you out of there. We're hanging some of Aunt Baby's pictures downstairs."

"OK." Walter stuck his wet hands out to Baby. "Pruned enough!"

Baby reared back. "Aack!"

The sound of tapping invaded Grace's sleep. In her dream, she is painting the Partridge family bus in bold blocks of colors, yellow, blue, red. Behind her, Shirley Jones and Susan Dey are building something, their hammers tap-tap-tapping nails into place. Susan stretches the chicken wire while Shirley secures it. A cage. Susan isn't sure they need it. Shirley is adamant. Grace can see the straining muscles in her forearms as she holds the chicken wire in place and nails it down. Despite the effort, her smile is syrupy-sweet, her voice musical. "Oh, Laurie. It's for the best. We can't be the Partridge family with her. We have to put her someplace safe, so we can sing, so you can sing. This could be your big break."

Grace opens her mouth. She wants to say, "No, Mother, please. You don't need to put me in there. I'll be good."

Nothing came out but a giant snort.

Grace woke up, startled. Lily and wet Walter stood over her, grinning. Lily held a hammer. "You were snoring." Walter giggled.

"I'm a bit tired," Grace said. She scowled and struggled to sitting. "Where's Baby?"

"Upstairs in the bathroom. She was watching Walter take a bath."

"Humph." Grace stared at the TV. *Gunsmoke.* "I thought we were watching *The Partridge Family.*"

Lily looked at the clock. "Two hours ago." Humming, she placed another drawing against the wall. Walter held it as she nailed it down.

Grace grimaced. "I'm a bit tired. That racket woke me up."

Lily grinned over her shoulder. "What racket? The hammering or the snoring?"

"Humph!"

"Grace!" Baby bellowed from above. "Grace!"

"OK," Grace muttered, then raised her voice. "Don't you holler at me! I'm coming." She braced herself to stand. Internal waters quaked.

"It's fine, Aunt Grace. I can do it." Lily leaped to the stairs. Grace subsided.

In the bathroom, Lily was faced with a stark-naked Baby, arms firmly crossed on her chest. She uncrossed an arm, pointed at the tub, recrossed it. Lily laughed. "A bath? You want to take a bath?"

"Pinkyellow."

"Pinkyellow it is then, Aunt Baby." Lily filled the tub with steaming water and braced Baby as she stepped up and in. Baby collapsed down; water erupted over the sides and down the overfill drain. Lily was soaked.

Nose to the water, Baby examined her submerged skin. "Pinkyellow." she nodded.

Lily gathered the Tupperware containers scattered around the floor and dropped them into the tub. "There you go, Aunt Baby. Have a ball. I'm going to change."

"Pinkyellow," Baby responded with a sigh. Beads of sweat crowned her forehead, grew heavy, and slid down her cheeks. Baby stuck her tongue out, stretching it sideways to catch the drops. Lily turned and left, her laughter echoing down the hall, Frank Sinatra suddenly silent.

By the time Lily returned to the living room, Grace was asleep again, sitting this time, head thrown back against the couch pillows. She woke up as the credits for *Gunsmoke* rolled up the screen. "Resting my eyes," she mumbled and rubbed her face. "Where's Baby?"

Lily smiled. "Taking a bath."

"Baby doesn't take baths."

"Well, she is."

"She doesn't like the water."

"She does now."

"Baby doesn't take baths."

Lily opened her mouth to respond, then closed it slowly. "She watched me and saw how fun it was," Walter piped up. "It's my fault. I'm sorry."

"Humph." Grace stared at the screen. Commercials, a promise of *Three's Company* up next. Stay tuned. Graces eyes strayed to the stairs, her ears strained. "This is something I have to see," she said at last. Walter, help me up." Walter pulled her to standing and settled back in to catch the show.

Grace watched from the bathroom doorway. Baby sank Tupperware with her fists, chuckling as the water overpowered the containers and sent them down to the bottom of the tub. She pulled them up full and dumped them over her head and laughed. "Hohohoho!"

"You old fool," Grace commented. "You're not a kid, you know."

"Grace!" Baby acknowledged her sister. "Pinkyellow!" Baby threw up her arms. Water rained across the bathroom. "Pinkyellow! Grace!"

"You don't take baths," Grace told her.

Baby wasn't listening. All of her concentration now focused on tugging the silver chain attached to the plug, then watching the water swirl down the drain with a lovely sucking noise. "Awk!" Baby scrabbled at the plug, fought the escaping water, and smashed the plug back into the drain. She turned the hot tap. Fresh water gushed into the half-full tub. "Hah!" She leaned back and chuckled. Steam rose in lazy wisps. Baby watched the water rush from the silver spigot. Carefully, she lifted her foot, reaching with her toe for the opening, finding it, pressing, pressing the toe in. Water shot everywhere, splattering the ceiling and walls, marking Grace at the door, attacking Baby's surprised face and suddenly flailing arms. "Gawk!" Baby sputtered and tugged.

Stuck.

"Blaa!" Baby's squeal was high, panicked. She yanked on her toe. The toe stayed; the huge body responded, sliding like a doomed ship, down, down and under the water.

Grace blinked, rooted to her spot at the door. This was it. She had all but given up. But here it was. Last chance. Opportunity washed ashore at her very feet. Grace was breathless with the surprise of it.

The surface of the water calmed. Baby lay at the bottom of the tub, her eyes wide open and looking toward Grace. Her short, gray curls straightened, waved like sea grass. Tupperware floated across her vision. She smiled. Grace smiled too, sad and hopeful. Baby opened her mouth and bubbles rose, caught momentarily in the hair, escaped and rose. Baby's smile faded, her eyes bulged. Her fists thumped and flailed at the side of the slippery tub. Grace's smile faded, too. This was it. This was it. The job finished. No more cage. Baby dead. Her too, soon. Both sunk in dark water. Together. Laurie Partridge would sing. No, no, not Laurie. Not Grace. Lily. Grace felt the breath in her chest expanding, burning, screaming to be let out. Grace was willing to hold it down forever.

Lily rushed past her, yelling, "Oh! Oh shit!"

Grace, knocked sideways, slipped in the wet, collapsed to the floor.

Lily struggled for purchase on the wet tile, hauled Baby up from the tub. "It's all right. It's all right," she sobbed. "I've got her. I've got her. It's all right." Water cascaded down them both. Baby's arms wrapped around Lily, threatening to drag them back under.

"Hoooo!" Baby's cry was the long, piercing wail of the abandoned.

"Shhh," Lily crooned. "I'm here."

Grace rose to her knees, let the air out of her lungs, slowly, slowly, until she was empty. This was it. She was through.

It is only two rooms, counting the bathroom, but the apartment is heaven to Grace. A twenty-minute walk to work. Perfect. She has lived in it one week. One week of total freedom. One week of New York. After her shift at the hospital, she wanders the streets, taking subways to different stops, acting like she has somewhere to go. This city is home. Everywhere is a place to go. She window-shops, picking out the smart clothes she will buy with her first paycheck, the swank restaurants she will eat in. Perhaps she should take up smoking, just so she can sit at a table and blow smoke, in one elegant rush, into the blue air above her head and squint with blasé disinterest at the other diners. It would be so, so...city. She will grow her fingernails and paint them red. Can nurses have red fingernails?

To get here, there were years of commuting for nurse's training, years of training at home, too. Dismantling the cage after Mother's death, discarding the diapers. Waiting until little brother Ted was away to college to start college herself. Then started the half-hour drive to class, back to the farm each lunch-time to check on Baby, feed Baby, take Baby to the toilet, wipe Baby, set Baby at the kitchen table with a pencil and paper, "Draw me a picture, Baby, a real good picture. Take your time."

There is the daily leaving a sandwich and a slip of instructions for Papa, who is forever out among his cows. Driving back another half hour to class, then repeating the trip at 5:00 p.m. Years of training, training herself, training Papa and Baby. All worth it for these two rooms, for this city, for this freedom. She is on her own. They are on their own. Like the Murphy bed that she seals up into the wall each morning, the niggling worry, the guilt, Baby, Papa are wrapped up tight, with hospital corners, and placed deep inside her. No, no, she will not go back. Not ever. Never. She doesn't call. Instead, she writes herself lists: wear something black tomorrow; visit the Metropolitan Museum of Art; shop for shoes, fish market. She has been here one week. She tells herself they are receding. Farewell.

When the call comes, Grace is still in her uniform. She sits on her bed, doing her toenails in Flaming Red, and carefully flips the pages of Vogue. The neighbors in the apartment to her left fight in high-volume Greek. Grace ignores them; she will not be drawn in ever again. The phone interrupts her halfway through her right foot. She carefully closes the bottle of polish before she answers. "Hello?"

There is no response.

"Hello?...I'm hanging up." As she pulls the receiver from her ear, she hears it. "Grace. I can't—"

Grace suddenly feels as if her lungs have shut down tight. "Papa! Papa! What is it? What's wrong? Is it Baby?"

Silence for an aching minute, then, "I can't—" The sob sounds like the scratch in a record album, ruined, irreparable.

"Papa! Papa, I'm coming!" As she shouts these words into the receiver, Grace is already slipping her wet toes into her pumps and fumbling for her purse.

"No. No…" *Her father's voice is no more than a cracked whisper when he finally responds. By then, Grace is long gone.*

The Buick is a relic, the most she could afford. She has hoped to use it as an excuse to limit her trips north. Now, she prays it will get her there so she can fix whatever the problem is, so that she can come back. Driving through thick darkness, Grace gathers her resentments to her, teases them from the tangled shapes of trees that slip by at the verge of the car's headlamps. A mother's rigid ignorance; a father's silence; a sister's and brothers' easy indifference, easy leaving. Baby. The complications of Baby's days; the taunts Grace has faced down for her, the explanations, the embarrassments; the stark love in her sister's eyes, the obligation. Grace weights each instance with anger, numbers them, carries them north.

It is dawn when she arrives. She sees them as she pulls into the driveway. They are down by the pond, Papa and Baby, gray in the early light. Behind them, the pond is black and slick as tar, repelling light. Around them, grass glistens with dew, Papa's pale head and Baby's dark, pearled too. Papa's brown plaid shirt, Baby's blue smock cling to their backs, wet. They are utterly still, a tableau. It is as if they have stood there all night, Papa holding Baby. Grace has never seen her father hold Baby so close. At all. There is a flash like a bright red alarm in her head, and Grace is stumbling from the car, screaming. "What's wrong? What are you doing down there?" *Grace runs.*

It is as if her voice awakens him. He moves the last steps toward the pond, holding Baby, leading Baby in an ugly, intimate dance. At the edge, he pushes her. Baby's arms flail, wheel in cool blue air, then stop and slip unresisting into dark waters. Running running, Grace screams. The pond at the bottom of Mother's garden is a million miles away.

There at last, not stopping, knocking her father aside, Grace jumps in, feels around with frantic arms and feet. Where is she? Where is she? A foot finds an armpit. "I've got her! I've got her!" *Grace pulls and pulls. Baby is dead weight in her arms.* "Help us!" *she gasps at the looming bank, the figure crumpled there. No response. Grace struggles in the sucking, peaty mud. Her shoes are swallowed from beneath her. She pulls and pulls. She will not let Baby go the way of her shoes. With each hard-gained step, the anger, the resentments loosen, slip away, sink in the fractured water. With them goes her separate, perfect future, until there is nothing left but the weight of this one body, this heavy love, Baby.*

After Baby is settled in bed, curled around a hot-water bottle, sleeping with deep, exhausted gulps, Grace finds she must collect her father from the banks of the pond. Walking back down, she hears the cows lowing in the barn, begging to be milked. She notices her uniform is stained tea-brown. She notices she is in bare feet, new pumps lost to the pond, her half-done toenails smudged lurid red, ringed in mud. Her father lies where she had knocked him. She crouches by him, turning him over gently. Something has happened here, too. A tremor runs unchecked through his right shoulder and down his arm; one side of his face seems collapsed, almost melted. He breathes as if he is drawing air through an impossibly long straw. "Oh, Papa," Grace whispers.

There will be no further negotiations, no second chance for either of them. This is it. Grace half carries, half drags her father to the house, calls the doctor to come, calls the neighbor about the bawling cows. She will sell them, every last one of them, send each with its separate name and personality quirk away. She will sell or rent the fields. She will have some money then. Not a paycheck, but money. What will she do with it? Grace sits in the quiet house, listens to its ticks, listens to the fitful breathing of her two patients upstairs. She will buy one of those television sets, something that makes noise, gives company, brings brightness into this house. She will buy that, and she will buy the biggest box of crayons she can find. For Baby.

TWENTY-SEVEN

*g*race woke in clear, early light. The white walls of her bedroom glowed a delicate pink. Tinted, too, were the hands she held up to examine. *I am pink,* she thought, bemused. In the pink. She listened to her body, heard no lap of rising waters. A fine silence. She recognized this. An ancient medical bubble surfaced. This was respite, a pause, slight, brief, probably the last. Yes, here as in the waning summer, a shortening of days. *Use this.* Grace watched the walls change from pink to pale gold to customary white. Minutes. Such a short time. Grace stirred, waited for dizziness, for pain, to subside. Butler, forever at her side, watched. "Get up, Butler. We have things to do."

At nine on the dot, Grace called her lawyer. "Elroy, I'm coming in. I want a will."

They all went. Butler was the instigator. In the past weeks, he had spent less and less time away from Grace, hardly leaving more than an inch or two between them. No one was quick enough to keep him out of the car once the door was open. Once in, he settled down, sandwiched into the front passenger seat with Grace, and grinned with accomplishment. Baby saw that Butler would be having a ride in the car. She wanted to come. Walter was enlisted to keep an eye on Baby and Butler. Lily was needed to sign papers. This trip would be a joint effort.

The lawyer's office was a tall Victorian on upper Main. His wife kept the front desk for him. A tiny, thoroughly gray woman who had

165

aged many times over since Grace had last seen her, she met them at the door and was immediately overcome by the size, number, and variety of their group. "Oh! Oh!" was all she could manage as Butler clipped past on the parquet floor.

"Ha! Butler!" Baby told her, clumping over.

"Ohhhh!" the woman managed, nose-to-nose with Baby's beaming moon face.

"Blue," Baby named her, patting her on the back, then suddenly crowed, "Butler pink!"

Butler barked once in response. Walter scolded. Lily grinned. "Passing through," Grace announced amid the pandemonium.

The oak door to the lawyer's inner office opened. The man who emerged was shaped exactly like his place of business, sturdily rectangular, impossibly tall. He dipped through the door, revealing a cap of silver curls peaked at the top and steeply sloping, down and out, to just below his ears. Curls trimmed his forehead. Bric-a-brac. Lily was seized by a fit of giggles.

"My will," Grace told him and proceeded past into his office, Butler at her heels. She sought the nearest chair and collapsed, gasping as a wave of pain rose to meet her.

Lily worked for control and followed Butler. Walter took Baby's hand and followed, too. No chair would accommodate Baby's wide bottom, though she tried every free one and even made Lily and Grace rise so she could try theirs. Grace rose wearily, waited for Baby, then subsided, closing her eyes with pain. Baby wandered the room, trailing Walter and touching everything, books, diplomas, piles of paper. She assigned colors. "Orange, green, purple." She put her hand on the lawyer's peaked head. "Greenorange!"

Lily was reminded of childhood games of "duck, duck, goose" and began grinning again. Then stopped. *This is serious*, she reminded herself, *you are becoming...what?* She squirmed on the too-hard seat, uncomfortable in herself.

"Elroy," Grace told him, "You get bigger every time I see you, and that wife just gets smaller."

The lawyer offered a pleased smile, eyed the wandering Baby. "You seem to have the same situation in your own family, Gracie."

Lily's eyebrows rose, her attention caught. *Gracie? Elroy?*

"I am wasting, Elroy. Cancer. Need a will."

Walter, suddenly rooted midstep, stared at his aunt, then the lawyer. He watched the comical man's smile collapse. He turned to his mother. "Walter," Lily said quietly, "why don't you take Butler and Baby for a walk around the block." Walter felt revolt rise in him, swallowed.

"Go on, now. It's OK. We have business," Grace told him, then nudged Butler's bottom with her shoe. "You, too, now. Go on. I'll still be here when you get back. Shoo."

Walter nodding, brows knit, pulled Baby to the door. Butler followed with obvious reluctance. At the door, Walter and Butler both stopped, and both looked back. But Baby was ready to go. Walks were always yellow. Leaving the lawyer's room, Walter registered the man's deep voice. "Grace. Grace, I'm so sorry. Is there—"

"Let's do this, Elroy. Can't be upright too long."

He had questions to ask and forms to fill out, things to know of Lily. Grace's attentions wandered. She stood and shuffled to the window. Standing in sunlight, she watched Baby, Walter, and Butler progress down the sidewalk. Behind her, Lily's voice provided a hesitant, musical patter. Connected by sound and sight to her family, Grace floated among dust motes, apart.

Halfway down the block, Butler rolled over and stuck his short legs into the air. He would go no further, the invisible umbilical cord that connected him to Grace stretched to its limit.

"I guess my permanent address is Aunt Grace's..." Lily's voice was low, uncertain. *Pinned down.*

Walter tugged on the leash. Butler simply slid down the sidewalk on his back, legs still hiked. Baby raised her face to the sky, mouth wide with hooting laughter. Grace thought she might feel that laugh's vibration in the air around her. The dust motes danced.

"Five-thirty...seven..." Lily struggled. The chair squeaked beneath her. Fingers tapped the armrests, the beginnings of some desperate tune. In the overlaying silence, Grace's ears waited for that first off-key note. Lily cleared her throat and tried to settle.

Baby suddenly collapsed next to Butler, lowered her nose into his belly. Mixed sun and shade threw patterns across Baby's wide back. Grace smiled. Walter threw his hands up and plopped down on the other side of the dog. He reached over and scratched Butler's exposed chin. A back paw worked the air in bliss. Walter's eyes crinkled with laughter. Grace put a palm on the glass, wished for a way through to that sun-spattered moment.

"Single...one child." Lily's toes took up the beat. Oak floorboards shivered.

A movement in the yard beyond the sidewalk caught Grace's eye. The neighbor was watching. Standing in pink-flowered gardening shoes with a hose in one matching pink-flowered glove, the woman stared openmouthed and frowning, forgotten water dousing her immaculate porch furniture. *YELLOW BOY, LEGLESS DOG AND FATTEST WOMAN ON EARTH VISIT VILLAGE. HAVOC ENSUES!* Grace thought and smiled to herself: *We will always be a scandal.*

"Grace," a voice recalled her to the room.

"Soaking her fancy cushions. Good," she told Elroy and Lily without turning from the window.

Neither knew how to respond, and so they watched Grace in her spill of sunlight, clinging to the window frame and looking out.

After long minutes, the lawyer cleared his throat twice. "I need your signature, Grace. Here and here. After that, this young woman here will be golden. Well, you know what I mean." He harrumphed and then raised his voice to a bellow. "Vida! Come on in here now and witness these signatures!" Lily winced. Frank Sinatra crooned. Vida scurried.

Later, as he ushered them to the front door, the lawyer took Grace's hand, stooped low over it, and kissed it. He turned to Lily. "Your aunt was an amazing dancer in her day."

Grace humphed. Lily blinked; in that second of blackness she saw Grace swirling across a darkened room, tiny in the arms of this house-sized man. "In my day, you nearly broke my toes," Grace said.

"Ah." The lawyer shifted, chuckled in discomfort. "Then I received the best of that encounter."

From the front desk behind him came the rustle of fingers through papers and a muffled squeak of disapproval.

"It's all too long ago to matter," Grace told him. "Lily, I could use your arm." Grace made her way carefully, carefully down the steps. She wanted to find Baby and Walter, wanted to sit on someone else's sidewalk and scratch Butler's belly. My moment, she thought, almost over…She settled for a near car seat shared with a wedge of fur ecstatic in reunion.

They are dancing. The room spins, a gleam of white and yellow light. The ceiling seems to arch away, the floorboards to dip beneath them. Laughter, music. Grace's red dress bells out behind her, ringing color through the room. A missed step, and they slam into the kitchen table. A chair skids across the kitchen floor, ricochets off the refrigerator, and clatters to the floor where the cage had stood such a short ago. Baby lets go of her sister and plasters hands to ears. Fear streaks like lightning across her face. Grace laughs, rubbing one sore hip. "It's OK, Baby. It's OK."

Baby's hands slip down her cheeks. She weaves slightly on her feet, desperately dizzy from the dance. Grace is an unfocused blur of red in front of her. Grace pirouettes on high, red shoes.

"Dancing, Baby. It's fun!"

"Ha!" Baby agrees and promptly vomits.

Grace is not quick enough to jump back. Her red shoes are splattered with Baby's dinner. She looks down at them over the bell of her too-tight prom dress. She can't help it. She laughs, laughs and laughs until tears well up and run down her cheeks, hit the floor and mingle with the mess there. Baby's smile is hopeful.

"Fun," Grace reiterates, scrubbing her cheeks. She steps out of her shoes and reaches over to lift the needle off the phonograph. "Don't you move," she warns. She knows Baby won't.

She goes upstairs, changes, takes a minute to pack the dress away again in the old dresser in the attic. Then she comes back to the kitchen, where Baby waits, unmoving, and cleans up her last dancing partner.

TWENTY-EIGHT

*W*alter tugged Butler by the leash through the woods across the road from the house. Lily walked backward, two steps ahead, coaxing. Sugar cubes rattled in the breast pocket of the man-sized, green work shirt she wore. She would feed the cows if they ever reached the field at the top of the trail. "That's my handsome guy! What a good boy! Good Butler! Come on, now! Good boy!"

Butler walked stiff-legged and resisting, his collar hiked up to his ears and chin. "For a little dog, you are very stubborn," Walter told him. "Don't you want to chase those cows?" Walter turned to his mom. "Is it useless yet?"

"Never. Come on, Butler! You can do it! Good boy!"

They shuffled forward another two feet. A far-off rustle attracted their attention. Butler's ears pricked at the possibility of a squirrel. The noise stopped. No squirrel emerged, but Butler remained alert for another second, then glimpsed the high, white flash of a deer's tail. He yanked back and out of his collar, then bolted. "Hey!" Walter held the leash aloft. The empty collar dangled.

"Oh, jeez," muttered Lily and headed off after Butler.

They could hear Butler off to the right and deep in the woods. The trees were huge and old, the undergrowth restricted to ferns. Last year's leaves rustled underfoot, a smell of loam rising with each step. Ahead, Butler's barking stopped and then began again sporadically, gaining a high, nervous quality. Lily finally saw him standing six feet back from the old wire fence that marked the edge of the property. His short legs were wide apart, his hackles raised. Seeing Lily and Walter, Butler rushed forward toward the fence, then back, barking wildly. Lily squinted, couldn't make out what it was Butler saw until a slight movement of the fence caught her attention. "Ohmygod! Walter, get Butler!"

Walter rushed forward, tackling Butler. The two wrestled in the leaves and ferns. "Stay still!" Lily's voice was a sharp hiss. Walter squashed Butler beneath him until the dog went limp with submission.

"What is it?" Walter whispered.

"A fawn." Walter could hear it in her voice: raw panic. A mother's voice. Holding Butler beneath him, he strained to see. The fence vibrated. Walter saw a splayed tangle of impossibly thin legs, a narrow, spotted arc of fur curled through one wire square of the fence and back through another. The tiny fawn was horribly caught. Walter could see how it had happened. It must have been following its mother. She went over. It had tried to go through, became stuck, tried to go back. The tiny hooves quivered. Scraped, bloody spots showed where the fawn had struggled. It panted, its tongue hanging out.

Walter squeezed his eyes shut, buried his face into Butler's fur. "No, no. Momma."

Lily couldn't remember his voice sounding so young, couldn't remember ever being called "Momma."

"Help it."

The words galvanized Lily into action. "Take Butler home, Walter. Bring back wire cutters. They're hanging in the toolshed. They look like big scissors with orange handles. Quick."

Walter wrestled the collar onto Butler, tugged him away. Once he was headed for home, the dog was willing. Walter turned once to look over his shoulder. Lily sat with her back against a tree, her face in her hands. Walter and Butler ran.

Lily sat, feeling the hard ground set off a quake in her stomach. She wondered about the fawn's mother…was she the noise Butler had heard? Had they frightened her off? Was she still nearby? Did she understand? Could she mourn? Lily rocked herself, tried to stop the thoughts, tried to wait.

Walter returned, breathing hard, sweat running down his face. He offered the wire cutters with trembling hands. Lily kneeled next to the fawn. One of its legs looked broken. Its head strained away from Lily. "Shh. Shhh," she soothed. She cut around the area where the fawn was entangled, engaging Walter to help in case the tiny animal struggled and impaled itself on the cut wires. The fawn remained still, its panting, its shock-bright eyes the only signs of life.

As Walter bent down each sharp wire, Lily slowly eased the fawn out of its tangle, careful to support its mangled leg. Once it was free, she cradled it against her chest; its head and chest draped down. She wanted to comfort it, heal it, take it into her skin and let it lodge against her beating heart. Walter reached out, slid his fingers along the soft fur of the back. "Will it be all right?"

Lily began slowly, gently walking. "We'll take it to the vet's. Maybe..."

Almost to the gate at the bottom of the trail, she felt it, a slight shudder, a sudden heaviness in her arms, a liquid warmth down her chest, across her arms. She looked down, stopped. The fawn's eyes slipped into sightlessness. Lily squatted and lay the fawn down in the trail. The front of her shirt was covered in the fawn's excrement, yellow-orange liquid, sharp-smelling. Lily recognized it, the color, the smell. Walter's diapers had contained just such gold when she had breast-fed him. "Oh, baby," she whispered to the creature. "We were almost there."

Walter stood close to her side. "What's wrong?"

"It's dead, Critter." In her grieving, she forgot, used the old nickname for her son.

"No." Walter's voice plaintive.

Lily stood, reached out to push the sweat-crusted hair from his eyes. "Walter, it was so tiny. It was just too much for it. The pain, the shock. It was such a late baby, Walter. Born too late. In a couple weeks, it will be freezing at night." Lily heard herself blathering on, couldn't stop. "It probably wouldn't have made it through the winter. It might have starved. This might have been better..."

"No." Walter ran.

"Walter!" Lily called, her voice weak. "Walter." Lily slid down onto her knees beside the small body. "I can't do this."

Walter climbed into the barn loft, collecting cats as he went. They mewed in protest but were too heavy with afternoon napping to put up a fight. He scraped a nest in the loose hay and settled in, gathering cat warmth onto him, feeling their heat and weight holding down the soaring ache in his chest. The skinniest of the black-and-white ones put a cool nose to the beat at Walter's neck, rubbed there. Walter was dry and empty and could not respond other than to hold them and keep them from going. His mind returned in flashes to the image of the fawn woven in the fence. Walter's body flinched. Cats raised their heads and blinked at him through narrow, sleep-glazed eyes.

The mother should have known better. She should have taken care. Walter wanted to go back, change it all, make that mother more careful. He stirred with anger. Cats complained. There was something here even more terrible, something his mind shied away from yet kept returning to. That small body draped over his mother's arms. He remembered the downward arc of its neck, the tiny, tiny hooves, splayed with tension, suddenly lax. He remembered its eyes, brown and bright, suddenly not. There was a leaving here too big to comprehend. The pain inside him constricted. Around him, the cats stirred, impatient, annoyed.

Had the baby been frightened? Walter wanted to go back. He wanted to place his cheek against the fawn's soft chest, its still-beating heart. He wanted to offer it his nearness, make it live. The cats roused themselves. They had had enough of the restless, zinging unease in the boy. They slunk off, tails high with displeasure, finding spots to settle just far enough away. Walter felt their going, a growing coldness on his chest, along his emptying arms, the press and release of each paw. He couldn't stop them. He was caught in that other moment of leaving, the fawn's giving over of everything. Then it came to him. Another leaving, not the cats', not the fawn's, not even his mother's ebb and flow, a leaving he had been told about but didn't really understand until now. Aunt Grace.

"*No.*" The barn echoed with the only word he had left.

Lily collected a shovel from the tool shed and buried the fawn deep in the woods, away from the fence that had killed it. With each bite of blade to earth, she swore she would take every inch of wire fencing off the property. When the hole was deep enough, she laid the tiny body in the bottom, took off her soiled shirt and covered it, spooning the dirt gently over the green bundle until it was covered. She sat a long time next to the grave, a numbness settling over her, prickling the hairs along her arms. She recognized the feeling, like sinking beneath some consuming drug.

She patted down the earth of the grave with her hands, noticing how the rich, brown loam made small clumps that rolled across her fingers, leaving narrow trails. Her hands felt immensely heavy. She struggled to her feet, hesitated, then left the shovel to mark the spot. She walked back to the house naked from the waist up. Once in the house, she pulled on a shirt and checked on Grace sleeping fitfully upstairs with Butler at her side. She gathered Baby from in front of the TV and scissors from the everything drawer in the kitchen. *Green Acres* protested behind her. In the barn, she called out for Walter. He didn't respond, though she knew he was there, could feel his weight on the boards above her, could see the sifting of hay through the cracks. The barn was filled with a vast silence.

"Walter!" Baby bellowed.

Silence.

"Green!" Baby needed Walter to know she was missing her program.

Silence.

"Walter, we're going to cut flowers and put them on the fawn's grave. I want you to come." Lily tried for firmness, couldn't find it in the overwhelming numbness. Her vocal cords seemed to sag.

"Walter! Walter!" Baby stamped a foot. "Green!"

Silence.

"Come on, Aunt Baby." Lily took Baby's hand and led her out to the flowerbeds.

Each carried an armload of late-summer flowers into the wood, Baby trailing behind, visiting her favorite trees, greeting their colors, until, ahead of her, Lily left the path and plunged into the deep woods. Baby followed. Ferns tickled her ankles. Baby smiled, *Green Acres* forgotten. The deep shadow under the canopy made her squint. There was a soft quiet in her, a quiet the color of the sky just above the sunset. Which crayon? *Wisteria*. "Lily. Bluepurple, Lily," Baby told her, struggling after with her load of blooms.

Lily marched on stiffly, leaden.

At the grave, Baby named the colors as Lily laid out the flowers: asters and phlox, lilies, sedum, black-eyed Susans, coneflowers, and Queen Anne's lace. "Purple. Purple. Yellow. Pink. White. Yellowyellow. White. Pink. Pink. Yellowyellow. Yellowwhite."

When she was done, Lily turned her back on the grave and led Baby away. Behind them on the floor of the dim forest, the mounded blanket of flowers glowed, gathering available light. Baby kept looking back, enchanted. Lily tugged and pulled wordlessly. Baby protested, resisted with stiffening legs, dragging feet. She left a trail of torn ferns. "Hohoho," she laughed to Lily. "Butler!" Her ankles were smeared green with fern juice. Baby stared down. "Green!" She picked up first one foot, then the other. "Green." Her mouth dropped open. At home, *Green Acres* lit the TV screen, unwatched. "Green!" Baby roared and charged forward, dragging Lily.

Back at the house, Lily noticed three things at once: no Walter; Butler at the kitchen door, skulking and anxious to be let out; and a smell, rank and pervasive, of human waste. Lily bolted for the stairs.

Grace was halfway down the hall, kneeling, wiping the floorboards with an already-soiled towel. She was naked, her nightgown and panties bunched up on the floor next to her. Her sleep-matted hair stuck up here and there in fuzzy spikes. Arrested at one end of the hall, Lily saw how thin Grace was. The skeletal arms struggled with the job of pushing the towel, the hipbones jutted, ready to rip through the translucent skin. Ribs showed down the length of her back. Lily knew that if she held her Aunt now, she'd feel each trembling rib…Each rib through the soft fur, vibrated by the frantic heart beating beneath. *Fragile*. Lily closed her eyes against the converging visions. Lily felt the leaden weight within her crack wide open.

Grace looked up. "Accident," Grace's voice strove for matter-of-factness but shook. "Nearly made it."

Lily rushed forward, lifting Grace so easily. "Oh, Aunt Grace, let's get you in a hot bath. I'll clean this up. I'm so sorry I wasn't here." *Failed!* No amount of flowers would cover this crime.

Just as Lily helped Grace slip down into the warm, sudsy water, Baby began to bellow below. "Grace! Grace! Ow! Ow! Lily! *Ow!*"

Grace lifted her head. "See," she managed weakly.

Lily ran.

The green itched. It burned. Baby dug her fingernails in and scratched with all her might. Red lines on green. The red stung. The green itched. On the TV screen, the Road Runner hooted "Meepmeep," blinked, and sped away. Lily raced down the stairs and into the family room, surveyed the damage. Wile E. Coyote fell through air. The ground rushed toward him. Boom. A cartoon mushroom cloud erupted on the TV screen.

"Oh, Aunt Baby, what's this? What have you done?" Lily ran her fingers gingerly over Baby shins, her brow wrinkled with worry: *What have I done?* "We need to get you into the shower. Come on."

"Meepmeep!" the TV urged her. Lily reached over and smacked the power button with her flat palm.

As she had for weeks now, Lily stripped and climbed into the shower stall with Baby. There was barely room for the two of them. Baby pressed her face up into the spray and gave gargly hoots of laughter. Lily squatted beneath the massive ledge of Baby's buttocks and, with washcloth and soap, began to sponge away the offending fern juice and blood. "*Ow! Ow!*" Baby howled wetly and stamped her feet, catching Lily's fingers underneath her heel.

Lily reared back and cracked her head on the glass of the stall. She slid to her butt, clutching her crushed fingers. Through the streaming glass, Lily saw Grace looking straight ahead, her face collapsed, her eyes lost, waiting to be found. Soap bubbles slid from Baby's ankles, taking with them the sting and itch. Baby pressed her face back up into the spray. "Fargfluf!" she gargled happily.

Lily struggled to her feet and began sudsing the rest of Baby, making wide arcs across her back with the washcloth, raising each arm and scrubbing there, coursing gentle circles for her belly and buttocks, each crevice wiped clean. Lily stopped, each familiar action suddenly foreign, and Baby a wild and dangerous landscape. The washcloth dropped from her fingers. Hot, salty tears mingled with shower water at the corners of Lily's mouth. The spray stung her, each droplet a tiny pinprick drilling into her skin. *I can't do this*, Lily's mind whimpered. Baby. Grace. Walter. *I can't do this. I can't do this all.* Each knifepoint sting of water answered, *Fail! Fail! Fail!* She stood there and took the beating, begged for an answer, prayed for Sinatra's sweet-smooth voice to slip into her head, to tell her what to do. Echoing shower, the pressing nearness of Baby, of Grace, the silent roar of needs, nothing else. Lily listened, despaired.

"Lilllly." Baby's voice was a high, wet whine. Lily noticed the goose bumps running across the acres of Baby's pale pink arms. The shower had turned cold.

The first time Lily runs away, she is six. She packs her red Bobby Sherman lunch pail with three pairs of panties, an undershirt, and four chocolate chip cookies. She waits in the old springhouse for someone to notice and call the cops. When it grows dark and a bat rustles awake in the black rafters above, she takes her Bobby Sherman lunch pail and walks across the dew-wet grass to the house. The kitchen screen door creaks. She can hear the TV on in the other room. Eddie's Father *on the tube. On the kitchen table a plate waits, next to it a glass of milk. One cold pork chop and a pile of peas, canned, melted butter congealed to hard, little dots on each sick-green surface. Behind her, laugh-track hilarity. Lily takes the Bobby Sherman lunchbox and the glass of milk up the back stairs and to her bedroom, eats the cookies and drinks the tepid milk. Next time they will notice.*

She leaves two weeks before her high school graduation, skipping all her final exams. She says she doesn't give a shit. It is the silence she is escaping. Since her brothers and sisters have left for college, the house has been heavy with it, a dark, oppressive weight of unspoken disapproval and disappointment, louder with each sibling's leaving. It floats, a laden cloud, above the bright, loud emanations from the TV, descending whenever the knob is turned off and the color fades to gray.

They agree only on Frank Sinatra, and even here the two sides, father-mother or child, must keep silent. Some acknowledgment from one camp of this shared enjoyment might cause the other to disavow. Then there would be nothing. Lily has tried to bust this silence wide open. She battles it with blue mascara and bubble-gum-pink lipstick and skirts so short that nothing is left to guess. The silence only thickens. She wants to slash through it with her purpled fingernails and scream, "What is so wrong with me?" But then what? When they opened their mouths to answer, what would come out? Everything? Nothing at all?

She leaves all that she owns and takes the Sinatra LPs, the Billie Holiday, the Bing Crosby and Lena Horne. This they will notice, she thinks. She uses the money she has saved for eleven Christmases and birthdays and takes a bus to New York City.

She carries the silence with her. She has not bargained on this. It parks itself in her room at the YWCA where she sleeps. It expands to fill the corners of the tiny cell, to muffle the sounds of rats in the walls. Always, she waits for her parents. The heavy box of stolen albums keeps the door closed against unwanted night openings, but it also holds the silence in, anchors it. It is her guilt, her pleasure. She finds a job bussing in a diner. She waits. They will notice, *she tells herself,* they will come. *If she listened to the albums, what would they tell her? She takes them to the library and uses one of the phonograph booths there. Frank Sinatra sings only to her. Listening, she is filled with triumph, with rage, with need.*

They do not come. What does it take? She listens and wonders. Frank Sinatra's voice rises and falls, a silvered, liquid sound. A sound receding. What now will she do to herself?

TWENTY-NINE

*W*alter sat in the hayloft, knees to nose, pinned under the realization of Grace's coming death. From distances, cats watched him with eyes narrowed, waited for him to subside so they could return to him. Walter rocked himself, a slight trembling motion. In the driveway, Grace's car engine struggled to start. Walter listened. The engine roared to life as if someone—*Lily*, Walter thought numbly, it could be no one but Lily—was in a great hurry…to be away. *Lily!* Walter was on his feet instantly. Barn cats streaked away.

"No! Wait! I—" Before he could finish the thought, he had launched himself, Flying Cat, from the loft and thudded into the piled hay below. Racing out the barn door, he could hear the spit of gravel from the tires. His legs pumped; his feet skittered on the dirt. His mind filled, became engorged with one thought, one word. "Don't!" He screamed it. Aunt Grace's car had bumped onto the blacktop and was roaring up the road. Walter chased it.

"Don't." He stopped at the crest of the hill, stood in the middle of the lane. He watched the car diminish, Lily's spiky head behind the wheel, not looking back.

"Don't," he whispered.

He could keep running, waving wildly, following. He looked back over his shoulder. The painted house glowed, its rainbow hues deepening with sunset. Parti-colored cows grazed there; small creatures peeked from safe trees; flowers bloomed forever. Grace and Baby waited. Walter looked down the road. The car had vanished. He could ask in town. Someone would have noticed Aunt Grace's beat-up old car, Lily clutching the wheel like a lifeline. They could tell him which way to head.

Twilight thickened. He heard the cows on the hill jostle and move toward milking, prompted by their tightening udders or the quality of evening light or instinct. No lamps went on in the house, its face vague and fading in the falling night. A car's headlights turned up the lane. Walter squinted, stood aside, hope filling his chest. The neighbor passed by slowly, waving. Walter's hand was too heavy to lift. He watched it pass until the red taillights turned a wooded corner. Standing in the dark, his chest emptied until he felt the night breeze blow through it, carrying his warmth down the road, trailing Lily. Walter shivered and turned and headed for the house. Light from the TV flickered from the front window, blue, silver, green, gray in the darkness, a Morse code meant for him.

Baby greeted him, hugely pleased. "Yellow! Yellow, Walter! Andy! Barney! Andy pink!" She was off the chair with a grunt and hugging Walter, enveloping him in mounds of moist, fleshy arms and padded polyester tummy and breasts.

Walter held on, let the hug and the roar of the TV fill him. A Campbell's soup commercial lit the dark room. Smiling faces. Family dinner. Family. *No Lily.* Walter's thoughts churned, threatened to drag him away. Aunt Baby needed him, needed him to turn on the lights, make the dinner, walk her to the bathroom, receive all the colors she offered...Aunt Grace needed him, needed more of him than even Baby. Lily needed him, too. He shouldn't have let his guard down, should have been watching her. Walter held on tight to Baby, burying his face into the stale Frito-smell of her belly, but now Baby struggled. Andy was back.

Walter let her go and watched the screen. Andy and Opie sat at the dinner table. Aunt Bea set two large platters of food on the table and sat down herself. Near the door, Barney eyed the food, unwilling to leave. He talked and talked, swallowing saliva, eyes glued to the food.

Every time Barney said something, Andy, Opie, and Aunt Bea would set down their laden forks and politely listen. Baby cackled.

"They should just invite him to eat, huh, Aunt Baby?" Walter commented. Baby roared as the forks dropped again. "Just feed him," Walter told the TV and headed for the kitchen, turning on lights as he went.

Walter pulled out bread from the box, peanut butter from the cupboard, milk and jam from the fridge. His hand hesitated over the jam jar. Aunt Baby had a condition, something about sugar. Dia-something. He remembered Lily's careful administering of food amounts and the shots that made Baby whimper. He wished he had paid closer attention. How was he supposed to do that? The jar of jam held midair, Walter considered. He had to be more careful. Lily had slipped away, but he would take better care of the other two. His job.

He set the jar of jam on the counter with a sharp smack. Peanut butter and jelly for him, something else for his aunts…something easy to swallow and not too sweet…Campbell's soup. He could do this, even the shots. Aunt Grace would tell him. From her bed, she could tell him, and he would do it. He reached down a can of tomato soup and pulled out a pot. He turned the knob of the stove to light and leaned back, grimacing. He hated the way the gas flame popped into life, always startling him no matter how ready he was.

Baby and Walter ate at the kitchen table. News squawked in the family room. Baby humphed at the TV, turned her back in disgust. Walter couldn't help himself. He listened for word of escaped Lily, careening cars, a Lily crash on the highway. Tom Paxton of *Channel 4 Fast Breaking News* wasn't telling, though. He chewed his sandwich and wiped Baby's chin every couple of bites, decided on a mug for their next meal. Baby chased pale oyster crackers through a sea of red, crowing in triumph whenever her spoon captured a prize. When she finished, Walter mopped her up and then poured the remaining soup from the pan into a mug for Grace. He placed it on the tray and added a pile of oyster crackers and a glass of milk. Baby watched, blinking at Walter through her glasses. "*Wheel of Fortune!*" the TV hollered from the other room. Baby's eyes widened, her mouth made a large *O* of excitement.

"Pat! Patpatpat! Orange! Vanna! Vanna White!" Baby lumbered hurriedly to her feet. Standing, a look of calamity rose in her face, she pressed her legs together, grabbed her crotch. "Oh! Ohhh!"

Walter recognized his aunt's need, felt an answering twinge from childhood memory. "Come on, Aunt Baby. You come upstairs to the toilet, then you can watch Pat and Vanna." Walter led Baby up the stairs. In the bathroom, he set the tray down on the sink and turned to survey his aunt. Baby stood in front of the toilet, her face scrunched in fierce concentration, her knees clamped together.

"OK. Go ahead, Aunt Baby." Walter pointed at the toilet. Baby didn't move. Her face became a vivid red. Her eyes behind the thick lenses bulged in panic. "Can't you do it yourself?" In Walter's voice an answering panic.

Baby moaned.

Walter inched over to his aunt and gingerly pulled up her dress. Acres of pink cotton confronted him. He grimaced and began tugging down Baby's panties. He was pretty sure he wasn't supposed to be doing this, could even go to jail for it maybe. Baby shivered, moaned again. Walter flossed the panties between Baby's clenched knees. *Who else would*, he asked the panties and yanked them over Baby's calves to the floor. He eased Baby back onto the toilet. Lily wasn't here. The thought made his chest contract like a fist. He watched the panic, the red, drain from Baby face. She peed and peed and peed and smiled at Walter. Walter smiled back, his chest loosening. *I'm here*, he told himself. He felt like a dad with his little kid in some public toilet. "Good job, Aunt Baby."

"Pat?"

"Yep." Walter nodded and hauled Baby back up. "Now Pat."

Baby made her own way downstairs, following the ratcheting noise of the turning wheel on the TV. Walter proceeded down the hall toward Grace. Halfway there, Lily's room beckoned on the left. Walter stood a long minute in the doorway, then stepped in, carefully balanced his tray, and groped for the lamp switch. The room wakened, the walls so carefully painted by Baby with their rising spectrum of mauve to pearl and their painted clusters of lilies. Walter caught his breath: How could she leave this?

Lily's PVT. MCCORKLE duffle bag was still tossed in the corner. Walter stood over it, Grace's dinner tray clutched in his hands, and gazed down. Hope rose from his toes like the tingling of an awakened limb. Walter scanned the room for other signs: the bed was unmade… wouldn't she make her bed before running away? The closet door stood ajar…Aunt Grace's record player sat open on the floor, darkness leaking into the room from the window above it. Walter blinked. No box of albums. No messy piles of worn jackets, their shiny, black LPs peeking out. *Gone.* Walter walked over to the bed and sat down. His hands shook. Oyster crackers slid around the tray. Walter eased the tray down on his knees. Stared down at the soup in the mug, watched the surface congeal to a thick, pink hide. He formed a careful pyramid of the scattered oyster crackers. He sat for a minute longer, listening to the burble of TV below, Baby barking colors at Pat, Vanna, and the spinning wheel. Taking the tray back into his hands, he stood, left the room, and closed the door.

Butler raised his head as Walter turned on the light in Grace's room. Grace stirred. "Walter," Grace mumbled, ran a shaky hand over her face. "I was taking a catnap."

Walter thought of the barn cats curled at his sides, on his belly, of their soft, buzzing warmth. Catnaps were good. "I brought you some dinner." Walter shooed Butler from the bed and set the tray down next to Grace. "Campbell's tomato soup. A warm and hearty American tradition," Walter quoted, then hesitated. "It might not be too warm… Aunt Baby had to go to the bathroom…"

"Where's your mom?" Awake and on the sharp edge of pain, Grace studied Walter and struggled to sitting.

Walter looked away. "She had to go get something." From below, an advertising jingle rose, whispered down the hall. "I'm filling in. She said, 'You fill in while I'm gone, Critter.'" It could have been that way; Walter could almost hear it. "Sometimes she still calls me Critter, but I don't like it anymore, because…because I'm not…" Walter dropped his head, examined his shoes. He swallowed, the saliva fighting him all the way down. *Go ahead,* he urged himself and raised his head. "She said that. She did. I can do it, Aunt Grace. I made soup."

Grace wanted to believe it, wanted to more than anything she had ever wanted in her life. "It looks delicious, Walter. I am a fan of oyster crackers especially. Put that tray right here, Chef. You can keep me company until your mom comes back." Words would make it true.

Walter smiled. "I can read to you! I'll go get something to read right now!" Walter rushed from the room, returned to admonish, "You eat, Aunt Grace!" His steps pounded out hope along the hall and down the stairs.

Walter returned with a pile of magazines to find Butler on the bed, licking an orange muzzle. Crackers sprinkled from the tips of his whiskers. "Butler! Bad!"

Butler's tongue curled up and over his nose. He was unrepentant. Grace chuckled, patted him. "He's OK. Just cleaning up. I ate most of it," she lied. "I saved the milk for those pills on the dresser. Hand two of them to me, Walter, before you settle in."

Walter carefully placed the two pills in Grace's waiting palm, put the glass of milk in her other hand, and watched her swallow with a jerking effort, then make a face. "There, now," she gasped. "What are we reading?"

Walter moved the tray to the floor, nudged Butler to the foot of the bed, and sat close to Grace. He smoothed an ancient *Weekly World News* across his knees. "Bat Boy is dating the cat-faced lady. See?" Walter pointed.

"That sounds important. Better start there."

Walter read. Grace listened, listened to the boy, to the distant TV, listened for the sound of Baby's heavy tread on the stair, for the crunch of gravel beneath wheels outside her window. Butler inched his way up the bed, unnoticed, until he wedged himself between his humans. The *Enquirer* shared secret details and stolen photos, fuzzy with distance, of some star's wedding.

Baby clumped up the stairs and wandered in. "Alex," she said, disgruntled. *Jeopardy* was not a favorite. She planted herself on the far side of Grace; the other occupants swayed and slid toward her presence. The *Sun* showed the reconstructed face of a famous singer and proclaimed, *MY PLASTIC SURGERY NIGHTMARE!* in bold red. Walter worked his way through the pile. Grace, her required listening narrowed to Walter and the dying hope of wheels, nodded and fought a drugged dozing. Butler snored. The *Globe* predicted the imminent end of the world. *WATCH FOR THESE SEVEN SIGNS!* Walter was down to the most worn back issues, the pages fragile after Baby's frenzied clipping. "The Fattest Man in the World is trying to find a mate," Walter told his aunts.

Baby, wide awake and avid, proclaimed, "Ho!" and pointed, jostling Grace awake.

Grace blinked, gazed beyond the light that pooled the bed, protected its occupants. *Darkness*, Grace thought...*the end of the world.* She reached across Butler and placed her cool, paper-dry hand over Walter's. "Is she coming back?"

Walter stared down at the glossy photos, the garish titles, the stories in black and white. *Let it be true*, he thought, let the fat man find his mate, let Bat Boy and the cat-faced woman live happily ever after, give the movie star peace, heal the scarred singer. *Let all the stories be true.* "Yes," he told Grace. He continued reading.

The hearing room is wood and small, two rows of benches and one table where Walter sits with the woman from the Department of Social Services. There is an empty chair at their table. Lily's chair. The judge sits at a desk that is not raised above the floor. She does not have a gavel. Only her black robes proclaim her as the one in charge. Walter cannot take his eyes off her. The dark skin across her cheeks glows in the overhead light. Her hair, lacquered in blue-black wings, pulls at her temple. She shuffles through papers and then checks her watch. Black eyes rise to survey Walter and the woman from DSS. The woman from DSS smooths the jacket of her gray suit, shakes her head with a slight movement. Small noises echo in the brown room: the brush of the DSS woman's hand along the material, the scrape of the judge's fingernails leafing through her pages, the soft rifling of paper, Walter's fast breathing...

"We'll give her a few more minutes." The judge's voice is deep, startling in the small space.

This is all wrong, *Walter thinks.* This is not the place for Lily. That's why she's not here. *He looks helplessly from the judge to the woman at his side.* This place is too brown and pinched. *He opens his mouth to explain. No words come out. He wants to tell them, tell the black woman and the gray. Lily is special; she is like a painting, like the paintings she has shown him upstairs at the museum. Close: she is specks of brightness, mixed up colors, chaos. You have to step back and back until you can see the picture, the beauty. There is not enough room for that here. There is no brown or black or gray in her. Only color and space. They need to know this, to understand about Lily. Walter's hand inches up his chest. If he raises it into the air, he will have to speak, they to listen.*

The door at the back of the room swings open. She is in tattered jeans and sneakers and wears a huge, orange scarf draped around her like a cloak. Her hair is gone, regrown to a stubble over her tender, pale scalp. It has been six months since Walter has seen her, but he would recognize her anywhere. Her eyes are jewels.

THIRTY

Ensconced on her barstool, Lily catalogued her faults and watched the parade of her many leavings rise from the bottom of her beer glass and break the surface of the amber liquid to disappear. This last one was the worst. Nothing could lift the weight of it.

Her hair still spiky wet from the shower, she had made sure Grace was safely stowed in bed, Baby happy in front of the TV with crackers and milk, the smeared, brown mess in the hallway mopped clean. She put the mop back in the hall closet, closed the door carefully, and turned to face the quiet house. With her back pressed against the closed door, she let the panic flood. Away, she needed to be away. Now.

The box of albums seemed the heaviest thing she had ever carried. It hindered her every step of the way, bumping into the bedroom doorframe, jamming against the hallway wall. On the stairs, it blocked her view of the steps. She felt with her toes for the step below, but misjudged on the last one, slipped and landed hard on her bottom, the box on edge in her lap. "Dammit!" she spat, shoved off the dead weight of the box and stood, legs shaking.

In front of the TV, Baby leaned back to see. The chair creaked like an alarm. "Lily?" She motioned to the TV. "Lily…meepmeep?"

Lily bent and scrabbled around the floor, retrieving records and covers. Her back and buttocks throbbed; her chin stung. Her ears seemed to echo with every noise the house held: the tick of the kitchen clock, the high-pitched laughter of Woody Woodpecker, the hum of the refrigerator, Baby's open-mouthed, nasal breathing, the sigh of the old house...Grace. The sounds roared in her head. She clutched the box to her chest. *Just you and me, Frankie.* Stumbling, she and the box ricocheted off the kitchen entryway. Two steps more, her hip connected with the corner of the table, the box tipping precariously as she rebounded in pain. "Let me go!" Lily yelled at the house.

"Lily?" Baby from the TV.

"Stay there, Aunt Baby. Watch TV."

The screen door recoiled too quickly as she shoved out, smacking her arm before banging behind her. Lily closed her eyes, held her breath, let it out slowly, opened her eyes again. In front of her were steps and grass and gravel, Grace's car, the road, the empty afternoon. A way. Behind her, the house was quiet except for late-summer wasps tapping at the windows. Lily was filled with the need to hurry, to be gone before her trailing thoughts, tangled in chairs and corners and Baby's simple questions, could catch up and stop her. She rushed to the car and shoved the box of albums into the seat next to her, leapt in after it and gunned the engine into life. Away. Away. Away. The words pounded in her chest as she struggled with the shift and lurched out onto the road. The length of the road, she wouldn't look back. She knew what she would see, the many-colored house, waiting. Away. A mantra. Away. A tune to live by. Frank Sinatra's voice urged her on, "Let's fly away, fly away..."

Lily drove to town, an act of reflex, the habit of months of trips to the drugstore, the farmer's market, the five-and-dime. The only traffic light in town stopped her cold. In the ninety-second delay, her life caught up to her. The light changed, and still she sat. What about Walter? What about Grace? Baby? Lily leaned her head against the steering wheel. The light changed to red again. *How does this happen,* she asked herself. Two cars lined up behind Lily's. Always. Green light. Another car joined the line. Always. A polite tap at Lily's window. Lily looked up, startled, unfocused. A middle-aged woman with graying hair and a face tanned from a summer of gardening smiled gently at her. "Are you all right?"

"What?" Lily's voice was edged with panic. "What did I do?"

"Nothing. I thought you might be in trouble." The woman pointed at the light. Lily looked up. The light changed from green to amber. In the rearview mirror, she glimpsed the line of cars.

"Shit!" Lily stomped on the gas. Grace's car roared through the intersection, leaving the concerned citizen standing, watching in mild perplexity. Legal traffic braked, giving Lily way. "What is it with this place?" Lily roared inside the car. "Why don't they just honk? In the city, they would have all sat on their horns! Or shot me! I need to be in the city! I need to be away! Away or shot!"

On the sidewalk along Main, people turned to the sound of muffled hollering coming from Grace's old car as it rolled by.

Lily didn't go to the city. She couldn't. They had burrowed inside her, Walter always there, Grace and Baby, even Butler. They had made a home in her core, and even though in her panic she had tried to expel them, still they clung. Some invisible cord was stretched tight. She was connected to Walter and Baby and Grace. She seemed to have run its limit and to have been snapped back. She was theirs. What would it take to cut free?

She went to a bar, the Red Dragoon. The building was two storied and as old as the town. A chipped, faded sign of a British Revolutionary War soldier hung over the door. "Perfect," Lily said and parked the car.

Inside, it was dark. There were six or eight locals clumped in companionable groups under low lighting. Farther back, billiard balls clicked. Heads turned when Lily entered, stumbling on the wide, uneven floorboards. A few had seen her around in her SPCA-shop clothes and aura-like dark hair, seen her walking on Main Street, seen her selling eggs and flowers at the farmer's market. A man at the pool table had once owned the plaid shirt she wore. Without knowing it, she was a local.

"Hey," the bartender greeted her noncommittally, waited. "What can I get you?"

Lily stared at him. "Beer?"

The bartender laughed. "I'm not even going to ask you which brand." He pulled a draft handle, Molson Light. "I've seen you around. You live with those two old ladies out east of town. That house is amazing." His tone conversational, he tilted the glass, watched the foam rise. "Who's the artist?"

Lily grabbed the glass and took a great swallow of beer. Her chest ached. "Aunt Baby."

"She must be famous."

Lily's smile was reluctant, sad. "Should be."

The bartender looked at her, smiled back. "So, what's with the hair? That some new style?"

Lily ran her hands through her hair, cupped her head in her palms. "I was Buddhist." Lily suddenly remembered the smiling nun in the monastery's reception room. *"Sign as a guest."* Lily's hand had hesitated over the form. *"I want to be an acolyte."* The nun had smiled, eyeing Lily's already-shaved head. *"Wanting and being are two different things. You will learn."* She had said it just like that, two different sentences. It had taken Lily days to forget to worry about what it had meant, days of uncomfortable otherness, menial tasks, squirming meditation, longing for that release after a needle, clawing failure. She had bled for Walter.

Lily looked up at the bartender, wondered: *What have I learned?*

He saw a question in her eyes. "Catholic," he answered.

Lily sought her beer, gulped. *Come, numbness,* she prayed.

"So, was...? You're not Buddhist anymore?" The bartender, head down, rubbed the ring where Lily's glass had been.

Lily shook her head, still immersed in beer. Where had she lost the thread? Forgot to practice?

"When I was eighteen, I told my mom I wasn't a Catholic anymore, and she laughed in my face. 'Too late,' she said. 'It's either waiting inside you or coming out in your life.'"

"I need another beer."

The bartender filled her glass. "All I'm saying is, it isn't that easy to break free. Every single thing I've done since that day has been aimed at proving her wrong. Look at me now." He threw his tattooed arms wide in the gloom of the bar. Lily eyed him. The bartender's arms dropped. "It doesn't matter. She says she hasn't lost hope. She says I was raised right, and it's just waiting inside. A soldier in God's army, she says." He helped himself to a glass of beer.

They drank in silence.

Outside, it was now dark; cars passed cautiously on the narrow street, their headlamps a moving swath of yellow on the far wall. Three couples came in, taking a table at the back. The place was filling up. Barstools scraped along the bar. The bartender moved away. Lily took inventory; she, too, was filling up nicely. "Nothing else in there," she mumbled to her beer mug. She announced to the crowd, "We need music in here!"

Heads rose, an embarrassed pause. Lily stood, waited for a wave of dizziness to pass.

"Frank Sinatra calls to us all!" She moved toward the jukebox. She noticed the smirks as she passed through the crowd, suddenly saw herself: *I am a comedy. The Lily Show.* Would Aunt Baby watch?

The jukebox contained hits of the late '60s, the '70s, a few notables of the '80s. Lily stared at the titles blankly. She wandered back to the bar. "I missed all those songs," she told the bartender.

"Missed them? Where were you?"

As Lily considered, a cascade of images rushed past: the disappointed faces of her parents, the dirty, desperate-looking apartments, the library cubicles where she read and read, Walter chewing on picture books at her feet, music playing, an insinuating croon guiding her thoughts, her movements. Away, she had been away.

The bartender opened the cash register and slid two quarters toward Lily. "Well, time to catch up, sister! You know what they say— live in the now!"

The bartender's idiot words, the smack of the register drawer closing, were like the snap of fingers before her eyes. She felt stunned, awakened. She felt the tug of some chord, some thread. The thread...the practice. About what? Not suffering, not running, not doing...Being now...being happy. *So easy?* The thin intent spun in her mind.

Lily stood. The beer sloshed inside her. It didn't matter. She felt suddenly sober, clean. She pushed the bartender's quarters back at him. "I'm not going to need these." Lily paid and headed for the door.

"Hey!" the bartender called plaintively. "Where you going?"

Lily smiled at him from the open door. "I'm going to try and follow your mom's advice. Going to be a soldier." Above her head, the bar sign swung, creaked in a fitful breeze.

Lily sat in Grace's car and listened. Silence, pure and weightless. Was this salvation…nirvana? Just living? What had she been doing all this time? She smiled. "We've sung this song too long, Frankie," she whispered. "Let's go home."

The mattress in her room is thin and hard. Lily sits on it, cramped with cold, unmoving. Every time the monks in their orange robes or the students in street clothes glide past her open door, Lily feels a slight, sharp breeze on her kneecaps. Frostbite, she thinks. Is this a lesson? What is it?

"I take refuge in Buddha." She is trying to memorize the sixteen precepts. Lily imagines she can see her breath, words coming out in small, white clouds from blue lips.

"I take refuge in dharma." Her bare feet are so cold, it feels as if her toenails will pop off.

"I take refuge in sangha." She has forgotten what sangha is…something… something to do with…? Two monks whisk by, laughing. Lily covers her knee-caps with her icy hands and waits for the corresponding blast. She wants to shout, I'm freezing here! *The passageway is empty again, and no one will hear. It comes to her then.*

"Sangha! The connection of all beings! Gotcha!" She basks in a moment of accomplishment that quickly cools. Three down, thirteen to go, the pure precepts, the grave precepts. Lily rushes through the next three.

"I will avoid all actions that create suffering. I will promote happiness. I will act with others in mind." Lily's teeth begin to chatter. She will not give in. She will not slip beneath her quilt until she has memorized them all. She closes her eyes. The rest of the precepts are specifics of behavior. Only one of these she knows by heart.

"I will not intoxicate with substances or doctrines but will promote clarity and awareness." Number five. She has said this to herself over and over for ten days now, every time the need of needle whispered to her, offered its seeming clarity…its refuge…its invading, false peace. Lily licks her lips, feels the air chill the

wetness, wills herself to focus. She opens one eye and peeks at the sheet of paper lying next to her on the bed, then closes it again.

"Number one. I will not kill but nurture life."

"Are you expecting a quiz?"

Lily's eyes fly open. At the door of her room, the nun who had checked her in stands watching her, a smile curving her pale lips. She wears a bright green, hand-knit sweater, chunky and warm, over her robes. Old Miss Sign-in-as-a-Guest, *Lily thinks.* Bitch, *adds Lily, then winces. How many precepts has she just broken? "I want to learn them by heart."*

The nun steps into the room and sits down on the bed next to Lily. "You are trying too hard. When you are ready, it will be easy."

Lily shakes her head. "Nothing's easy for me."

The nun smiled. "There must be one thing…"

Lily thinks. The prick of a needle, the slow, sweet sinking…No! Not that. That was not easy. It comes to her then, his face, small, pink with heat, sweat-shiny beneath spiky golden-haired halo tufted with couch cotton, sticking out from behind the dusty, brown couch in their first apartment. "Boo," the little face said. She remembers all of him emerged, filthy-footed, spaceman-print pajamas, grubby, open hands. An ecstatic lunge into her arms.

Lily smiled back at the nun. "Walter."

"That's enough." The nun took off her sweater and placed it around Lily's shoulders. "That's a way, a start. There is no end."

THIRTY-ONE

F rom her bed, Grace heard the attic stairs being pulled down, the struggle of feet on the rungs, the slide of a heavy box above. Around her they slept undisturbed, Baby, Walter, Butler. Light feet descended the rungs of the attic ladder, a pause, then Lily appeared at Grace's bedroom door. "I've been missing a slumber party." Lily smiled at the cluster of bodies illuminated by the bedside light. Baby slept flat on her back, mouth open, glasses askew. Walter and Butler were curled like bear cubs on the other side of Grace's diminished form.

"We were reading the magazines." Grace raised a foot slightly. Bat Boy's face slid.

Lily walked to the bed, bent to run fingers through Walter's hair. Walter squirmed and scratched his head in his sleep, then threw an arm over Butler. Butler gave a sleepy growl, rabbited with his back feet a time or two, then sighed with content. Lily sat down at the foot of the bed, adjusting the clutter around her.

"You're back."

Lily nodded.

"He said you would be."

"Did he believe it?"

Grace didn't answer but adjusted herself painfully, carefully in her narrow space, then said, "Heard you upstairs."

"Storing some things…albums."

"Sinatra? For good?"

Lily looked down at her hands holding magazines. The World's Fattest Man grinned back. *Number Four. I will not lie but be truthful.* "I hope so, Aunt Grace."

Grace smiled, shifted with pain. "Well, that old red prom dress came back down. I was glad. It was time."

Lily echoed Grace's smile. "Maybe it was." She thought of her parents' reaction. *The Lily Show.* The World's Fattest Man smirked up at her, a comrade. Baby's jaws worked as if chewing, then dropped open again. She snored. "Should I move them to their beds?" *I will be a soldier of life, a red dragoon.*

"No. I like it. You could hand me my pills, there on the dresser."

Lily stood carefully so as not to disturb the sleepers and retrieved the pills. "Have you been waiting for these a long time? Aunt Grace, I'm sorry."

"No. Walter got me some a while ago. They must have fallen asleep. I lost track...I was visiting."

Lily smiled. "With Walter and Baby?"

"No. Other family. They come to me...my sister Kate brushed my hair every morning before school when I was little." Grace's fingers moved over the covers. "I can still feel that brush on my scalp. I thought she was the cat's meow back then."

Lily watched the movement of Grace's fingers. "That's hard to imagine. You don't seem that close..." *Number Six. I will not speak of others' faults but speak out of loving kindness.*

Grace looked up at Lily. "Time's not always a friend. Memories become colored by everything that follows."

They sat in quiet. Lily looked down. Beyond the pool of light created by the bedside lamp, her toes dipped into darkness.

"Now, your father, he was the brains of the family, youngest, smartest. When he was just a mite, he stole my new transistor radio and took it all apart. I could have killed him...two days later, there it was, back together on my bedside table." Grace shook her head, felt the pills working their magic. "When I close my eyes, I see them all, jumbled up, young and old...Mother in her garden, hands black with soil. They come to me. Different than I expected. Better than I judged."

Lily reached out, took Grace's hands, watched her eyes glaze with relief.

"Papa died...I was selling off the herd..."

Lily waited a second, then prompted, "The herd?"

Grace laughed, a soft cough of noise. "I found this list...all the cows by name...looks...habits...personalities...'Enid is quiet and good but not an overly friendly cow.'" Grace laughed again, softer still.

Lily smiled.

"In that neat, schoolboy hand of his...cows were his religion." Grace was floating away, but there was something else, something still to be said. She focused on Lily's face. "Why couldn't they take that care with her?"

Lily felt the tears gather behind her eyes. *Number Nine. I will not harbor anger but forgive. So many life lessons.* "I don't understand about families. Why can't..." Lily swallowed and tried again, "I want..."

"Family...religion," Grace shook her head, whispered thickly. "Same...devotion...a long haul..." A picture rose in Grace's clouded vision: *Mother's blue dress is dark with wet, her eyes wild. The smell of river is thick in the kitchen. Somewhere Baby wails, a high, lost sound. "She's saved, Grace! Saved!"*

A scrap of some old verse came to Grace. She focused on Lily's face, pearled as if in dream. "Only the faithful get to the..." Grace closed her eyes and slept.

Lily let Grace's fingers slip from her grasp and smoothed her hands over the covers. "Sleep, Aunt Grace," she whispered. "Oblivion. You're welcome to it." Lily reached over Baby to switch off the lamp, her arm's shadow sliding across Baby's face.

Baby's lips chomped and pursed. "Purple," she breathed.

Lily felt the color, moist and warm, sighed onto the tender underside of her outstretched arm. The tiny hairs there trembled with the gift. Lily curled up at Grace's feet. She slid a hand beneath Walter's sleeping form. A steady, human rhythm pressed her palm. A small continent of warmth rested there. She wanted this, would fight for it, this religion, this promised land.

These were the last days. Baby would color them. She carefully pulled from the box each crayon, one after another, laying them in a neat row across the kitchen table. She picked two or three at a time and, holding them together, drew zigzags or swirling spirals or shaded blobs that faded to nothing on the big square of butcher paper. Lily watched, fascinated. The picture pulled Lily in, surrounded her. She wanted to run her fingers over it, feel the subtle dips and whirls, find the safety of its message. *Tell me, Baby...*

Baby tried. These were the last days. Baby knew them; they flowed from her fingers, drifting days of textured colors. Here in the kitchen were mornings of bright and cartoonish laughter, yellow, red, green, three matching milk mustaches; Walter feeding the chickens, then Baby chasing them, arms aflap; Lily's momentary, happy laugh at the back door. Late evenings were precious-jeweled tones, violet and ocean blue, the three of them under a red plaid blanket on the couch, watching Don Knotts tremble with fear in *The Ghost and Mr. Chicken.* Lacquered, bright moments, brittle, brief, ready to crack. In Grace's room a grayness filled the air, pale but palpably present. Baby saw it. If she stuck out her fingers, reached out from the spot next to the bed where she and Lily and Walter sat with Grace, off and on all day, she felt it, the soft gauze of gray, its fine graininess, like sand, slipping through her fingers.

In Baby's own room, a better color, a soft, shining pinkness that her body gave off each morning as she played the new getting-dressed game with Lily. When Baby finally allowed it, Lily, lying on the bed, feet dangling, would uncover her eyes to see bright, pink life glowing through a white-and-orange-daisy dress and Baby's coquettish swirl causing madonnas to lift and float from their tacks on the walls. Then, just for Baby each morning, Lily said the bright, bold new headline words: "My gosh! You are so beautiful, Aunt Baby! That is the most beautiful dress I've ever seen. If Andy Griffith saw you, he'd steal you away and marry you in a minute." Pink-and-yellow joy!

Around Walter, a midnight blue had knit itself, soft and insular, a layer of fur. It was the deep blue of his first coming to the house. Walter was sad. He was sad about the fawn buried in the woods and about Grace and about his mom who had run away and come back but for how long, and sad about Baby whose days seemed the same, but couldn't be, and sad about Butler and the cats and the chickens that didn't know anything and could die at any minute. He was sad about playing Flying Cat, leaping and leaping into the air, and sad about floating on the still, stained water of the pond, because he couldn't know where he would land or if he would sink.

Baby saw it, saw the colors, saw Walter's blue, Lily's quick flashes of brilliance, green, red, orange, purple, saw Grace's seeping gray. Baby was yellow, yellow and pink, pink like Andy who would see her and steal her away and marry her. Baby had a secret. Baby knew something. Grace should know it too, but Grace was too busy with gray, and Baby couldn't tell the others. She didn't have words, only crayons. So she sat at the kitchen table and drew the last days and colored them in. When she finished the picture, they would know.

At Grace's insistence, hospice was called. Lily's days of carrying Grace to the toilet and back to bed were over. Such a light burden, once gone, left Lily's arms bereft. The nurse, Molly, swept into their lives. "Ha!" Baby said, looking her over. "Greenyellowgreen."

"My favorite color," Molly answered. It was decided. Perfect.

She was slight and strong, with crisp, silver-gold hair that shed its own light. Standing next to her, helping when she could, Lily felt like some dark-furred forest dweller, large and awkward, a moose maybe. To Walter, Molly was cheerful and matter-of-fact, a source of information on the outside world, a hand parting his insulation of fur. "School starts in a week. You'll have a great time," she told him. "Lots of great kids in this town." Walter's heart stirred. Another leap.

With Grace she was skill and relief, a catheter, a morphine drip. This gift and touch, Lily's hand, Baby's, Walter's, Butler's breath on her face, were all that tethered Grace in the flow of her dreams and memories.

Baby fidgeted. Too much sitting in gray. Time to paint. She stood from her spot at Grace's bedside, stomped to the far wall, and slapped its aged, white surface. "Yellow."

"I don't think..." Lily's voice was tentative.

"Yellow." Baby slapped the walls again.

Grace nodded, a slight movement of the head. She would acquiesce in this, too, let Baby have it, the work of her days, the flow of her life, the tenor of her thoughts, the walls that surround her: *I give all this.* When the time came, she gritted her teeth against the pain and silently let herself be carried the long journey down the hall and stairs and settled onto the old couch with her morphine and her dreams and Butler on her chilled feet.

The painting took all day. First the trip to Pete's Paint with its discussion of color chips and brushes and rollers, cans and cans of myriad colors to be mixed and carried to the car, while Walter at home held tight to Grace's hand, watched cartoons with the volume on so low, the characters mimed their antics from the screen. Then layer upon layer of paint, Baby brushing the corners while Lily rolled the walls, Lily all the while perplexed at Baby's choice. A break for lunch, for the glucometer and Baby's shot, another later break for dinner with Grace in front of *Get Smart*, then back to paint. The upstairs windows were all opened wide; a cross breeze carried the fumes and Lily's questions from the room.

The next morning, Grace was carried upstairs. She blinked in the sunlight pouring into the room. White. The walls, fifteen years brighter, but still white. She thought of Baby hard at work on Lily's room and Baby putting the finishing touches on Walter's night sky, she thought of the odd-numbered years of touching up the great canvas of the house, she and Baby on rented scaffolding high above the hard earth, clinging to the bright face of Baby's whims. Grace felt tears of frustration build behind her eyes. All that pain, each movement an agony…a night on the couch when she was dying…all those years… for white? So little?

Once in her bed, she gazed upward. Here was a small change, at least. The ceiling was yellow, a deep, wet, peachy yellow, like the first bite into juicy, summer fruit. A tug of memory: a shared, stolen sweetness, Baby's pink tongue licking sticky fingers…*Yes*, thought Grace, *I could lay here and stare up into this a while longer.* It was enough. It would always have to be enough. Grace smiled. "Baby…" she nodded as she spoke.

Baby ran her fingers lovingly over the white wall. She pointed here and here and here, spots all around the room. "Yellow, yellow, yellow, yellow, yellow, yellow." Grace's eyes were closed. Printed on her eyelids was a figure…*who?* Baby's voice receded. Baby slapped the wall hard. "Grace! Yellow! Yellow!"

"Shhh," Lily soothed. "She's tired, Aunt Baby. She's sleeping…she loved it, Aunt Baby. I know she did. She's just so tired." Walter nodded in encouragement and sought his mother's hand.

Baby humphed and clomped over to Grace's bed, stared down at Grace's gray face, her thin, gray arms and long, gray fingers, still, all still on the white sheets. Color color color. All was color. Baby wasn't finished. She had secrets to tell, stories to paint. Now the real work began. She stomped out of the room. They would see color. When she was through, they would know.

Grace woke from her dreams to Molly's cool fingers on her wrist. Her body floated. "I was dancing…" she whispered.

"In a freshly painted room, I bet. Take a whiff. Take a look." She laughed.

Grace opened her eyes. It was late afternoon. A golden light carrying hints of green from the hill across the road angled through the window; in the room, smells of cows and grass and paint drifted with gilded dust motes. Lily, with Walter in her lap, his growing-boy legs dangling long, sat in the chair next to Grace's bed. They hardly seemed aware of her waking; they looked away, mesmerized. Grace followed the line of their sight. What little breath was left to her caught in her throat, her eyes filled. Baby was painting.

With the ease of a dancer, Baby circled the dozens of open paint cans on the floor. Using her once-white smock as a palette, she dipped and wiped and dabbed, adding to the pictures on the wall across from the foot of the bed. The wall was just over half covered, a large space remaining directly across from the foot of the bed. Separate paintings, each with its own, uniquely painted faux frame, a museum of moments, memories, gifts. Around each painting, dashes, streaks, arcs, and swirls, abstract patterns of pure color exploded like shouted comments. The rich yellow of the ceiling bathed the paintings, the hurried splots and splashes between, with a pale gold.

Baby worked furiously, her back to Grace. The fat on her upheld arm jiggled, swayed; a sweat stain showed dark down the back of her dress. Grace saw it all through smeared vision, each movement, each painting, each event of hers and Baby's life, wet and new on the walls of her room. In the far left corner, a small child pressed a red-mittened hand against the palm of an older girl, dark haired and hollow eyed. In another painting, its richly baroque frame still gleaming wet, the child, older by a few years, offered a white box of crayons. Next to this, a starkly modern frame held a picture of a young woman crayoning the walls of a cage.

Baby stepped back from her latest offering. Grace saw two girls, younger and older, running naked through a medieval wood, silver moonlight filtering through the high branches of trees and lacing their flowing, dark hair and the curves of their bodies. It was too much, too much offered, too much to accept. Grace moaned, heard Molly next to her tap and adjust the flow of morphine, felt the morphine's welcome tug, the call to memory. The wall faded to white.

Grace woke off and on to see the walls being covered around her, Walter and Lily always beside her, watching, sometimes Molly too, entranced as the others. Baby painted, hardly stopping to eat, squeezing her knees in sudden surprise at the needs of her body. At these times, Lily rushed her off to the bathroom, checked her sugar, administered a shot. Baby bent with her smock drawn up over her hip, panties down, impatient to be back to color. TV was forgotten. Andy could wait. The story was here, on these walls, in this room.

The paintings mixed with Grace's dreams in a fragmented parade of memory, truth, and hope. Here she danced, the red dress a vibrant splash around her slim waist, over there, she held wildflowers in one fist and seemed to be pointing out each bloom to a young, smiling Baby. Framed in purple, Walter sat in a pile of hay and barn cats, his mouth wide with laughter. A somber line of rainbow-hued cows made their way through twilight to milking, surrounded by a frame composed of full milk bottles. Within the boundaries of a brilliant yellow frame, Lily balanced on the thin spindle of a record player, her arms flung wide, midwhirl. Grace saw herself, older, standing on a hill, Baby at her side, sugar cubes in their outstretched hands. In another, Baby, Walter, Lily, and Grace sat on a blanket in deep grass, flowers around them, butterflies above. In yet another, Baby and Grace on hands and knees, side by side, their large rumps great mounds of matching, stretched daisies in orange and green. In front of them a small shed, a small, sad face just visible in its interior: Lily in the doghouse. Paintings of Baby and Grace with ice cream, a younger Baby with crayons at the kitchen table, Grace watching, a broad, proud smile, Baby in the yard, scattering chickens.

Each time Grace dropped off, each time she woke, new pictures appeared. She heard Lily whisper to her son, "Look, Walter. We're part of the picture. We're here forever." Grace turned her head to speak to them. They had disappeared. In their place, Don Knotts grinned in black and white; Maxwell Smart smirked under the Cone of Silence with a smiling, waving Baby, and the pig from *Green Acres* sat on Grace's couch and watched TV with Lily and Walter. The steps of the Metropolitan loomed near the door to the hallway. Instead of the building, they led to an enormous portrait of Van Gogh's shoes. Near the west window, Baby and Grace stood before a Madonna and Child, Lily the Madonna, Walter the Child. All four wore matching yellow coronas. On the other side of the window, Grace and Baby sat, heads together, reading *Weekly World News*. Bat Boy smiled up at them from the pages. Baby and Grace in shades of green. Baby and Grace in neon pink. Baby and Grace. Grace closed her eyes against it, this outpouring, so overwhelming. All this given, all this returned. But in that temporary darkness, visions came, voices whispered. *Baby and Grace. Grace and Baby.*

As Grace ebbed, the walls exploded with life, her life, Baby's, Lily's, and Walter's. Grace woke a last time in evening's leaving light to the wall moving around her, the people there murmuring, shifting. She focused momentarily. It was only the nurse, Molly, and Lily clearing paint cans from the room. Directly in front of her, Baby worked on the last piece of open wall, a light directed harshly on her frenzied activity, the vibrating bulk of her frame, the fragmentary splashes of color that her movements revealed. Grace glimpsed a cluster of green leaves, a fleshy elbow, a patch of dark fur. Walter sat on the floor at Baby's feet, cross-legged, elbows on knees, chin in hands. Grace watched his body dip with sleep, his bony elbows wobble on his knees, his thin back pull sharply erect. Lily scooped him up, led him down the hall to bed. Grace saw the muscles work along Lily's lean calves as she walked him down the hall. There was a new clarity to Grace's vision, a brightness.

Baby stepped back, the brush dropped from her fingers to the floor. "Yellow," she mumbled to herself. She turned to Grace, grinned to see her awake. "Grace!"

Grace saw there was not a bit of Baby that was not covered with paint: her smock, her arms, her round, soft cheeks, her dentures, the tufty ends of her gray hair, streaked lines and daubs and splotches and spirals. She was a canvas, an abstract.

"Grace! Yellow! Yellow!" Baby stepped aside so her sister could see this last picture, last story. "Yellow! Grace! Hohohoho!" she hooted and threw her spattered arms wide. "Yellow!" a bellow of triumph. Grace's color.

Six feet from Grace's toes, their favorite village street stretched away, astoundingly real, the gray-pebbled asphalt, the rows of staid, old, white houses with dark shutters; the graceful, ancient oaks and maples, thick with a late-summer green that cast a dappled light on the sidewalks below. Grace and Baby walked there, their backs to the viewer. Grace, short, fat, and iron hair tightly curled; Baby huge beside her, soft, gray wisps of hair askew. Their arms were linked, and beneath that union, Butler trotted, ears and nose skyward, proud. The hems of their matching dresses, Butler's pert, furry bottom, the leaves of the trees, all seemed to sway in time, to set the whole room, the whole world, rocking to their rhythm. In all her life, Grace had never seen anything so, so *perfect*. She could step into it, take Baby's arm and walk away.

Grace swallowed, her mouth worked. Lily was at her side, leaning down. Grace looked into Lily's eyes. "I tried...tried to kill..." The words, so hard to find, to give up. "Should have...my job...Baby."

In Lily's mind, an image of the bathtub, Baby's blue eyes staring up through water, Grace crouched by the sink. "No. No, Aunt Grace." Lily gathered Grace's hands in her own, brought them to her cheek, to her lips. "You wouldn't."

Grace could feel the slight warmth of Lily's words on her fingers. She shook her head, opened her lips, struggled. Where were the words? How could she make Lily see? She fought this last battle, to pull together the splotches of sound, to pattern their slight hues of meaning. "She chose me."

Grace sensed Baby at her other side, smelled the sharp scent, felt the wetness of paint-smeared fingers on her face. She couldn't turn to Baby. There was no movement, no words were left; she couldn't interpret this leaving, couldn't explain or apologize. No words were left. Her vision filled with the picture, the colors. *Grace and Baby. Baby and Grace.* She was absorbed.

Baby sits at the kitchen table, coloring, Butler's fat tummy warm on her toes. She is drawing family. Midnight blue *Brother Bill,* spring green *Adrianne, Little Paul. Baby smiles.* Purple mountain's majesty *Paul. They are coming. Family always comes. All the colors mixed together are brown. Baby has found this out. That is why it is important to remember their names, to keep them separate. Every crayon has its own place in the box. Baby knows them. She is the keeper.*

There will be pink ham and pinker ambrosia. Pink as Andy Griffith's smile. Lily says. Good. When family is gone, taking their colors, Walter and Lily and Baby will visit the trees and climb through the woods and feed the cows their sugar. At Lily's voice, Butler will chase the cows. Baby will laugh. Lily says. Then they will open the jar and let Grace out. She will dance with the wind. Lily says.

Grace is not in the jar. Grace is not in the house, not in the barn where the cats make white and black and tan and orange puddles of softness for Walter to sink into. Lily says Grace is gone, and her words when she says this come out brown. Grace is not gone. Baby knows gone. Grace's mother and father are gone. Grace is never gone. Grace is away. Grace goes away to school, to dance in a red dress, to work in a funny white dress and shoes, to shop for oatmeal and rainbow sprinkles and orange juice and greengreen peas. Grace always comes back. This is the yellow secret. Not a secret. It is there on the walls of Grace's room for everyone to see. Walter comes. Lily comes. They are yellow. Yellow comes and stays. Grace will come. Baby will wait. She will sit at the kitchen table. Butler will sit at her feet, a purple tickle on her toes. Baby will use her crayons. Baby will color the days.

34339090R00118

Made in the USA
Lexington, KY
02 August 2014